Beautiful INK

NICOLE REED

Beautiful Ink
Copyright © 2014 by Nicole Reed

Published by Nicole Reed

Cover Design © Hang Le
http://www.byhangle.com/

Photo Image by Tyler Seielstad Photography
http://www.maketimestop.com/

Edited by Lisa Aurello

Formatted by Angela McLaurin, Fictional Formats
https:// www.facebook.com/FictionalFormats

Find out more about the author and upcoming books online at nicolereedbooks.com or facebook.com/authornicolereed.

~This is for those who carry a piece of their soul inked out lovingly on their skin.

Prologue

"Do as I say, when I say it," he forcefully commands. "Turn around and put your hands on the chair behind you."

I slowly pivot on the balls of my feet. He doesn't have to tell me to grip it tightly: my fingers curve over the back of the metal chair instinctively. Thousands of tiny chill bumps cover me in dread at the thought of my naked body on display. My heart throbs in a frantic rhythm, this moment the torturous accumulation of years of anxiety and apprehension.

His heavy breathing sounds frighteningly close. "You are not allowed to fuckin' move."

My eyes clamp shut. I am afraid of the consequences I have wrought. My tongue darts out of my dry mouth, wetting my cracked lips. I should have taken the water when he offered it earlier. The last harrowing fifteen hours have been an emotional train wreck, and just when I think things can't get any worse, they do.

I don't hear a whisper of the leather until it rips into the center of my back. The cracking sound against my skin reverberates all around me.

"Ahhh," I cry out, the white-hot pain sucking the air out of my lungs. There must be small metal spikes lining the belt, because they stab excruciatingly into my flesh. I almost let go of the chair, until I remember his words not to move.

"That's for the year I woulda gave you my name," he says, directly into my ear, but loud enough for everyone else to hear.

I didn't think I could shed another tear, but at the sound of the pain laced through his voice, my eyes swim with them. Even after this, it kills me to know that I hurt him. Many seconds pass before the next strike slams across my sensitive butt cheeks. My knees go weak, making it harder for me to stand. A cry escapes me from another assault of the metal and leather, this one stinging worse than the last. I dig my fingers into the cold metal of the chair, silently praying that I can hold myself up.

"That's for the year I woulda made our dreams come true."

So many memories assault me along with his belt, memories both sensual and evil. I want to open my eyes, but I fear what I would see in his gaze. The grief in his voice already rocks me to my core.

My screams echo around the room when he delivers two consecutive swings of the belt. His torture finally beats my body down, and my knees buckle, roughly sending me to the concrete floor. My eyes open in time to see red splatter across my arms, staining my already colorful skin. His unerring aim catches the exact spot as the first, slicing deeper into my flesh. I choke back the bile that threatens to erupt.

"Get up," he growls.

I force myself back to my feet, bowing my head, and bracing myself for his words as much as his strikes. My tears represent the agony of defeat that I don't want to give him.

"That's for the goddamn year," his voice breaks midsentence. "I woulda gave you my child."

Any inner strength I have left vanishes at the words torn from his mouth. His feet stand before me now and I have to see him. My eyes lift from the ground to stare directly into his dark, penetrating gaze. The room and those in it fall away and I only see him. This was once my friend. My family. My lover. My savior.

"*Our* child," he whispers through gritted teeth. He leans down to deliver a tender kiss upon my chapped lips, his tongue soothing them. His actions surprise me, the antithesis of his words. I watch him move slowly back. The look of desolation in his eyes is more than I can bear, so I close mine.

His backhand catches me completely off-guard. The searing pain explodes across my jawline up to my eye and has me staggering backward. The chair scrapes against the floor, following me several inches. I stare at the blood-splattered ground, blinking my vision back into focus. I hear the sound of his heavy shit-kickers as he moves behind me once again.

The voice in my head screams enough. I am too close to my breaking point. I wouldn't have lived through the earlier offer of the bullet to my brain, but I am not sure I will physically or mentally survive this agonizing persecution.

The next whip of his belt catches me against the soft flesh of my legs and on the underside of my rear. Quivering uncontrollably, I completely lose my balance, finally relinquishing the chair. He jerks my elbow up, making it easier to steady myself. His foot kicks out to knock the chair across the room away from us. My stomach threatens to rebel at the feel of something wet and warm running from my back, down the crease of my ass, slowly over my legs. I glance down to see drops of crimson silently rolling over my feet to encircle them. He tosses the belt so that it lands in it.

Our joint harsh panting is the only sound between us. He painfully tugs me backward to him, further lacerating my torn skin. The smooth texture of the leather rubbing against my back prompts another scream of pain. His jeans roughly grind against my buttocks.

"No," I say over and over, but make no attempt to move, knowing it would cause him to order more of this torture.

"Do you know what it's like to pretend it's your face on every girl I kiss?" The sound of his husky voice whispers softly against my ear. "Wanting it to be your body under me every time that I fuck someone."

A violent tremor racks my system. His words are making me sick and I whimper as I feel his fingers brush across my wounds. They tenderly wrap around my body, and I look down to notice him painting the letters "HHMC" across my heaving chest in my own crimson blood.

"Blood in and blood out," he says, kissing my neck in between his words. "Your fuckin' choice. But know this: it is forever now my blood that runs through your veins. And I will drown you in it before I let you escape me again."

ONE

January 2008

My machine vibrates softly against my palm. I grip it tightly, adding last minute touches to the piece I've been working on for the past four hours. The black ink and ruby red drops of blood seep through my client's pale skin. I gently wipe them away and ease my foot off the pedal that controls the power, to preview my artwork.

The tattoo is flawless in its design. A crimson burst highlights the background perfectly. My heart swells with pride knowing that another beautiful masterpiece came from deep inside of me, that I am still capable of tapping into and releasing the art from within. A smile meant only for me stretches the corners of my mouth.

Tattooing is more than a job, more than a hobby. It is an intimate, emotional, and powerful thing to be marking someone for life. I am giving over a part of myself forever. In return, I am fully in control of my world and everything around me, if only for that small gap in time.

When a piece is carefully thought out and has meaning to my customer, it has double the value to me. I am tied to the art in blood and ink, a part of my soul to be admired by countless others or hidden to be savored only by the wearer. I was destined for this calling. It has been my salvation and redemption from a past that would have destroyed the beauty waiting to be unchained from my soul.

I reach for my spray bottle of antiseptic soap to give the area a quick mist, drying it carefully with a clean paper towel.

"That is the shit." My customer grins at the Chinese water dragon wrapping his cut bicep. It is fitting considering he is a current Olympic-gold-medalist swimmer. He swivels his arm back and forth while still sitting in the chair, trying to get a better angle to admire it.

"There is a mirror on the back wall," I say, indicating the area over my shoulder. He stands to get a full glimpse, while I inspect my art at a distance. It gives me a chance to see if I missed any shading or line work in the reflection. My lips curve upward in pride when I notice that it is about as perfect as possible and that he is obviously sporting "The Look." It is the only gratitude that means anything to us artists.

I turn in my chair to clean my station, but not before catching a flash of light from the corner of my eye. "Hey,"

I exclaim, glancing back to see him taking a picture in the mirror.

"Sorry," he replies, winking a dark eye at me with a sexy smile. "Need to update the Instagram. Fans love it."

I slowly nod, my heart beginning to thunder at the thought of a picture. *Of me.* What are the chances that I am in the mirror's reflection? *Calm down, Keller.*

"Ginger, at the front desk, will go over all the necessary care instructions," I say, standing to wrap the tattoo in clear plastic wrap. I jerk my head, indicating the reception area. He pays no heed to me, seemingly in awe of his new tattoo. He shrugs his shirt on while walking toward her.

Now that I'm able to release my hand from its rigid grasp, my fingers literally throb from the last couple of hours of work. They stick to the latex beneath the rubber gloves, slick with perspiration. I roll my stiff neck from side to side, releasing the pent-up tension. My current euphoric state of mind that my work brings me unfortunately doesn't transcend to my physical being. Not moving for long periods of time is one of the setbacks of tattooing. You have to know your own body's limitations, and four hours without moving is definitely mine.

As I organize my area, the tattoo shop comes alive around me once again. The inner workings of my mind seem to cancel out the people and noise while I'm tattooing. When I finish, they flood back in and I am ripped away from the world of skin and art—my escape. But if I have to be torn away from the passion that feeds my soul, other than owning my own shop, this is the best place imaginable.

Screaming Ink has the perfect layout. It is wide open with its circular floor plan. Silver metal plating covers the walls with art designs cut strategically throughout. When clients enter the front door, they are greeted by our receptionist, Ginger, who just happens to be my first real girl-pal. After listening to the customer's choice of body art, either piercing or ink, she matches each client with the artist who best suits.

I glance over to our waiting area where clients sit in plush black leather chairs, enjoying the 360-degree view of all the tattoo stations. When it's their turn, they will be directed to one of the six workspaces located around the back wall, separated by half partitions. The owner loves the shop having a large open area, but at the same time, the division of our chairs affords privacy for the artist and customer.

As I clean, I listen to my co-workers who freely discuss the latest Xbox system as they sling ink. Most of the guys and girls I work with seem to be the biggest gamers outside of the shop. Chatter overflows with spawn camps, fragging, and something about getting Leeroyed. This is one of the main reasons that I keep mainly to myself—my childhood never held such luxuries like playing video games. I'm ostracized once again for the upbringing that even now I hide from.

I turn to throw away the plastic baggies that cover my equipment from being saturated in blood plasma and ink mist. Beginning my mental checklist meticulously followed after every tattoo, I dispose of the tubes and ink caps before placing my needle into the sharps container. My area now only needs to be wiped down with a strong medically approved antibacterial agent to be ready for my next client. I know that I need to check my client schedule. It would be a miracle if this were my last one for the night.

My eyes glance up to check the time on the black Kit-Cat clock, its revolving eyes and wagging pendulum tail keeping watch over the shop. I groan when I notice the time. In this business, 10:00 p.m. is sometimes just the beginning of a crazy evening, especially, on a busy college campus like this one. I head toward the front, stretching my arms out in front of me. The whisper of my name slightly slows my pace. I stop, glancing at the first station on my left.

"Keller, that dragon was tight," Malik says, glancing up at me with those pale green eyes of his marking my every move. He doesn't wait for an answer, placing his machine back to work on his current living canvas.

It has been three years since I took that moniker. I feel more like a Keller than a Helen any day. And just like the name that I was given twenty-one years ago, and the name that I stole, I am trying to prevent the limitations from my past from dictating my future. I may not be blind and deaf, but at one time I was, inside. The name was fitting when I ran. It made sense in the madness I was escaping. And now I am Keller; she is me.

I view Malik's work. His gray and black shading is more

vibrant than other artists' colors. I am in awe of the way he brings his art to life on the skin. An extraordinarily gifted tattooist, he worked beside some of the top celebrated names in the business before opening his own shop. A small tingle of something within my body vibrates at his bass voice. It has been a long time since I've been attracted to anyone, but getting involved with my boss cannot be on my radar, so I shut it down big time.

"Thanks," I reply, smiling shyly at him when he looks up at me again. My social awkwardness is a side effect of my family. I glance back down, walking to the reception area. And even though my eyes are trained directly on the floor, my feet still trip over nothing. Good job, *Grace*. To be so fluid at my job, I'm horribly clumsy in everyday life.

I met Malik about a year ago when I stumbled, literally, through the front door of his tattoo shop. I was scouting a new location. At the time, I had been living in Virginia when an old friend of my family drunkenly ambled into the shop while I was working. His being severely inebriated saved my ass. It gave me a much-needed head start to run—straight to a little college town in Ohio.

In this business, it's hard to get a job tattooing unless you detail where you did your apprenticeship and of course, job references. That is a little difficult when you are on the run from your shady past. The type of past where you pray every damn night that the things you have witnessed and personally experienced haven't left you irreparably broken. I left everything behind except my art. I couldn't leave the art, and even now I know it will be my ruin. When I ran, I risked everything to not be the person I was most afraid of being, what that life would have demanded I become.

When I fell through the door that day, I had no idea that I had found my new home. I gave my regular lie to Malik that I was on the run from an abusive ex-husband and his sadistic warped mind, the "Please, Mister, save this lost little girl" spiel. And of course he bought it, like most everyone before him. After four years on the run, the last year here is the longest time spent living anywhere since I left home.

I approach the front desk to find it empty of Ginger or any clients for the moment. She must be on her smoke break. Ginger is the first true friend I have had in years. She knows there is more to my past than the little I have given her, but she never presses me for any of it. My secrets are held tightly within. The life I now fight for and the lives of others depend on my continued silence.

My index finger presses the return key on the keyboard to clear the blank screen of the computer so that I can view my schedule. Yes! I can't contain the happiness of not being booked for the rest of tonight. My head and hips involuntarily bounce to the deep bass of the music playing from the speakers overhead. The lyrics roll silently off my tongue as I block my schedule, wanting to get a jump on the first weekend I have had off in months.

"Are you done for the night?" A deep, masculine voice says, suspiciously close behind me.

I whip around to find Malik. My body freezes at the

intensity dwelling in those translucent eyes of his. He has never asked for more than I've been willing to give. It seems like he wants to ask me out, but he does not cross that line with employees. I have heard him utter on several occasions to fellow coworkers, "You don't shit where you eat, boys." Yeah, I get it. It is the hardcore truth, especially regarding your boss.

"I don't have anything scheduled right now. I'm kind of hoping to head out of here early," I say, biting the inside of my lip. "If that's okay with you?" I know he likes to keep all the chairs filled. No artist, no customers.

"Girl, you know it's good with me," he says, nodding. His thick black dreads bob up and down with the movement of his head. He uncrosses his sinewy arms.

I can't help but appreciate the array of countless tattoos visible on the light brown hue of his skin. He raises his hand toward his mouth, rubbing the dark, manicured hair of his mustache down to his goatee. Those eyes of his never leave mine.

"Any certain clubs you plan on hitting up this weekend?" His cheekbones slightly darken at his own question.

"Nah, not really," I answer. I nervously drop my gaze to the ground. "I may stop by Lowry's before heading home." My own plain brown eyes slowly rise back to his. I watch him nod, then finally look away. He releases a loud exhale.

"Yeah. Be careful, okay? School is back in session and these kids are restless from this cold-ass weather. Drives 'em a little stir crazy. Know what I mean?" Malik turns to look at the schedule on the computer screen. He drags his finger across the keyboard, his silence confirming that we should end this crazy conversation.

"Sure. Yeah," I reply. My own pent-up breath releases in a loud whoosh. Well, it sounds loud to me anyway.

I know that walking away is the best closure, so that is what I do. The woman in me begs to turn back around to invite him out or at least back to my small apartment. But I do neither. Instead, my self-preservation kicks in into high gear and I do the sensible thing, which is to leave him the hell alone. I slide my leather jacket on before locking up my toolbox where I keep most of my everyday supplies. My machine I take home with me inside my rolling suitcase, never knowing when I may have to run. I mutter my goodbyes on the way out as I drag it behind me. Malik nods while everyone else yells "'night" back.

A full-body shiver racks my frame when I step out into the frigid night air. Winter is definitely upon us. The frozen ice crunches underneath my black boots as I move toward my car. My eyes scan the perimeter, seeing more than the average person normally would. I watch carefully and listen closely, the way most people instinctively take their next breath. The world narrows and I see the streetlamps lighting the road, illuminating the drunks and partygoers who line it while listening to the clash of rap, rock, and country music drifting out of the different bars. The pop-pop of a Harley-Davidson motorcycle engine always puts me on edge, which thankfully I don't hear tonight.

"Hey! Wait up, Keller," Ginger says, opening the door and letting it close behind her. She starts out in a run before almost slipping and busting her tiny ass on the ground. Her hands wave furiously in the air while she tries to maintain her balance. Her high-pitch shriek shatters the silence around us. "Freaking, ice. It's colder than a witch's tit out here," she yells.

"Uh, are you okay?" I ask, unable to hide the amusement in my voice. She nods, walking toward me again.

I stop to wait for her. Ginger cracks me up on a regular basis. First off, you never know what color the girl's hair is going to be. As of right this minute, it is a bright canary yellow with burnt orange tips that reach well past her shoulders. It's her eyes, though, that are the most visually stunning aspect of her appearance. The violet contacts she wears are so unnatural that people are dumbfounded for minutes when she first meets them. Her incredibly tall height makes her skinny body seem more willowy than lanky, and she doesn't have a single piercing or tattoo on her virgin skin. I have heard from the moment I started working here that she is planning to get tatted, but that lily-white skin of hers remains unmarked.

"Are you heading over to Lowry's now?" Ginger's strange eyes seem to almost glow in the dark. We both walk over to my rundown Honda parked across the street from the shop.

"Yeah, I think so. What time are you getting off?" I ask, lugging my tools to my trunk to lock them up.

"In about an hour, if we don't get too busy. I'll meet you there," she says, craning her head to see who is out partying

We both turn, walking back toward the sidewalk in front of the shop. Lowry's is located two doors down from here. It's a small bar where most of the locals hang out. Well, mainly the non-collegiate ones.

"Call me if dickhead is there. I'll need to prepare myself to administer a serious butt-kicking since he hasn't called me. No text or nothing. Nada," she says, nudging me with her bony elbow.

Dickhead refers to one of the bartenders at Lowry's whom we both knew was a dog before she even decided to take him home—fleas and all. He evidently rocked her world and now will not call. I say good riddance, but then again, my recent history of unintentional celibacy doesn't really warrant comments from this corner. I keep my mouth shut and just listen like a good friend should.

"I will. Just remember, though, that you attract more bees with honey. It all depends on what statement you're trying to make," I say, hopefully giving her good advice while knowing I am the biggest dork ever. This friend stuff is hard, but I love having someone close to me. I try to sound like it's second nature, having a girl who's a friend, but in all reality, I'm lost as to what to say or do.

She looks confused for about two seconds before

16

shaking her head. "Whatever, Keller. Just call." She turns to walk into the shop.

Well, I thought it sounded good. I head toward Lowry's, sidestepping several shady characters hanging out in front of the bars that line the street. I chant in my head that they don't scare me; this is my life. They can't find me. I force myself to think of something else. Ginger attends the local college, working toward a Bachelor of Arts degree. I have seen her amazing charcoal abstract art. It is sensually dark, actually stirring deep emotions within me—some that I prefer remain locked tight inside. But that is what makes her such a great artist. Her art evokes feelings in me that should never see the light of day… and memories of a certain dark-haired boy that are too painful to remember.

I step into a doorway that has a sign proclaiming *Lowry's* across the outside and a neon beer sign in the dingy window. This small dive is the only place where I feel almost comfortable, other than Screaming Ink. When I look around, I see the roughnecks that I am accustomed to, not the college kids in my everyday life who flash me their virgin skin, marring it for the experience and not the magic.

My skin has been marked in two ways: freely and by force. Both were life-changing experiences. One should have scarred me, forever branding me with hatred for this passion of ink and art, but instead showed me the beauty of choosing living artwork. Every piece that is tattooed on my body will have significant meaning to me whether I'm nineteen or ninety. Even the one that wasn't my choice is a painful lesson in remembrance.

The high-pitched voices from the live girl-band, carries through the small, dank, dark bar. It is cramped with bikers, punks, emo dudes, and hardcore chicks. Anyone who feels and looks different finds anonymity amongst others here. If not for the colorful tattoo sleeves completely covering both of my arms, my numerous chest pieces, and several back tats, I would look like every other college coed walking this campus with my dyed jet-black hair barely reaching my shoulders and toned, lithe build. But with my tats, nose piercing, little black tube dress, matching leather jacket, and killer biker boots, no one gives me another glance. I'm just one of them. I might look the same as those I run from, yet I'm radically different. No one owns me, nor controls my actions here. They don't dictate my future or signify my past. I revel in precious freedom amongst strangers who feel like old friends.

I find an empty barstool at the end of the aged wooden bar. A cloud of thick cigarette smoke burns my eyes and clogs my throat. It wears off only seconds before the bartender comes over to take my drink order, smiling at me. Thankfully, it's not the dickhead, but a familiar female bartender. I am sure she doesn't know me by name, but recognizes me as a regular.

"Cherry Coke, right?" she asks, the rings in her thin eyebrows, broad nose, and mouth a matching bright fuchsia tonight.

"Yeah, thanks." I reply, giving her a smile for remembering my drink order. Especially, considering I don't drink anything heavier than soda.

I shrug my jacket off of my shoulders before letting it slide down my arms. My hands catch it so that I can lay it on my lap. I contort my body sideways on the barstool, watching the enigmatic band on stage. It is the first time I have ever heard them play and I'm surprised at their immense talent. The beats are solid, the melody a darkness that blends with the occupants easily.

"Can I buy you a drink?" A voice asks over the music. "I'm a sucker for a girl with flames tattooed on her arm."

I glance over at a fine male specimen leaning on the bar. He is definitely my type with his rough exterior. Tattoos cover the majority of his skin that I can see, including his bald head. His preference for facial piercing is a definite turn-on, but it is the kind look in his eyes that is usually the most attractive feature for me. And as much as I want to accept, something cautions me to decline. I've said yes to his type before, only to find that something stops me from sharing my body and mind, just as I don't share the secrets I hide.

"No, thanks. I'm waiting for someone," I say, smiling at him.

He nods, seeming disappointed. Yeah, you and me both, I think to myself. My eyes find the tattoo he is referring to on my upper arm. Red and orange ink shade inside black outlined flames, carefully designed so that they come together to form a heart in the center. They were lovingly inked on my body years ago. Not my first tattoo, but one that reminds me of a painful time in my life. I stare at it. The memory it evokes takes me back to somewhere long forgotten and by the time my drink arrives, I'm already transplanted to the past I can never escape.

TWO

June 1998

Stepmothers are stupid with a capital "S" and so are dads who never come home, I think to myself as I wipe the dumb tears away. I slam the door to my and my little sister Tara's room, locking it behind me. My hands automatically cover my ears, ignoring whatever Paula is screaming on the other side.

"Some wady called looking for daddy today. She said it's his new gwaddam girlfriend," Tara says, her lisp worse when she gets upset. She is pretty smart for a five-year-old.

I remove my hands and step away from the closed door. That would explain what crawled up Paula's butt and died.

"That claptrap better quit yelling," I say, marching back and forth across my room. I have no idea what a claptrap is, but it sounds a lot like Paula.

School ended for summer last week and I hate being home all day with her. Today started out good because I went swimming at Holden's house with his best friend, Mikey. Tara can't swim, so Daddy says she has to stay at home. Holden's daddy and my daddy have been best friends since they were little.

Holden says that Ward told him that he is my protector. Ward is his daddy, but for some dumb reason he calls him Ward. I tell that crazy boy that just because he is three years older than me don't mean he is my boss. He is stupid if he thinks he can tell me what to do. I'm almost taller than him by a half an inch. He complains that he hasn't hit his growth spurt yet, but whatever.

"You little shit! Open this damn door right now!" Paula yells, the sound of her fist pounding on the other side of the door.

I jump back, the harsh sound scaring me a little. Lately it seems she gets madder and meaner the more she drinks. She hates me—I know she does. I try to stay out of her way, making good grades and stuff like that. But I don't know why she doesn't like me. She grinds her teeth when she looks at me sometimes. I hope they break off in her mouth one day.

"Helen Rudder, you open up this instant," she screams.

"Go, Hels. She won't hurt me." Tara begs, reaching for my arm and looking up with fear in her matching plain brown eyes. We both also have the same blonde hair as our mother did. Maybe that is why Paula hates me. She has nasty black witch's hair. I bet she wishes she had princess hair like ours. No, that can't be it. Tara has the same and she doesn't seem to bother her like I do for some reason. It has to be something else about me.

"She can kiss my A double S!" I let a loud yelp out. A burning starts inside of my chest. My breaths seem to come faster like I've run for a long time and I want to hit something. I never curse, but for some reason I think now is the perfect time.

"Pease, don't say that, Hels," Tara says, looking over at the door like a scared, old cat now.

"I hate her, Tara. One day somebody's going to hit on her and I'm going to laugh like…" I pause, not knowing what I'll laugh like. "Like a… monkey. And I don't know why you are being such a chicken now. She never touches or yells at you." Inside, I secretly hate that she likes Tara and not me. It makes me mad at Tara sometimes. I march over to the window and slide it up, hoisting myself up to straddle the ledge. I have long legs like my momma did and it makes it easier to climb in and out.

"One day, I'm going to be bigger than her and then let her try to scream at me," I mumble through gritted teeth. Taking one last look at Tara, I shake my head at her. "Don't let her in. Give me a couple of minutes then shout through the door that I went out the window. Follow me if she doesn't leave you alone. Okay?"

"'Kay," she replies, giving me that little kid smile with two missing front teeth. No tooth fairy visits for us, like I hear other kids talk about at school. It's not fair.

I turn and drop to the ground only a couple of feet down. I start to run, looking back to make sure Paula isn't peeking out of the window, when my body slams into something or someone.

"Girl, where the hell are you running off to now?" Daddy asks, grabbing hold of me.

My heart wants to beat out of my chest. I look down to see his greasy hand tightly gripping my arm. He jerks me nearer toward him, the smell of stale cigarettes and beer on his breath makes me want to puke. When he holds me tighter, I'm too close to the stink and stain of oil from the cars he works on at the garage, that cover his t-shirt. My eyes follow the patches up his black motorcycle cut to see his face. His skin scrunches together like one of those wrinkly dogs that run wild in the backyard.

I remember when I was little how his eyes were like the blue of a summer sky. My momma once told me if it weren't for those damn eyes, she would have kept on looking. I never knew what she would have kept on looking for though. Now his eyes are bloodshot most of the time. That is what Paula calls it anyway. We both turn our heads toward the single-wide trailer when we hear her yelling my name.

"Paula's mad 'bout something," I murmur.

"That bitch is always pissed at something I'm doing. She knew the life when she said I do," he says, letting me go. He reaches into the pocket of his cut for his cigarette and lighter. "She's more of a fuckin' headache than she's worth." I watch him place the smoke in his mouth.

When he flips the lid up on the lighter, I stare at the flame that appears. The orange and red colors look so angry within the fire, both fighting each other to be the brightest. He brings it to the tip of the cigarette, burning the end before closing the lighter. I look up into his face again and watch him blow out a white, fluffy smoke cloud.

"Go back in there and say you're sorry. Get her off the warpath and my damn back," he commands.

"Hey! I didn't do nothin' to her." I stamp my flip-flop against the sandy dirt. Something gritty squishes between my toes.

"Nobody said you did, kid. And I really don't give a fuck. Get your little ass in there and smooth this shit over. Nobody's getting supper with her in this mood," he says, the cigarette hanging out of his mouth as he speaks.

My daddy scares me. Not that he has ever hit me, but I know he wouldn't hesitate to give me something to cry about. I stare up at him. Somehow him not touching me at all is scarier than if he hit me all the time.

"Fuckin' females. Worthless, the lot of 'em." He turns to walk toward his motorcycle. He loves that thing more than me. More than Tara.

My ears hear the words that he mutters. He doesn't care about me. He has never wanted me, or my sister. It feels like I have swallowed a big, fat cotton ball and it's stuck right in my throat. I hate him. I hate Paula. I wish he weren't my dad.

I turn and dash for the woods. My small feet carry me faster into the trees behind the trailer park. Every few steps, I stumble so I put my arms straight out at my sides, trying my best to keep balance. I hear Daddy hollering, but it doesn't stop me. His screams push me deeper, but I stay clear of the swamp. A batch of thorny weeds whips against my knees, lashing painful scratches across my chicken legs, but I keep running. They hurt less than her slaps and his words.

Paula is drunk as a skunk. She has only been his old lady for the last two years, but dated him for much longer. Tara, my little sister, was not even a year old when my dad first brought her home. I guess I was about seven at that time. My real mom died in a motorcycle accident when Tara was only months old. My dad went through our home madder than I had ever seen him and tore down all of her pictures, including the ones with us in it. I hid one underneath my mattress, a photo taken at the hospital of my mom, Tara and me, surrounded by my dad's friends, the Hell's Highwaymen Motorcycle Club.

My dad spends more time with those dumb guys than he ever has with any of us, including Paula, the puke head. The only time we get to have with him are dinner some nights and when he takes us to cookouts at the clubhouse next to Dawson's Garage where he works. The club is the Hell's Highwaymen Motorcycle Club or MC. My dad said that he and Ward started the MC back when they were teenagers. Ward owns the garage and built the clubhouse. He says they're the only family that matters to us.

I race until I don't hear her or him screaming my name anymore, only the silence of the woods, which creeps me out. The sun is starting to fall and I am not sleeping out here in the dark. I don't want to be alligator bait. I have never run from my dad in my life, probably because he's usually never home. There is only one place that I can go and be safe.

By the time I walk through the clearing to Holden's house, I'm out of breath, but I'm happy I made it just in time. The sun has gone and hid from the daytime again. Hold's home is a big two-story house that seems huge compared to mine. I stop to watch his mom, Sage, folding clothes as she removes them from the wire hanging between two trees. Her midnight hair whips around her from the wind that is picking up. She wears tight blue jeans and body-hugging shirt like all of the other MC old ladies who like showing off their boobs. Paula calls her the HBC or head bitch in charge, and actually seems pretty scared of her. Sage has always been nice to me, but I don't want her to notice all the bloody scrapes that now cover both my legs. They really hurt and I don't want her or nobody touchin' them.

There is a trellis—Hold calls it that—placed next to his bedroom window. I slowly climb up the white wood frame, ignoring the twinges of pain from the scrapes. My arms shake by the time I crawl through his window and land directly on top of his twin bed. The boy always leaves it open in the summertime for me to climb through. I've been escaping here for years. His parents know it and he says that they're cool that I come here.

I take my once-pink flip-flops off and sling them to the

floor. A hiss escapes me when I accidentally brush my hand against a long, thin cut that reaches from my knee all the way down to my ankle. Something wet slides down my cheek. I hurry and wipe it away. Stupid tears.

My head hits the bed hard, like a ton of bricks, as I lie down. The painful scratches rub against his blanket, but I ignore it, curling into a ball to face the wall. I stare at the motorcycle posters, burying my nose in Hold's pillow. His sheets always smell so good. It's the same scent as the baby powder I used to sprinkle on Tara's butt as a baby. I think his mom changes them all the time. Paula washes mine once a month if I'm lucky. Maybe, I can get Hold's mom to show me how to wash mine and Tara's.

I turn my head toward the door when I hear it creak open and rush to sit up. Holden walks through in his blue pajama pants, matching t-shirt, and toothbrush. He stops when he sees me on his bed.

"Bitch Paula again?" He shakes his head when I nod. "I can talk to Ward like last time. See if that helps. My mom said she better not lay a hand on you," he says. He starts to say something else but stops when he sees my legs. I watch his face turn redder than a tomato and his blue eyes widen so big, they remind me of those plastic alien eyes. "I am going to kill her myself. Did she do that?" He points his toothbrush toward my legs.

I violently shake my head back and forth. "No, I ran to get away and the weeds got me. Don't you dare say anything, Holden Lee Dawson. Do you hear me?" The last time he did, my dad cussed Paula out so bad that he made her cry. Things were better for a week, before they turned the worst ever. I swore I would never mention any of it ever again.

"You better not be lying to me," he says, pointing his toothbrush at me again.

"I wouldn't lie for that pig," I say, knowing I would in a heartbeat if it meant she would leave me alone.

"I don't know why your dad lets her treat you like that. It's not right, Hels." He places his toothbrush down before walking over to switch off the lights.

"It doesn't matter. When I get bigger, I ain't gonna live here anyway. I'll take Tara and go far, far away. You just wait, Hold. I'll marry someone rich and famous. We will have a big 'ole house, fancy cars, and nice clothes. Better than Jenny Smith and her stupid friends."

"Scoot over," he says, sliding next to me on the bed. His voice sounds like he is mad at me. "You don't know what you're sayin'. You're just a little kid."

"I do too know what I am sayin'. I am eleven and you're only three years older than me. That don't make you smarter. I make all A's." I draw my fist back, letting it go to punch him in the shoulder.

He rubs it, pretending it hurts, while shaking his head at me. "No, you don't. The club is our life—yours and mine. Ward has told me that we are the future and he is setting it up so that we'll have all those cool things you want. One day, I will be running the club and you won't have to worry no more about Paula. And you will have everything nicer than what Jenny Smith and those mean girls have. I promise you, Hels."

"I hate Paula," I whisper, tired. "I hate him."

"I know," he says, quietly. "Listen, tomorrow we'll hang out and swim off the boat ramp all day. We'll even take Tara with us. Okay? Just lie down and go to sleep."

I watch him crawl underneath the covers. We both lie still, next to each other, staring at the fluorescent lights of his glow-in-the-dark planets stuck on the ceiling. The sound of his breathing comforts me. Hold is my best friend. None of the other girls around town talk to me. They never have. He has been the only friend I have known other than Tara, but she is just a baby.

Once his breathing slows and I know that he is sleeping, I quickly grab hold of his hand. I wish that Tara could feel as safe as I do right now. The stupid water starts to fill my eyes again and I shut them tight. I keep them closed, praying silently that the pain in my chest that is making me shake all over doesn't wake Hold.

The sound of doors slamming and loud angry voices wakes us. I leap up first, sweeping my long blonde hair back from my face and the dreamless sleep from my eyes.

"What is going on?" Hold asks sleepily. He yawns while sitting up in his bed. His black hair stands straight up all over his head. I watch him run his fingers through it, mussing it worse than before.

"Don't know." I look out the window to see that it is still dark outside. The sound of someone's feet pounding up the stairs scares me. Holden's door swings wildly open. We both jump when it slams against the wall behind it.

"Thank fuck's sake," Ward whispers, his massive body blocking the doorway.

We both watch him stumble into the room and fall heavily to his knees. He lowers his head and clutches at his chest. His big, muscled body trembles like he can't stop it. Hold's mom runs in next. Sage looks weirdly at Hold and me before falling on the bed, reaching out to roughly grasp both of us. I notice the red of her eyes and the tears that overflow them.

Something strange is happening here. I pull away to look over at Ward. There is this sadness that creeps me out coming from Sage, but it's Ward who scares me. He is running both hands over his face, down his long, dark beard. I can't help but notice he has on the same clothes that my dad always wears. A white t-shirt covered by the club's black leather cut and jeans. The difference is the word "President" patched on his chest where my dad's spells "Vice President."

"Come here, darling," he says. Ward's big ham hands motion for me to come to him.

Ward isn't someone I have been around a lot in my life, only at cookouts at the club where all the kids like myself are told to scat and every once in a while when he is at home and I'm here with Hold. He mainly ignores me, which is okay, considering he's kind of scary. I have never

31

had a reason not to like him, so I slip out beneath the covers, tiptoeing over to him. He offers his hand, pulling me tightly in for a bear hug that swallows me up. My nose wrinkles at the smell of burning fire that covers him.

His voice sounds gruffer than normal, almost like he has a sore throat. He clears it several times before speaking in my ear. His humongous body shakes against mine. Is he cold?

"Helen, there is something I need to tell you, girl," he starts, but pauses before continuing. "There was a…" he stops once again, his voice sounding weird. "I need to tell you something." He pushes me gently from him, gripping my scrawny arms in his large hands.

With Ward on his knees, I am eye level with him. Large tear drops pool in the creases of his scraggly face, shocking me for a minute. Something bad has happened. Something really, really terrible. Men like him, like my dad, never cry.

For a minute, I don't want to hear it. I want to scream at him to shut up. Just don't say it and whatever it is can't be real. My heart starts galloping wildly in my chest, hurting from near bursting. I jerk away to try and break free from his hands, but he doesn't let me.

"Don't say it." I scream, bucking my body back to make him release me. I don't know what it is. I don't want to know. I shake my head back and forth, closing my eyes tightly together. Keep them out! Don't listen, I tell myself. Don't feel. Adults lie. My own tears flow from the corners of my eyes. A black monster grows in my belly, eating all the blood and guts inside. I whimper, feeling it now, an emptiness. Something inside of me is missing. Lost. Gone forever. "Tara," I whisper, the air leaving my lungs. My knees buckle and I fall, damaging my already shredded legs.

"She's gone. Paula. Your dad," he quietly says, his voice sounding as broken as I feel. "A fire. Everything burned to the ground while they slept. That cunt probably fell asleep with a cigarette in her drunk-ass hand. My brother Sam… my… gone."

Ward stands, leaving me frozen on the floor. I can't breathe. I. CAN'T. BREATHE.

He walks to the door, facing away from us. "We thought you were in there, too, but when they couldn't find a fourth… we hoped you were with Holden. Now don't you worry, girl. I have connections. You're one of us. The Hell's MC is your family and we take care of our own. This is your home now."

I don't hear his words. I can't look at any of them as my entire body starts shaking. My teeth chatter, snapping together so loudly it clangs in my head. I can't stop it. My baby sister. The one who never had a mother to love her, no memories of her like I had. Her sweet breath as she lay next to me at night, scared as I was, never knowing what tomorrow would bring. Her giggle that was magical to hear, because she hardly ever got a chance to laugh. Please no. NO! I rock back and forth, trying to stop all these memories that crowd my brain.

"Please give her back." I wrap my arms around my knees, praying to a God that doesn't know me. No one's ever took me to that church place on Main Street where he evidently lives. My heart hurts. Ward's words reached in and snatched it right out. I'm afraid to look down, knowing I'll see the big hole where it used to be. I forget all about the scratches from earlier. "Just give her back!" I scream at the ceiling.

I feel someone roughly grab my arms, lifting and turning me, hauling me tightly against something hard. His bony chest feels larger than life and I latch on. He is the only person who has ever been there for me, the only one to never hurt me, the only one I can possibly allow near me now. My only family. Holden.

Chapter THREE

January 2008

Anyone who cleans on a day off should be shot. Accordingly, my bathroom has not been scrubbed down in my rundown one-bedroom apartment for months—if ever. I stand to stretch my back muscles out, noting that a popping sound accompanies every bend. Damn, I am a hot mess. I can't help but notice my tired reflection in the oval mirror above the sink. My doe eyes, which are normally enhanced by the tilt at the corners, are dull and lifeless. I look more like the Beast than Belle, with my hair sticking out around my head, a reject from the 80's hairband days. You know it is time for another dye job when you can see the blonde bleeding through the black locks, looking too much like gray. *Eek!*

Fatigue shouldn't be plaguing me, with the time I took

to rest this weekend, but Friday's trip down memory lane has prohibited the sleep that should have taken care of the blue bruising underneath both of my eyes. Ginger joined me at the bar for drinks after she got off that night, but I was already wanting to leave. My head was filled with too many thoughts that I couldn't share, leaving me with nothing to say to her.

Saturday was much better. Ginger came by and we spent the entire day shopping and hanging out… and laughed so hard I almost peed my panties, especially when we gossiped about the weirdos who came into the shop that week, and which hot boy in a perfect world we would hook up with. It was great, but now I have to reap the consequences of putting off the cleaning. I turn to walk back into my bedroom, blowing away a stray lock of hair that continues to fall in front of my eye. The sound of my cell phone ringing changes my direction, and I walk to retrieve it from my bag. When I glance down, I see that it is Malik's number. My head cocks in interest.

"This is Keller," I answer, chewing on my lip in excited expectation of his impromptu phone call.

"Hey, girl. Sorry to bother you, but I need your help," he says, using his no-nonsense business voice.

Not interesting. Like any good employee, I know what that line means when the boss calls on my day off. I try to hold my groan in unsuccessfully.

"Listen, I've got three guys who didn't show up for their scheduled chairs and I desperately need to fill them. I've got a waiting room full of clients and two artists available including myself. Please Keller, come save my ass," he begs. I can imagine him tugging on one of his dreads as he talks. It's what he does when he is pissed that other asshole employees don't take their jobs seriously.

I whine a little before answering him. I know he can't see me, but I roll my eyes dramatically as I stomp the floor.

"Keller," he starts.

"I'm coming. I'm coming." I chant. Now I am pissed that I even answered the damn phone. What was I thinking? What? That he was going to ask me out, or something like that? It takes me only seconds to press the end key, but minutes to calm myself to keep from throwing my cell phone across the room. It's not the phone's fault.

I march back into my bathroom to turn the shower on to warm. The only positive about that call was no more cleaning. I have an honest excuse from myself. It doesn't take long to wash up, and even a shorter time to get dressed and ready. I'm not really a girly girl. Fortunately, I was blessed with my mom's natural beauty, needing little to no makeup. The Cherokee Indian blood that ran through my ancestors on my dad's side leaves a yearlong sun-kissed look to my skin. I thankfully washed a load of clothes earlier this morning so I grab a pair of clean skinny jeans to pour my body in and I add to that my "It's Not Ink… It's Art" t-shirt. It pretty much says it all.

On the way out, I grab a can of Diet Coke before leaving my apartment. I'll need all the caffeine I can digest for the duration of the day. My mind is so full of the list of chores that I had planned on accomplishing that I miss the bottom step, and my feet fly outward. I grunt as my not-padded-enough butt lands on the concrete ground hard, sending shooting pains ricocheting up my spine. The wind is knocked completely out of my chest, forcing me to gasp for air. My soda stains the ground in brown bubbles around me.

I remain motionless in a stunned silence for what seems like an eternity, before busting out laughing. It hits me that this is a life of normalcy—from the weekend rushing by, to my cleaning my home on a day off. Now, getting called into work is the oh-so-freaking cherry on top. I have been so caught up in myself, in this life I am making, that I realize I have relinquished some fear of my past. It is a miraculous moment and I am no longer pissed at getting called in, but excited to get to work.

The day flies by in a flurry of stencils and ink. It seems that everyone decides that they want a tattoo today. Around lunchtime, it starts raining, turning the wet drops into a sprinkling of snow showers. The colder the weather becomes, the more people who roll into the shop. Tattoo artist love drunk nights and rainy days. It's considered our rush hour. Most of the pieces requested are very simple. Normally, I would spend time painstakingly ensuring my client is one hundred percent emotionally invested in the tattoo he or she is getting. Well, that is, until it's rent time and the waiting room is packed with serious spenders. Then I think to myself, come on, big money.

I am lost in a palette of colors, etching my own private world and doing what I love best. The hum of my machine is sweeter than the ambient music. I could live the rest of my life doing only this. It is worth the cramping and sore muscles at the end of the day. Some of my clients chatter relentlessly through the process while others respect the silence. I can ignore them both to do what I do best: tattoo.

At some point, darkness falls outside. It is my only recognition of time passing. I have just finished my fourth tattoo and take my time to clean since the rush has slowed. My niche is more fine lines and photorealistic art. I love the realism brought to life on my canvas, but lately script pays the bills and does not take me as long to complete.

"If I tat out one more pussy tenderfoot, I am going to scream," Billy says, referring to the clients who cannot handle the pain. She is the only other female artist in the shop.

I look over to see that we are all in between customers. Billy wipes down her station while Malik looks at something on his laptop.

"The last motherfucker cried the entire time. I really don't see how you can block that shit out," she says, looking pointedly at me.

"It's a gift," I say, smiling at her.

"My girlfriend had her clit tatted and pierced without making a sound," she huffs, obviously priding herself on the fact.

"I also heard Rachel likes to be gagged and tag-teamed," Malik says, cutting his eyes to me. He shakes his head before looking back at his laptop screen.

I muffle my laugh, but not before Billy gives me the evil eye. We all know about Billy's girlfriend because she is pseudo-famous in the adult entertainment business.

"Her job is strictly for dicks and real life is about the chicks," she says.

"At least you got the plural part right about dicks," Malik says.

These two are closer than their bickering indicates. Billy is the Caucasian female version of Malik, with her smooth, heavily tatted skin and long, bleached-white dreads that cover her head. She is also pierced in every possible place imaginable, which includes two massive gauges in her ears. She has never revealed her age, but I would guess it to be around twenty-eight—same as Malik's. They joke constantly, showing love for each other with their snarky comments.

"Hey, at least I got a date to the prom. I don't ever see anyone with you two losers. And we all know that Malik will never ask only-the-lonely Keller out anyway. Plus, you wouldn't say yes if he did. Losers," she says, sitting back in her own chair while smiling at us.

A burning heat flushes my cheeks and no doubt they would be fire-engine red if I looked at a mirror. Why did she just say that? I anxiously glance over at Malik to see him glaring at her. What do I say? *As if you would say anything, Keller.* An awkward silence permeates the room, except for her foot swinging loudly against the chair.

"C'mon, you two. You act like nobody has bloody eyes in their sockets. Malik looks at you like he wants to eat you for breakfast and you look like you either want to let him or run. I am leaning more toward running." She looks directly at me. "For the sake of the shop, please just fuck and get it over with."

"Step carefully, B," Malik says, his voice a low rumble.

"Geez! Can't anyone take a joke up in here?" Billy gets up, reaching for her jacket. "While we are slow, I am going to grab us all some subs for dinner."

I watch her stroll up to talk to Ginger before walking through the door, plowing through a group of guys coming into the shop. I am almost afraid to look at Malik because of the embarrassment coursing through me. *Wow... just... wow.*

"You know, I could fire her but for only one problem," Malik says, placing his laptop down to stand.

I clear my throat before answering. "What's that?" My voice comes out gravelly and deep. Oh, no. I am not meaning for it to go all sultry.

"She is one hundred percent correct," he says, shrugging his shoulders.

"But you're never going to ask me out. Are you?" I ask, knowing the answer before he opens his mouth.

"No," he says, after a moment's pause.

I am more relieved than disappointed, which surprises me. The attraction between us has always been strong—I guess in more ways than one. I always thought that when my life became settled, if it ever did, something might possibly happen between us. But now I know for sure. It is more comforting to be assured that I will not lose him as a friend by messing it up with anything else.

"Good," I say.

"Huh?" The look of confusion on his face is priceless.

I laugh, only because I cannot hold back my reaction from his comic expression. I don't imagine that Malik gets rejected much, if ever.

"I'd much rather have you for a friend and boss than be just some ex and unemployed," I say.

He walks up to me, his head shaking. His hands rest on his waist.

"True that. Look, I have never pressed you for your past and I won't. Ever. But one day, you will meet someone who will break all your barriers. When you need that friend, come find me. I will always be here for you, Keller," he says, leaning in to whisper quietly against my ear. "You feel me?"

I nod, knowing that he is wrong. I will never let my barriers down, because the day that I do, will be the day that I die. That is what happens to foolish people. He slowly leans back, letting me see the sincerity in his eyes.

"Hey guys, I have your next clients up and ready." Ginger announces. Her words connect us to reality.

Malik turns away, nodding to Ginger. I do the same. I

guess Billy did us both a favor by forcing us to clear the air. I owe her a big thank-you when she gets back—and money for dinner. The sound of Malik's customer greeting him prompts me to look up at my next client. Great. Just what I need—another frat boy who has a hard-on for a tat.

He smiles before reaching me. Several strands of brown hair escape from underneath a gray beanie. I can't help but notice his defined muscled chest that he proudly displays, letting it peek out of his semi-unzipped black hoodie, no shirt underneath. Douche alert! However, I have to give him mad props for sporting some sexy, hip, threadbare jeans.

"Hey," he says, offering his hand to shake.

I look down at his outstretched arm before glancing up at him. He's got at least five inches on me. I would guess probably around six-two or even taller. And handsome in that scruffy, college-boy way—all chiseled jaw with just a hint of a five o'clock shadow, which seems to float most women's boat, but so not me. He looks confused when I don't grasp his hand. For some odd reason, I don't want to take it. I guess I'm over this everyday type of client, but this is what pays the bills. So I plaster a smile on my face and reach for the hand that he still offers. My small one slides into his, and I instantly jerk my arm away. I don't like how his size dwarfs me. It reminds me too much of someone who I'd rather never think of again. I resist the urge to wipe my hand against my jeans.

"Hi. What tattoo are you getting today?" I ask, almost too quickly. I turn away from him to walk toward my workstation, listening closely as he follows behind me.

"Something really simple. A date. I was thinking all numerals in black ink," he says.

I stop and change direction to look at him after that statement. *Oh my God.* Is he for real? Does he think I'm stupid? Like I am going to spell out all the numbers? Maybe he thinks I'm going to Egyptian hieroglyph his ass. Stupid college boys always assume I am dumb just because of the number of tats covering my body. I may not have a high school diploma, but I have life lessons that would outsmart them any time of the day.

"Uh, numbers. Just simple numbers is fine," he stammers, as I move toward my area obviously ignoring him

I have already prepared my space for my next customer, so I indicate for him to have a seat. He slowly sits down and I watch him look nervously at my instruments. Ah. He really is a tat virgin.

"Is this your first tattoo?" I watch his body language for signs that I can talk him out of it. For some reason, I do not want to ink him. I can't explain it. It definitely could be his body size, but for the life of me, I have no desire to touch him.

"Uh… yeah," he says. His face pales when he glances up at me. "I'm not a big needle fan."

He actually has russet-colored eyes. I've used that particular shade to paint a thousand times in my lifetime, but have never seen someone with eyes that match it exactly. I stare into rich brown irises that have a reddish-orange tinge around his pupils. His eyes are deep-set with a slight slant at the corners, hinting of someone exotic down the family tree. I catch myself gazing stupidly at him. *What are you doing, Keller? Snap out of it!* My inside voice screams at me.

I look around to see if Billy is back. She would kill me for trying to pawn off another tenderfoot on her. I glance over to see that Malik is already gearing his machine up to tattoo his client. Taking a deep breath, I return my eyes to his. He is still staring at me.

"You know, I always advise my customers to be one hundred percent sure before getting a tattoo. If there is any doubt, then you should go home and think about it for another twenty-four hours. That will give you time to decide if this process is for you or not, especially now that you have seen everything for yourself." I gulp in air, saying all that in one rushed breath.

I watch closely for his reaction, and it surprises me. Instead of the nervousness that I expect, I now feel a calm radiating from him. I'm not sure where it comes from, but it throws me into left field.

"Well, that makes me feel better," he says, his voice revealing a slight Southern accent.

"What does?" Now I am completely and utterly confused.

"I am guessing that date tattoos are fairly simple and easy money makers," he says. "Am I right?"

"For me they are," I answer honestly. I have no idea where he is going with this.

"Well, you could have taken my money and slapped the tattoo on, but instead, you took the time to possibly talk me out of it. And offer good advice," he says, with a crooked smile.

"Does this mean you're going to wait?" I ask, eagerly awaiting his answer.

He pauses before answering. "No. I'm ready. But, it was nice of you to throw that out there at the risk that I could have walked away."

Damn. In fact, double damn. I take a rush of breath in and sputter a cough out, choking on my own saliva.

"Are you okay?" He stands to try and pat me on the back.

I hold my hands out while moving, not wanting him to touch me. My eyes water from the force of my coughing fit. I barely hear him speaking as he shoves my bottle of water into my hand. In between barks, I take large swallows. The water washes away the tickle in the back of my throat and hopefully the stupidity that is invading my brain. Finally, I am able to speak. "Thanks," I say, barely choking the words out.

"You're welcome. I couldn't let my artist choke to death before I benefit from her talent." He obviously is trying to make light of the situation.

I take several more gulps of the water so that I don't have to reply to his comment. The time actually allows me to think. I can tattoo numbers. I have tattooed so many of them I could do it in my sleep. It should be a breeze. I can't remember why I was even sweating the situation before. Is it my time of the month? It would explain my overly emotional climate this weekend.

"So, you want month, dash date, dash year?" I ask, looking around for the cap to the water bottle.

"Yes. Is this what you are looking for?" He holds up the top.

I nod, reaching for it. My hand hesitates before taking it from him. I try to maneuver myself where I make sure not to touch his long fingers. The whole situation is just ridiculous. My hand actually shakes as I place the top back on my drink before sitting down. I reach for a pair of latex gloves, stretching them on.

"Ginger should have asked you if you had any allergies to latex," I say, needing to immerse myself in my world of art to escape this idiot I'm becoming. "Do you want any particular font?"

"Yes, she did and no, I don't. No allergy and no special font. Whatever you think looks best," he says, sitting back down.

"Where do you want it?" I glance directly into those eyes of his.

"On the left side of my chest," he answers, not hesitating for a second and then his voice drops an octave. "Over my heart." The answer is one I can tell he has carefully thought about.

I don't miss the pain showing deep within his eyes. It calls to me, to my own personal brand of torment. I know what it's like to be connected to something that scars you to the bone, never leaving, always right underneath the skin waiting to get out. I quickly turn away, closing my eyes to steady these off-kilter emotions threatening to expose me. I don't want to share that with him, not with anyone.

"Okay. Beside you is a piece of paper and pencil. I need you to write down the date exactly how you want it and I'll draw something up for you," I say, not looking at him. Having clients physically communicate what they want helps me confirm what they are asking for, especially if I were to tattoo incorrect information. This could help cover me.

In only seconds he hands the paper to me. I reach for some of my stencil paper and stand up to outline some different numerical fonts. Neither one of us says anything into the silence we create. The music playing overhead and the buzz of Malik's machine are the only sounds between us. I take as much time as possible, without being obvious, to stabilize my emotions.

"What's your name?" His voice breaks up the monotony.

Didn't I tell him? I usually introduce myself first, but nothing has been the norm this evening. "Keller," I answer, looking down at the stencil I am still working on.

"Interesting name," he replies.

"Mmm," I say. Though I aimed for a response, it sounds more like a grunt.

"How long have you been tattooing? I hope you take it as a compliment when I say it cannot have been for too long," he says.

I turn my head ever so slightly to look at him. He is sitting back comfortably with his feet up in my chair. His arms are crossed loosely over his chest. It is hard to explain why I have so much experience at my age. People never understand when you tell them you started tattooing at fifteen and that you did it almost every day of your life. When most girls were worried about boys and makeup, I was worried about lines and shading. Not to mention sterilizing my equipment, praying I wouldn't accidentally prick myself, and catch half the diseases the dogs I worked with carried.

"Long enough," I answer. When I am finished, I walk over and hold the stencils out for him to preview.

"Those are good. I really like the first one," he says.

I nod again and turn to cut out the one he chose. "You can take off your hoodie now," I say. I can't help myself when I sarcastically add, "Guess going shirtless is a college fad these days."

"I wouldn't know; I'm not a college student. I'm shirtless because I came to get a tattoo on my chest and figured it would be the easiest course of action—not to mention less painful. I normally don't walk around without a shirt on. I'm not that big of a douchebag," he says, taking the words right out of my mouth.

"Sorry," I mutter, sufficiently put in my place. I take my gloves off and then replace them.

"Why did you do that?" He nods toward my hands.

I know immediately what he is referring to. "I don't want to cross-contaminate any bacteria, so this is part of the process. I should have told you earlier that if you have any questions before and during tattooing to please ask," I say.

This time he nods at me. He removes his hoodie, revealing more of that immaculate chest of his. I've heard of a six-pack, but damn, this guy looks to have double that. Guys who have a body like this work out religiously. That is not a turn-on for me. A gym is a place of punishment in my book; however, I do like viewing the results.

I grab a razor to shave the area, removing any hair from the site—not that he has a lot. The stencil is the tricky part: it has to be positioned symmetrically. I slowly lean down to place it where he requested, right above his left pectoral. My hands slightly shake as I smooth it out over his hard body, applying enough pressure for it to stay. His eyes stray to mine. We are only inches apart. My heartbeat thunders loudly in my head, deafening all common sense. He stares intently into my eyes, searching for something. I should be afraid. Horrified even. Instead, I am curious, a notion almost too alien for me to experience. What did he say his name was? I can't remember if he told me or not.

"What did you say your name was?" I ask, not moving a centimeter away from him.

A puff of air warms my face, the scent of peppermint on his breath is strong. I breathe it in, letting it fill my lungs.

"I didn't," he quietly says. "It's ah… It's… Vin," he

stops. His eyes look away from mine, almost like he is questioning what he told me his name was.

Thank goodness I am not the only one flustered. He looks back up at me and gives a nervous laugh. I guess the idea of getting the tattoo is getting to him. This happens to almost everyone.

"Don't worry. Everyone gets nervous," I tell him, leaning back. "Go look in the mirror and see if it is placed where you want it."

I watch him get up and walk over to look at his reflection. I enlist great restraint in not letting my gaze drift downward to his denim-covered butt, but instead watch his reaction in the mirror. His hand hovers over the stenciled outline. He turns back to sit again.

"It's exactly where and what I want. Let's do this," he says, rubbing his hands together.

"If you are sure," I reply. "Okay, I'm going to go over some basics." I point to the surgeon's steel tray where my equipment sits on a couple of paper towels. "These are my two different machines." I tell him while assembling everything. "One is called a liner machine and the other is a shading machine. You will note that both the needle and tube are in individual, sterilized, unopened packets for each one. This is because they are disposable and will only be used for you. You will see that everything is covered in plastic baggies, including my machine and cord. This is to protect my equipment from the mist of plasma and ink. Again, it helps to ensure no cross-contamination. I am going to pour some black ink in the cap sitting out and we will be ready to go." I place my bottle of ink back in my box after using it. "Any questions?"

"Not yet," he says.

"Alright." I sit down on my rolling stool, sliding next to him. We are both about eye level now. "Just sit back and try not to move. If the pain becomes unbearable, just let me know. We can stop and take a break." I dip my tube into the ink, pressing the power pedal. The humming of my machine completely calms me, reminding me this is what I do best.

I rub a little Vaseline over the stencil and begin the outline. My mind forgets who he is, concentrating on making my lines perfect. I give myself over to complete perfection. Every tattoo, no matter the simplicity, deserves everything inside of me. The numbers display a flair of my artistry in every curvature, my own signature that others can try and replicate, but will always be only mine. My inquisitiveness begs to know the significance of the tattoo. It is a date from ten years ago. I can't believe I haven't asked what it means.

"Can you tell me what the date signifies?" I ask, not taking my eyes away from my work. At first he doesn't answer. I know that many times my clients aren't willing to speak of the meanings behind their particular art. I respect that. On my body resides more than a few with meaning I will never share with anyone.

"I lost someone whom I loved very much," he says, pausing for a second. "My mother actually."

I wait for more of an answer, glancing quickly up to see

him looking at me. I touch his chest with a paper towel, blotting away the blood and ink while I work. My mind wants to ask him for an in-depth explanation, but I can't. I won't.

"Have you ever lost someone whom you loved more than life itself?"

I'm caught unaware at his very personal question—I am actually gutted by his words. I release the pedal beneath my foot, not looking at or answering him. The silence is more pronounced between us without the sound of my machine. I am afraid to glance at him: my insides freeze at his question and my steady hand shakes.

"I'm sorry. I should haven't asked you that," he says, leaning to speak directly into my ear.

My eyes shift upwards to his, our mouths only inches apart. "I guess I asked first. Yeah," I say. "Hasn't everyone?"

"I was admiring your tattoos, especially, the one on your right forearm. For some reason, the bird cage with a pair of angel wings locked inside spoke to me of some type of personal loss." He looks down at the spot to which he's referring.

I glance down at the tattoo. No one has ever guessed out loud what it might allude to before. It is almost as if someone has ripped off a piece of my clothing, baring me to the world. I need a minute—or ten. I push my chair away from him. He has jolted me viciously from my secret world of art.

"Listen, I am evidently way out of line," he starts.

I hold up my hand to halt his words. My instinct is to run when anyone asks too many questions. Unfortunately, I cannot walk away unless I want to redress my entire area. I have to be sensitive to contamination issues. He starts to sit up, but I stop him.

"Sit back," I say, pointing at him. I slide my chair next to him. "You want to know about my tattoo?" I don't wait for an answer. I press the pedal down, putting needle to skin. For me, it's easier to talk about the tattoo than specifically about whom I have lost. "That tattoo is meant to represent someone I love very much. While on this earth, they are trapped in a life not of their making. The angel wings are a representation of their inner goodness, too good for the world they were born into. If you look closely, there are small feathers that are falling to the bottom of the cage." I am shocked at what I just revealed. It is not like me to share something so personal.

"There is no door on the birdcage," he says.

"No, there isn't."

"Is that on purpose?"

"Yes."

For the duration of time, he doesn't utter another word. I wipe his tattoo down before sliding my chair back to preview my work. Hallelujah! I am finished.

"You done?" he asks.

"Yep. Take a look at it in the mirror and then I'll wrap it for you. You'll be ready to go." I watch him walk over to inspect his tattoo. It looks aesthetically fine to me. Should someone ever glance upon it, he or she will see only a date, but for Vin it will mark a time that forever scarred his soul. Never to forget. As I start to shift my eyes away, I catch his in the mirror. They stare directly back at me. I see more than just the color now, something that scares the bejesus out of me. A connection. His hand hovers over where I just tatted him. He mouths "thank you" in the reflection. I nod before standing.

He walks back over. Without saying anything, I carefully place a strip of plastic wrap over his tattoo. I tape each side down. The entire time, I can feel his eyes boring into me.

"Ginger, at the front, will go over all the necessary care instructions. You can head that way when you're ready," I say, turning so I can begin to clean my area. I look over to see Malik still working on his customer while Billy pierces another, singing the lyrics to "Soul to Squeeze" that is playing overhead.

"Keller, would you like to have coffee sometime?"

His voice surprises me for a second. I look over and don't hesitate before answering him. "I'm sorry. I stay pretty busy." My heart doesn't skip beats; it skips entire lines. I feel like I am going to hyperventilate, not because of his question, but because I want him to leave.

"Did I do or say anything to piss you off? If so, let me make it up to you. I've been pretty nervous tonight, with getting my first tattoo and might have said something to offend you accidentally," he says, placing his hoodie back on and zipping it all the way up. "I'm here on a work project and I only know a few people in town."

"We aren't allowed to date customers," I say, which isn't a lie. It is the truth. Sort of. Malik has warned that it is not a good idea; however, it's not a policy or anything. I busy myself at my station so that I don't have to look at him.

"That's the great thing about coffee—it doesn't have to be a date. C'mon, just say yes. Put me out of my misery. Two friends having espresso... lattes... cappuccinos... whatever you women drink these days," he says, smiling.

"Whatever we women drink these days?" I ask, sarcastically raising my eyebrow at him. "I drink black coffee, thank you very much."

"I am digging a deep hole for myself," he says, uttering a nervous laugh. "Okay, I think I'll stop there and say thank you for the tattoo. It is absolutely amazing. I don't think I'll ever experience it again, because I'm a wuss. But hey, never say never, right?" He starts to walk away, before stopping and slowly turning around. He begins to say something, but pauses and shakes his head before looking once more at me.

Something happens. I cannot explain it. But when he looks at me for the last time, something deep passes between us. An electrical current runs through my body, heating everything in its path and I know something uniquely different is passing me by. The question is, will I let it? Minutes tick away with neither of us saying anything—my definite answer. He finally bows his head, then turns to walk up to Ginger to complete payment.

I turn back to finish cleaning my station. A large wad of

emotion is lodged in my throat. I look down at my arm, at the tattoo that caught his attention. It is hard to run from my past when it is clear for the world to see. I must have wanted to share it the only way I knew how, the only way that didn't get me, or the people around me killed. It is really fitting considering a tattoo started all of this—and could have been the reason I ended it all.

FOUR

October 2001

He is the biggest idiot that I know. I stand looking at him, wanting to throw everything in my hands at his big head. And considering it is every single one of my textbooks, I really could knock his stupid ass out. Which is probably what the dumb lug needs—someone to knock some sense into that dense brain of his.

"Calm down, Hels," he pleads, backing up to stand behind his motorcycle. The sunlight bounces off his chrome wheels, blinding me for a fraction of a second, but doesn't douse my anger.

"What do you mean you quit school? It just started only months ago and you're a freaking senior," I say, trying my best to hold back from yelling. We both stand in the almost empty school parking lot. The single-story, redbrick building, proclaiming Harmony High School across the front in ugly metal letters, looms in the background behind us.

"You know how much I hate it." He tosses his arm back toward the school in dismissal. "I don't plan on going to college. Ward really needs me more at the garage." He shrugs his shoulders. "Look, I'm goin' to get my GED— it's not like I'm ignorant. I have more important stuff that I need to be doin'. And if you're worried about your ride to school every day, I am always goin' to drop you off and pick you up. Ward knows and is cool with it."

My first textbook whizzes directly over his head.

"Hey, you almost hit me," he yells, looking surprised.

"There is no *almost* about it: I missed on purpose. You're the one who taught me to throw a baseball hard and true. You should know I don't miss."

"Hels, calm down."

"Holden Lee Dawson, you march yourself straight into the school counselor's office and sign yourself back up for classes."

He runs his hands over his buzzed cap of black hair. Slowly, he raises those big baby blues up to me, his square jaw stubbornly set. "I'm sorry, Hels. Not goin' to happen. I've tried for months to talk to you about this and you didn't wanna hear it. School isn't for everyone."

"It is if you want to get out of this hellhole. You're smart, Hold. Don't waste it. Education is everything for people like us or it should be. I want us to both go away to college."

"Hels," he says, dropping his voice low. "We've talked about this. It's not goin' to happen. Not for me, anyway. I wanna be a part of Hell's Highwaymen. It's my legacy. The MC is not only my family, but my way of life. I'm not ever leavin' Harmony. It's my town… it's my blood." His face turns red at his declaration.

"You are so dumb!" I stamp my foot, my black Converse smacking against the pavement, and turn to put my books in my backpack. After a minute, a tanned hand reaches over my shoulder, holding out the book that I tossed at his head.

"You're so cute when you get mad," he whispers, his words tickling the back of my neck.

"Shut up or I'll show you cute when I slash your tires," I say, sweetly. I squirm to get away, before dooming myself to look back at him.

His laugh is the only answer I get, but it's his single damn dimple in his left cheek that melts my heart every damn time. Seconds later I hear the deafening roar of a motorcycle approaching. I glance up to see one cruising directly for us, screeching to a stop in front of Hold. The rider switches the roaring motor off before stepping to the ground, and removing his helmet.

"Hey, man," Mikey says, nodding at Hold and completely ignoring me. "You finally quit this hellhole for real?"

"You know it, brother," he says, stepping up to Mikey and giving him that half hug that I see the MC guys always do.

Mikey wears the black MC cut, but he isn't patched yet. On the back of his vest, instead of a large patch of a motorcycle riding through flames with the name Hell's Highwaymen printed across the top, his patch only reads "Prospect." This means that he is a member in training and does whatever the club wants him to do. I've heard Hold say they do the shit work, which to me seems like they must clean the toilets at the garage. *Yuck!*

"Well, get ready to inherit the kingdom. It's just the beginning, brother. One day we will run this shit." Mikey claps him on the back and laughs.

I know what that means. Now that Hold is quitting school, he will get his own cut. I once heard Ward tell him that barring any problems, he will be a prospect for a couple of years before quickly rising in rank. Ultimately, he will become the vice president before taking over Ward's position as president.

Ward is always secretly talking to Hold about the stuff he's working on for the MC to be financially set when Hold is in charge. I eavesdrop sometimes, not always on purpose. He talks a lot about letters and numbers. Something about M-4's, and AK-47's, types of guns I guess, and another thing he calls the ATF. He gets really mad when he mentions that. And sometimes he talks about a safe house off of Route six. I'm smart enough to know that I shouldn't know anything about that place and keep my mouth tightly shut.

I don't know anything about Mikey. He seems okay but as we have gotten older, Hold keeps his friends separate from me. It kind of hurts my feelings, because he must be embarrassed about me for some reason.

"Is this your new piece of ass?" Mikey turns to look at me and I watch his eyes widen.

Within seconds, Mikey's shirt is bunched up in Hold's hands and he is lifting his skinny butt off the ground.

"Shit, Hold," he says, nervously reaching for the grip that Hold has on him. "I didn't know it was her. Man, she grew up."

"Watch your mouth, Mikey," Hold says, releasing him.

Mikey quit school when he and Hold were, like, in the tenth grade, so he hasn't seen me since I was in middle school. That was about the time when I wasn't allowed to be around any of the MC guys, unless they were in my grade at school. I go to school and literally come straight home every day since I have lived with Hold's family. It's not that they make me, but my one comfort is my art. I only go out with Hold; otherwise I sit in my room and draw.

"Are you coming to the cookout tonight at the garage?" Mikey walks over to get back on his motorcycle.

Hold glances weirdly over at me, before shaking his head to Mikey. "Nah, I'll probably just watch a movie or something."

"When you get that cut, you'll be expected to be there, brother," Mikey says, then looks directly at me before looking back to Hold. "Enjoy your free time while you still can." He tilts his motorcycle helmet on, roaring the bike to life at the same time Hold starts his up.

The idiots both rev their engines loudly, the motor vibrations shaking the ground beneath us, and the pop-pop unmistakably the sound of a Harley-Davidson. Mikey nods before riding away. I drag my feet toward Hold's hand that offers me my helmet. I knew this was coming. I figured it was going to happen last year and was, in fact, surprised when it didn't. When he passed all of his classes, I hoped he would see it through and graduate this year. I thought wrong.

I slide the helmet on, buttoning the chin strap, and swing my leg over the back. Once I am sitting directly behind Hold, I wrap my slender arms around his trim waist. So many girls would die to be in this very same position, but not me. Hold is like a brother and definitely my one and only friend. I have lived with him and his parents for almost four years now, since they took me in. Sage, his mom, treats me great, but there is something that doesn't feel right between us. She is not home most of the time, so it's not a big deal anyway. Evidently, she runs the office at the garage and stays busy with club business. Ward is nice to me, but, thankfully, I don't see him much.

We zip down the street on his Harley-Davidson 1200 Sportster that Ward bought him for his sixteenth birthday. I place my chin on his shoulder and watch the world rush by. For me, riding on the back of a motorcycle is as natural as walking is for most people. I like the adrenaline that pumps through my body as it vibrates underneath me. The wind whips renegade hair that escapes from my helmet. Just the thought of not being encased between the walls of a vehicle is freeing. God, I love being on the back of Hold's motorcycle.

My mind goes back to Hold quitting high school. The problem is twofold. I really want out of Harmony, Florida. It's not your typical touristy beach spot. No, Harmony is a small declining coastal town located on the Gulf of Mexico. We do have a main street but it consists of only a few sorry stores that yet manage to stay open for business, including Edna's Flowers, Sarah's Seaside Treasures, Beanie's Pawn Shop, Big Papa's Subs, and finally Hard Ink—plus, more empty rundown storefronts than anyone cares to count. The Harmony PD is at the end of the street, and Mom & Pop's Supermarket sits two streets over along with the Shack, and across from it is our only gas station whose storefront sign dangles crookedly from its roof, knocked half down by the last hurricane. Even the palm trees that line the sidewalks look dreary in this pathetic town. Dawson's Garage sits on the outskirts all by itself and past that is nothing but marshy swamp and alligators for miles. We are a long distance from any large chain stores, over an hour's drive from the nearest Wally World.

It has been my dream since I was little to leave this place in the dust. Education is the key to success and I am trying my best to achieve this goal. Even in ninth grade, I'm taking all advanced-placement college courses. I have been drawing since I was little and the school counselor thinks I can get some type of academic or art scholarship.

The other issue with Hold quitting is how alone I will be.

You are so selfish, Hels. You know how miserable the boy is.

At school there are three separate divisions: the "richie rich" kids, the poor ones, and the future Hell's Highwaymen Motorcycle Club spawn, better known as the MC'ers. If you're a rich kid, you don't mess with the MC'ers because they're more than likely also in the poor category and your parents smartly warned you to keep your distance. The poor kids don't even look at us because they know trouble when they see it and that sums up Dawson's crew. And, well, the MC'ers, all five of us left in high school, don't talk to me because they fear Ward Dawson like they fear Satan. God forbid that I do some ungodly thing like stay out and party with them and Ward finds out. They would get blamed.

So now I'm pretty much cut off from the entire world. My one confidant is deserting me—how unfair. I need a friend, and since he is it, he needs to stay. Tonight is Friday. I have all weekend to try and convince him to come back. Surely there is something I can do to persuade him.

After taking all back dirt roads home, we finally arrive at Hold's house. I hop off the motorcycle, wrenching my helmet off, and head straight inside on a mission. The screen door shuts behind me, when I hear someone.

"Hold? Hels? Are you guys home?" Sage calls out.

I follow her voice into the kitchen. "We are," I answer, smiling at her. "Do you know what Hold did today?" I sit down on one of the bar stools, combing my fingers through my long, wayward blonde locks.

"Baby girl, you knew this was coming. Holden is old enough to make his own decisions and he is only taking care of business, just like his father. I know you're unhappy about it, Hels, but you have to look at the big picture," she says, walking over to stand in front of me. Sage is very beautiful for her age. Hold gets his blue eyes from her, but in his I see kindness where Sage's shrewd ones seem to always gauge me. "I take my position very serious as Ward's old lady. This town looks at me like a dirty biker whore, but I'm the goddamn glue that holds this entire operation together and I plan for my son to have it all one day. That is why it's so important that you understand your place. Let's pretend that you're Hold's old lady…"

"Which I am not," I say, interrupting her. I place my folded arms against the laminate countertop in front of me.

"Okay, which you are not… *now*."

"Or never will be." The top of her heart tattoo located on her fleshy breast draws my attention. That had to hurt. At the sound of her clicking her tongue, I glance back up.

"Doll, never say never," she says, patting my cheek. "But if you were Hold's or anyone else's old lady, it would be your responsibility to support him no matter what. We bury deep our own feelings and expectations to support theirs a hundred and ten percent. We exist only for their happiness. You truly get what I'm sayin'?"

I do and I don't. I see what she is saying, but I am leaving this forsaken hellhole and plan on never becoming anyone's old lady. Ew. Gross. It just sounds disgusting and totally doesn't fit into my future, but I can't tell anyone about it. Hold told me it was very important to never tell anyone of my plans. Only him. And to never, ever say anything negative about the club. I nod, letting her believe what she wants. Sage has always been nice to me, but I know she has to be strong to be married to someone like Ward.

"Okay, kiddo. I'm going out for a while. There is a frozen pizza in the freezer for tonight or you and Hold can order one. Look in the kitchen drawer for some cash." She leans over to kiss my cheek, the sweet smell of her perfume tickles my nose. "Always remember, what is best for the club is the right thing. The club needs Holden working full time at the garage now. He wants it, so why not? Don't give my baby boy a hard time about this," she says, smiling at me before grabbing her keys to leave.

What is so great about the club? When I was a child, I didn't have a dad because of the club. It came first— before me, before everything. Even now, the club is taking my only best friend and his future. What is there to love about that? The problem is that Hold doesn't see it that way. He never has.

I look up as Hold busts through the kitchen door.

"I'm starvin'. Fix us some snacks, will ya?" He walks over to the sink to wash his hands.

My mind starts racing. "I'll fix your favorite batch of

homemade chocolate-chip cookies if you enroll back into school on Monday. In fact," I stand to walk directly up to him. "I will bake them every day after school until you're sick of them. Deal?" I finish, smiling up at him. He finally hit his growth spurt a year ago at sixteen, shooting up to over six feet tall. That was the year that all the girls went gaga over him, including goody-two-shoes Jenny Smith. She even tried to befriend me in hopes of getting close to Hold, but I'm not stupid. Oh, no. I finally told her where she and her snotty friends could stick it.

"Then I would weigh five hundred pounds and look like Hound. That fat fu—uh, dude can barely fit on his bike. No thanks. I'll stick to my off-brand premade chocolate-chip cookies," he says, drying his hands with a paper towel.

I reach over to grab it from him, throwing it quickly in his face. His stunned expression gives me the head start that I need. With a screech, I race through the kitchen, swiftly dodging chairs, but Hold quickly catches me around my waist. I twist and scream as he throws me over his shoulder, carrying me into the living room. My hands beat rapidly against his solid back, which doesn't seem to be doing me any good.

"Let me down, Hold," I beg. My face is hot from being upside down.

He drops me hard onto the leather-covered couch, and then swiftly begins tickling my sides while sitting down next to me. I laugh like a deranged hyena while maneuvering to try and get away from him without success. I hit his arms, which have thickened slightly with the weights he lifts every morning in his room. My shirt rides up and I immediately feel his fingers against the fleshy curve of my abdomen. I can't help but notice the moment he realizes that he is touching my bare skin, his blue eyes darken, and he changes the motions of his hands. The sounds of our childlike laughter that filled the room only seconds ago, comes to a dead halt. His fingers now slowly trace small circles. His breathing also sounds faster to me.

His eyes look down into mine. Something doesn't feel right. I'm old enough to know what happens between girls and guys. I hear all the latest gossip on which freshman lost her virginity and to whom. The girls at school especially love recapping what Hold does on the weekends, making sure I listen to all of it. Like I care. Hold is my brother and he doesn't think of me like that. I certainly don't think of him like a boyfriend. But the way he is glancing down at me doesn't seem very brotherly. I sit up, pushing away from him, sliding to the other end of the couch. I smooth my hair back, tying it in a knot behind my head. He blows out a long, loud breath of air.

"Are you ever going to grow up?" he murmurs, rubbing his hand back and forth over his shaved head.

"Excuse me? What does that have to do with anything?" I kick my foot out to nudge his leg.

"Okay, this is going to be super uncomfortable, but I have to ask," he says, finally looking at me. "What... how do you feel about me, Hels?" His face turns three shades of red.

"Well, when you're not being a weirdo, like right now, I love you. You know that." I shrug, not really wanting to have this conversation.

He clears his throat. "Like… how do you love me?"

"You're so stupid. You know that, right?" I start to get up, only to have him tow me back down next to him. His hands hold me in place by my arms, which we both know I could totally get away from if I wanted to.

"Answer me," he says. "This is important."

I look to see his knee bobbing up and down, which usually indicates he is nervous about something. What is going on here? What does he want me to say?

"Uh… I love you… lots?" I say, questioning where he is going with this.

"Damn it," he says, letting me go before standing. "Never mind—forget I even asked. I am going to take a shower. A cold one." He storms out of the room, not looking at me again.

I let my head fall back against the cushions on the couch. Hold and I have always been close, but the older I get, the harder it is to be just us. If it weren't for him, I would never have made it past that first year after Tara and my dad died. He held me together. I wanted to die for the things I had said and thought that night. I convinced myself that I willed that fire, but Hold wouldn't let me believe it.

He looks after me, making sure that kids at school

never have anything negative to say. He even makes sure that his mom buys me the coolest clothes, so that I never feel like the poor white-trash orphan girl. I see him trying so hard to make sure everything is fine. In the last couple of years, I have to almost force him to go out on the weekends instead of staying home with me.

I love Hold, but not like a boyfriend. I love him more than that—I love him like he is the only family I have left in this world. I know the difference. Jake Carrity is one of the most popular boys in my grade. When I see him, my heart beats really fast and my stomach fills with tiny butterflies. It's almost like I can actually feel their wings flitting softly underneath the skin of my abdomen. These feelings I have when I am around Jake are everything described in the romance books I read. And I think I have caught him glancing at me a time or two, which is amazing considering he is part of the rich crowd. It could be my imagination, but I really hope he sees me.

I hear the sound of the water running upstairs. I don't know what Hold wants from me. It could be a guy thing— hormones for all I know. For now, I am going to pretend like it didn't happen. I think that is best for us both. At the sound of my stomach rumbling, I get up to go find some junk food. I bring a snack up to my room, hiding from Hold because of the craziness on the couch. After finishing, I lie down and listen to music, trying not to worry about what he asked.

Around dinnertime, I take a quick shower before heading downstairs to find Hold. He wasn't in his room when I went to look. As I walk into the kitchen, the home phone rings.

"Dawson residence," I answer, pressing the cordless phone against my shoulder.

"Helen, it's Ward. Put Hold on the phone." His deep voice over the line makes me jump.

"He's not in the house. Let me check outside, sir." I place the phone down on the countertop before opening the backdoor. "Hold," I yell, looking around the yard. "Holden."

"What, Hels? I'm working on my bike," he shouts from somewhere behind the house.

"Ward is on the phone," I holler back. The sound of him swearing, then his feet rushing around the house, is my only warning before he charges past me.

"Sir?" he answers. "Yeah, can you give me about twenty minutes? Yes, sir. I'll bring it straight to you." He hangs the phone up.

"Everything okay?" I ask him, shutting the backdoor.

"Yeah. Ward needs me to bring something to the garage. They're having a cookout tonight and he can't leave. Club business."

"Do you want me to fix a pizza for us while you are

gone?" I really want to get things back to normal with Hold.

"Man, I am really tired of pizza. I could go for a nice, juicy hamburger. You want me to pick some up at the Shack on my way home?"

That actually sounds really good, but I remember that it is Friday night. And it's football season. Everyone will be at the Shack—a local hamburger joint—after the big game. I have never been allowed to go to the Shack on a weekend night because evidently it gets rowdy as the only entertainment for teenagers in this podunk town. I'm sure Jake will be there. He plays junior varsity football, but I know they all hang out after the varsity game. That would be so cool.

"How about I ride with you and we both go by there on the way home?" I smile sweetly, fluttering my eyelashes at him.

"Quit doing that. You look retarded. You know you aren't allowed to go out until you're sixteen. This is Mom and Ward's rule, not mine."

"I'm not going out, dummy. I am going to get food with you. Big difference. C'mon, Hold. Please," I whine. "Pretty please with a cherry on top." I clasp my hands together and all-out beg him.

He looks at me, unsure, before scratching his head. "Fine! Alright. We'll drive the truck and you'll stay in it, while I drop something off at the garage. Afterwards, we'll stop by the Shack and order our burgers and leave. We are not staying. Deal?" He places his hands on his waist like he means business. *Sucker!* He is such a pushover.

"You got it!" I take off running to my room to get dressed. I squeal on the way up. What do I wear? Ooh. Ooh! Sage bought me the coolest blue-jean miniskirt. I also have the soft pink mohair sweater that goes great with my blonde hair. I slip on my ballet flats before arranging my hair back in a loose ponytail. With one last look in the mirror, I rush downstairs, plowing straight into Hold who is standing at the bottom.

"Whoa, what are you wearing? I told you that we aren't staying at the Shack and I mean it, Hels," he says gruffly while looking at my attire.

"I know, but I thought I would look nice just in case."

"Just in case *what?*" He narrows his eyes at me. "Or should I ask *who?*"

Great. Now he looks pissed. Boys. "Nobody," I yell, charging past him and out the front door.

I hear him locking up behind me while I climb into his truck. It's a little Toyota that Ward also bought for him. He slings open his door and hops in. Before he turns the key in the ignition, he places something wrapped in brown paper on the seat between us. As we start down the road, he finally breaks the silence.

"I don't want to fight with you," he says, his voice sounding sad. Don't be mad about the school thing. I can't change it now, even if I wanted to."

"I know. Why does everything have to change the older we get?" I glance over at him as he drives.

"You know, some things are worth getting older for,"

he says, a small smile playing across his lips as if he knows a secret.

I know exactly what he is talking about. "Keep it to yourself, *Hot Lips*. Cecily already shared that particular story with the entire school." I laugh at the expression of shock he turns to give me.

"What? You didn't know that your dates are talked about all over school? Please," I say, rolling my eyes. "People love for me to hear the latest. It's like they think we are together or something. Stories about your sex life don't shock me, Hold."

He doesn't say anything for a minute. I watch his hands grip the steering wheel tightly.

"It doesn't bother you?" I can barely hear his question because he says it so low.

"It's not like I want to hear it, but..." I pause for a second. "...it doesn't bother me," I answer honestly. With the bright moonlight shining into the car, I can't help but notice the look of disappointment that crosses his face. "Should it, Hold?" I ask only because now I am confused.

"Look, can we change the subject?" He switches the radio on. Blurry by Puddle of Mudd plays loudly out of the speakers.

I sit back and listen to the music. The lyrics speak to me. I shut my eyes tightly and wish for the road to open up, swallowing me whole. Neither one of us says anything into this awkward silence. I feel the truck start to slow down, and the clicking of the blinker alerts me to where we are. I open my eyes to see the chain-link gates are closed, blocking the entry to the garage, which is next to the Hell's Highwaymen clubhouse. Hold turns in, rolling to a stop before them. He lowers the window when two prospects walk over to us, one of them Mikey.

"Wassup," he says, giving them a mock salute.

My ears perk up, anxious to know what it is they are saying since they seem to be mumbling to each other. The idiots congratulate him on dropping out of school so he can work in this grease pit. One of the guys says something about him being included in club business now that he will be here full time. The longer I listen to these two talking to Hold, the angrier I become.

I ignore them to look down the long half-mile driveway to see it currently lined with more bikes than I care to count. With all the outside lights on, I can see people loitering around the clubhouse and the garage at the end. The garage is a one-story building with five distinct garage doors for business. There is a large sign above it proclaiming, Dawson's Garage. Next to it, is the clubhouse, which is where they all hang out and some even live on the second floor. It is a two-story building with a matching silver tin roof. Several fluorescent neon signs line the windows, advertising alcohol, motorcycles, and outlines of naked women.

"I am just dropping a package off to Ward," Hold finally says, showing it to them.

They nod before walking over to open the gates, sliding them back so we can enter. Hold drives toward the garage, stopping halfway to park besides the tree line. I watch him switch the ignition off. Hold takes the keys out, tapping them on the steering wheel. He looks to be deep in thought.

"This shouldn't take long," he says, fidgeting with the key ring before looking up at me. "Stay in the truck. Don't get out. Got it?"

"Yes, sir." I playfully mock-salute him.

"You are such a smartass." He smiles, grabbing the package before turning to open the door.

I watch him walk the rest of the way to the garage. It's weird to place the boy I grew up with against this man he is becoming. His body is changing and it is crazy when I think about it. I developed early, lucky me—not. I didn't want boobs at thirteen, but they sprouted right out. When you have a small body and big boobies like mine, you just look funny. I don't care what people say, though. Sage says I will appreciate it one day. Whatever.

I jump when I hear a loud popping noise outside of the truck. I turn to glance through the trees and see a large clearing where someone looks to be shooting fireworks: blue, green, and red burning streaks of light explode to sparkle and fizzle throughout the dark sky. With every launch, it lights up the night, illuminating the throng of black-vested men standing around. Some surround a large fire with red Solo cups in their hands. My eyes take in the scantily dressed women scattered around, mainly rubbing their big boobs against the seemingly drunken Hell's Highwaymen.

Every few seconds, I see men who are not wearing a

cut. These guys are considered "friends-of-the-club" or better known as club lackeys. They want to be in, part of this brotherhood, but just don't really hack it. I know all of this because even though my dad never really talked to me, I listened and learned. I kept thinking one day I could show him just how much I knew about the club and he would be proud. I wanted to love the MC as much as he did, but instead, it left me hating something that took him away from me.

I turn to see Hold talking to a few guys, before stepping into the garage. I fan my face, noticing how warm it is becoming inside the truck. My hand blindly reaches for the key to switch the ignition on for the air conditioner, when I realize Hold took the darn keys. Dummy. When fanning doesn't help, I pinch the front of my sweater—tugging it in and out to get some air flowing. I think about rolling the windows down, but they are power only. Damn it. I should not have worn this sweater, even though it's a lightweight one.

When my overheated body feels close to exhaustion, I open the door. Thank goodness that it is a breezy night. I turn, facing outwards, letting my feet rest on the soft ground. The cold air blows softly against me, cooling my overly warm skin. My eyes close in sweet relief. The chorus of men's deep voices surrounds the night along with the fireworks crackling overhead.

"Hey, pretty lady," a male voice says, far too close to me.

My eyes pop open. A young guy stands a few feet away.

He has shoulder-length, dirty-blonde hair with a matching goatee. I guess he's good-looking, if you like them scruffy. My eyes travel up from his jeans to his white t-shirt, instantly noticing he doesn't wear the Hell's Highwaymen cut. That vest means everything to these guys, and they go nowhere without it, which means he is just a friend-of-the-club.

"Hi," I answer.

"Why aren't you partying with everyone else?" He drunkenly stumbles closer to me.

"Why aren't you?" I ask, shrinking back against the seat.

"I had to take a piss and didn't want to go into the garage. Not my scene, if you get what I mean."

Yeah, I do. It probably *means* that you don't rate high enough to be welcome in the garage, I think to myself. I nod my head, hoping he will just walk away.

"Are you here with someone?"

"Yes, he should be back any minute," I say. He moves so close to me, I can actually smell the sour liquor on his breath. My stomach churns: it is a bad reminder of my father. "Please back away, so that I can close the door. It's getting a little chilly now."

He grabs my arms so quickly that it literally stuns me. Something tells me he is not as drunk as I thought.

"Do you have a tattoo? Are you marked by your men?"

What the heck is he asking? Do I have what? Am I marked by who?

"No, I don't have any tattoos. And what men are you

talking about?" I'm confused by his questions, but my heart nearly stops at seeing the evil glint in his eyes at my answer. I go from offended to being completely scared in two seconds flat. I don't want to look away from him, but I need to see if Hold is coming back.

In the second it takes for me to glance at the garage, he drags me swiftly away from the truck. I open my mouth to scream, but before I can, he hits me hard, his palm cracking loudly across my cheek. My left eyes feels like it is going to burst out of its socket. The excruciating pain radiates from my face down my body.

"Scream and I will do that again," he says, his voice low and menacing. "Next time, I'll knock you out, bitch. I can bust a nut either way."

His words scare me. He drags me into the woods, the opposite direction from the garage. I know that I need to scream, but if he does knock me out, nobody will find me. *Think, Helen.* Helpless tears fall down my face. While he drags me with him, I look down in search of anything I can find to hurt him. Before I can come up with a plan, he throws me to the marshy ground, covering me quickly with his agile body. He places his filthy smelling hand over my mouth, sufficiently blocking any cries for help. My stomach heaves at the scent of vomit. I try to buck him off, but he is much bigger than I am. His body lies flat over mine, pinning me to the dirt and leaves beneath me.

I tremble with fear, my eyes frantically searching for help. I know that my time is running out. I scream beneath his hand, but it only comes out muffled. His fingers on his other hand pinch my inner thighs painfully while he tries to tug them apart. He lets out a string of curse words and I'm not sure if this is to try and still my movements or if he is trying to find my panties. I spread my hands on the ground, praying something sharp can help me. My fingers blindly search without success. When I can't find anything, I bring them up to pummel his back.

"Quit fighting, bitch," he threatens quietly in my face. His sick smile makes me want to puke.

Everything is happening so rapidly. I fight hard, but I don't feel like I am getting anywhere. In a moment of desperation, I get my teeth around a small amount of flesh that imprisons my mouth, and bite down hard. He rears back, his hand retreating, and giving me a chance to scream loudly. I hear it echo through the night at the same time the fireworks colorfully explode in the sky above me, the thunderous bang obviously drowning out my calls for help.

He leans up to straddle my body, before bringing his hand down to deliver a second blow. His vicious slap causes my ears to ring. It seems like minutes tick by before I can hear anything else. The taste of metal in my mouth turns my already sensitive stomach. These seconds give him plenty of time to tear my panties completely off. His fingers roughly palm me, before trying to force their way inside. I jerk back from him, but he only laughs while he unzips his jeans.

My head swims with lurid images. I know and don't know what is coming. He is going to take my virginity. He is going to hurt me. My tears leak toward the ground. Accepting my fate, I close my eyes. The sound of a grunt is the only warning I have before I open them to see that Hold has launched himself at my attacker. Their fists pound each other, the next one sounding louder than the one before.

Someone is screaming. I look up to see a man obviously yelling for help over his shoulder. Several others finally make it through the trees, running toward us. They reach where Hold is pounding his fist into my attacker. Sandman tries to restrain a feral Hold. I watch one of them open his phone and I hear Ward's name mentioned. My chest feels weighted down as precious air eludes me. Is this what it feels like to have a heart attack? My vision blurs completely, leaving only shapes of those around me.

"Hels, look at me. Damn, I think she's in shock," Hold says, but his voice seems too far away to save me this time.

FIVE

February 2008

The older I get, the faster time passes me by. Some days I am afraid to blink, knowing that time is a rare commodity that I don't have a lot of. Not that I am worried about my life ending. Dying is the least of my worries. Being found would be a fate worse than death, the thought of reentering the life that I fled my darkest nightmare. He would make my life a living hell.

I should have moved on by now. The two warnings I received when I first ran were not to stay in the same place for long and not to tattoo. I tried to heed both. At first I took up odd jobs as I moved from place to place. After the second year of running, I even ghosted some college classes, blending in with the crowd to audit art and writing courses at a local university, and, for a small amount of time, it helped fill this clawing emptiness in my soul. But then one day I realized it wasn't ever going to be enough. Tattooing gives me a reason to keep going, a hope that human nature isn't all evil, and that people can still shape their own destiny. I decided returning to it was a risk worth taking.

It's dangerous to stay this long in one place, but the life I am trying to build is worth just a small amount of danger. Just a little longer, I think to myself, looking out of the small, busy café's glass window. I blow gently on the cup of black coffee in my hand, not wanting to burn my lip as I did only moments ago.

Hurried people pass by outside as I sit and watch. A light blanket of snow covers the ground, making the small town look like a postcard greeting. It seems like I am in a fantasyland with everything being relatively normal. A magnificent dream of a life I never imagined, but my greedy heart longs for more. That daydream includes a home I would go back to after having my cup of coffee, with a husband who has a regular, everyday job and the two small children who mirror us both.

A small pang of heartache grips my soul. I should be content with the piece of heaven that I'm experiencing now, instead of wishing for something that will never be. I could never be selfish enough to draw someone into this hell of hiding.

My mind quickly drifts back to that night at Screaming Ink over a month ago and a certain customer who I have tried to forget about. I haven't seen or heard from him since that first meeting. It is better this way. I don't get involved ever. The times I have come close are the ones where I quickly packed my bags and left town. Not that I want to get involved with him—he certainly wasn't my type. I only felt bad because he said he didn't know anyone in town. I know too well that feeling of isolation and could have at least had a cup of coffee with him.

I test the dark liquid filled to the brim inside of my cup. It has cooled just enough for me to taste the bitterness that I crave. My eyes shut in ecstasy at the jolt of caffeine that hits my system. I think I love my cup of joe just a little too much. Especially, considering I have a small teacup permanently inked within one of my sleeves to depict this addiction. It was much more feminine to get instead of a mug.

My eyes take in the busy Monday morning crowd, getting a caffeine fix right along with me. This spot is a hub of the local crowd. You can identify the college students by their backpacks or total aloofness with their headsets blocking the rest of the world out. The business crowd is evident by their dark suits and the frenetic way they rush about, cell phone in hand.

Then you have the loners like myself. We don't keep banking hours or worry about our GPA. Nobody or nothing to rush off to. No, you know exactly who we are because we have never fit in. The rejects. The never-haves. We sit back to enjoy the cup in hand, either wallowing in our aloneness or envious of something we can't have.

A glimpse of neon green catches my attention. I turn to

see Ginger bouncing in, her new shade of hair color blinding everyone. It is only mere coincidence, since she doesn't know I'm here. I know she has classes on Monday mornings. She chats up people while in line, whether they want to or not. I think most are so entranced by her pansy-colored eyes that they are sucked into her conversation regardless.

After paying for her coffee, she turns to leave when she notices me. Her elfin face lights up in a smile and she walks my way. I can't help but return her exuberant grin.

"Hey, you," she says, dropping into the chair across from me. "I forgot that you have the early shift."

"Yeah," I say, yawning. "I was there last night until after midnight. I had to finish that sleeve I've been working on for months."

"Malik said that it was going to be badass," she says, taking a sip of whatever is in her cup.

"It is." I designed the sleeve entirely myself for this girl who works at one of the local diners. She saved for months and we worked on the concept the entire time. What she ended up having was the entire story of Snow White depicted on her arm. Not the Disney character, but this angelic, mystical tattoo of love, friendship, and loss.

"Mmm, I really need to set up an appointment to get mine done with you."

I glance over my cup of coffee at her while taking a drink. "Oh, right," I say, sarcastically. "What are you getting again?"

"I am still thinking it over. You know, it's a really big

decision and I don't want to rush into something I will regret." Ginger's face flushes pink, which clashes with her green hair.

"Girl, I think you need to just give it up. Malik is not going to fire you over not getting tatted, if that's what you are worried about."

"No, no," she insists. "I want to. Really, I do!" Her tone emphatic, I'm not sure if she is trying to convince me, or herself.

"Did you go out this weekend?" I ask, giving her a slight reprieve.

"Yes. And since you had to work and couldn't join me on my escapades, I of course found trouble. Again."

"Not the douche bartender," I say, already knowing the answer.

"He has a nice ass. It looks really good in jeans," she says, guilty.

"What am I going to do with you?"

"Not let me freak out over him not calling me after the best sex I have ever had. And I mean ever, ever." She starts to say something else when I notice her looking at the front of the café. "I know that guy. How do I know him?" I watch her face scrunch up as she tries to remember.

I give a slight laugh. Knowing Ginger, he's somebody she took home who didn't call, which boggles the mind. She is a beautiful, intelligent woman... well, minus the hair. I take another sip of coffee while she stares someone down.

"Oh, well," she says, shrugging her shoulders, then looking at her watch. "Damn, I am going to be late for class. I don't work today, but I'll come by the shop afterward. See you later, chica."

"Later," I smile and watch her hurry out. I worry that I have become too close to Ginger. My smile evaporates at the thought. I convinced myself that it was okay to have a female friend. I have always longed to have that bond with another young woman, to know what I missed as a girl—a sisterhood that I lost. My eyes tear up at the thought. It is a pain that never goes away. Until this day, even the thought of losing her robs me of oxygen. It's like living with no air.

"Are you okay?"

That *voice*. I glance up into brown eyes. *His.* A sheen of tears clouds my vision and before I can blink them away, a single one falls. He watches it travel down my cheek. And I don't see his arm move, but suddenly his finger imprisons it on the tip. Our eyes meet again.

"Keller, right? Vin," he says, placing his hand on his chest.

I nod at his question. He remembers my name?

"Can I sit?" He doesn't wait for an answer, but moves to the chair across from me. He places his cup of coffee down and then leans toward me with his elbows resting on the table. "Black coffee, huh?"

Wait, what? I watch him point toward my cup. He wants to discuss coffee? I bring the back of my hand up to wipe my eyes and clear them before looking at him. Today he has a black wool cap covering his head and matching coat over jeans.

"I remember how you like your coffee," he says. "It's how I take mine also. Can I get you some more?"

"No, thank you," I murmur. I feel like he has once again witnessed something too personal to share. Yet, I make no move to stand and leave.

"You working today?"

"I have to be there at ten," I say. I turn to watch the snow flurries now coming down outside.

"It's beautiful, isn't it?"

"Yeah."

"I'm from the South and we don't get a lot of the white stuff. Mainly we get a lot of black ice. You from here?" He leans back in his chair while taking a sip of his coffee.

"I'm from all over." I give him the truth from the past four years.

"Military brat?"

"No, orphan."

He takes another sip of coffee, looking perplexed at my answer.

"What part of the South?" I ask, wanting to change the subject.

He grins, placing his cup back on the table. "I was born in Lafayette, Louisiana." His voice lowers before he adds. "I grew up on the bayou, living with my grandparents. I dropped the Cajun accent a long time ago. I went to school up North on a scholarship and realized pretty fast that no one across the Mason-Dixon Line could understand a word I said."

"What did you go to school for?"

"Well, I received a degree in architecture. I thought I would be the next Brunelleschi, but instead of designing some dome in Italy, I was only shooting for an NFL dome," he says, laughing.

I don't have any clue as to who or what he is talking about.

He clears his throat. "I guess you don't know or care who Brunelleschi was?"

"Nope," I answer.

He nods. "Anyway, I realized that I shared the same passion my grandfather did for restoring the interior of old houses. So I called him up, went to work for him, and I have been doing it ever since. I am restoring a house off of Cedar Street, a 1904 Victorian in the Art Nouveau style. It has these amazing stained glass windows throughout. Right now, I'm scraping off yards of white paint that someone used to mutilate this ornate staircase. Can you imagine?" He shakes his head and sits up in his chair. "I'm boring you, aren't I?"

Actually, he isn't. "No, you're passionate about your work. It shows." I trace the top of my cup with my finger.

"Is that how you feel about tattooing?"

"Yes, I feel lucky to be able to wake up each day and go do something I enjoy."

"Do you draw or paint in your spare time?"

"I do," I say, nodding my head. "I specialize in portraits."

"Really?" He looks surprised. "No unicorns and rainbows?"

He has a natural joking nature. I see it, as he gives me a slow smile and wink of his eye.

"Sadly, I have tattooed many unicorns and rainbows on sober idiots, but in my drawings the only time you will see a unicorn is if he is farting a rainbow. Or the rainbow could be strangling the unicorn. Either works for me," I say, not cracking a smile.

He laughs. "So tell me about yourself. How did you get into tattooing?"

Electric chills run the circuit of my spine. Every possible warning bell goes off in my head when someone questions me on anything regarding my past. Ginger finally stopped after I shut her down time after time. In the past, when someone would start asking, I'd go running. I know everyone isn't going to necessarily turn me over to those who hunt me, but I can't take any chances. My best guess would be that there is a large sum of reward money offered for my *safe* return, safe being a loose term.

"I really need to be getting to the shop," I say, standing and reaching for my jacket on the back of the chair.

"Let me walk you," he says, rising.

"That's okay. It's just a block over. I am sure you need to get back to working on your house." I slide on my jacket before adjusting my scarf.

"It can wait. Great thing about being your own boss—I'm a one-man crew most days. I actually live there while I renovate, so sometimes I even work twenty-four hours when the mood strikes me." He places his hand on the small of my back, guiding me out of the café.

I try to think of something to railroad him, but before I do, we are already walking down the sidewalk, side by side. Our elbows intimately touch. When I notice, I quickly inch away. Snowflakes fall carelessly all around us as we stroll.

"Looks like they've de-iced the cement, but I would still watch your footing," he says, glancing over at me.

I nod, looking back. Our height difference has him almost hulking over me. This would normally bother me, but strangely it doesn't at this moment.

"So, where were we? Ah, yes. You were going to tell me how you became a tattoo artist." His elbow closes the gap to nudge mine.

"I used to draw when I was little, so it came naturally," I say, not following it up with anything else.

"That's it? That's all I'm going to get? Really?" he says, grinning at me. "What about your childhood? Where are you from?"

I stop, turning to look directly at him. Several brown wisps of hair escape from underneath his hat. My own newly colored raven locks blow in the frigid wind.

"Look, I don't really talk about my childhood. I lost my family and I ended up an orphan—nothing special or magical about that. I survived and here I am. Nothing else really to say," I say, turning to march angrily to work.

"Hey, wait just one minute," he says, reaching for my arm to spin me around.

My struggling to jerk away from his hand only causes

me to lose my footing and fall intimately against him. Heat radiating from his body warms mine, calling me to inch closer. He must have sanded wood today. He actually smells like the large trees I used to hide in when I was a child, a woodsy scent. Very clean. Very manly. Very sexy.

"I want to get to know you—that's all I am asking. No more, no less. I have never met a more infuriating human being, much less a woman, who didn't want to talk about herself. You really must be missing that gene, which I must be crazy for even mentioning."

"Why?" I whisper, wanting… no, *needing* to know.

"Why what?" His eyes gaze deeply into mine. "Why do I want to get to know you or why I must be crazy for mentioning your missing gene?"

I roll my eyes at him. "The first."

"I have no clue, but considering how many times I have thought about you these last couple of weeks…" he lets go of me, placing his hands in his jean pockets, and shrugs his shoulders. "Something about you calls to me, like my houses do."

I move away from him, his words stinging a bit. "What? Do I say fix me? Is that why I am like your houses?" I narrow my stare. How dare he?

While we stand there, a snowflake floats gracefully down upon my cheekbone. It's almost as if time slows. His hand lifts toward my face, capturing the crystalized water as he did the tear earlier.

"Even the heavens weep with you," he says, looking at me. "What made you cry earlier? Do you need to be fixed?

Remember, they are your words, not mine."

"I'm fine," I say through gritted teeth. "Listen, it's been very nice knowing you, but I'm not interested. Not now. Not ever. Have a nice day." I spin around and head toward work.

"Keller," he says, halting my movements.

I stop, but don't turn around, composing myself the best I can. He hit some sensitive spots. So much inside of me suddenly feels raw and exposed. I slowly rotate my body so that I am now looking at him. His black wool attire is a stark contrast to the white falling around him. I take a mental picture. This is how I will sketch him. This is how I will remember him. I have a book of all the people who have passed in and out of my life these last several years. The title across his page will read, "Asshole."

"Vin," I say back to him.

"We will see each other again," he says, before turning to stroll away.

"Don't bet on it," I call to his backside. He only waves his hand in the air.

I storm down the sidewalk like a woman on a mission. Anger bubbles up inside of me. How dare he? Who says that? A creeper, that's who. Normal men don't threaten single women. That is just insane.

I swing open the door to the tattoo shop and stomp in. Malik's head pops up as I come rushing through. I mutter obscenities underneath my breath. I squint my eyes at him as I pass, blaming him for just being male.

"Want to talk about it?"

"Nope," I answer back.

His quick laugh is the only answer I get. I start setting my space up, ignoring everyone else around me. My first appointment is at ten-thirty this morning so I actually don't have time for these feelings that course through me. I am going to put Vin out of my mind for good.

SIX

October 2001

My eyes flutter open when I hear low voices speaking around me. I first see an old wooden dresser next to where I am lying. The bed, where someone must have put me, has a matching head- and footboard. There is one thing I know for certain: it is not mine.

"Look, man, she's awake. Somebody get Hold," a strange male voice says.

The sound of feet running on the hard floor, coming closer to me, reminds me of another time—a horrible time. My heart starts racing and I sit up. This time Hold bursts through the door, throwing himself on the bed. He wraps his arms around me, and the entire evening floods back into my memory. I start to shake when I remember what happened. Hold saved me from being raped. Oh, God.

"Shh, it's okay," he whispers, cuddling me closer to him.

I don't even realize I'm crying until he says that, but then the tears flow faster. I let the sobs escape from deep inside of me. I start explaining what happened, about the truck becoming hot, and then opening the door to cool down.

"I know. I took the goddamn keys like an idiot. I didn't know it was goin' to take me that long. Everyone was congratulating me for comin' to work full time at the garage. It's all my fault," his voice breaks with emotion.

"I shouldn't have opened the door. You told me to stay in the t-t-truck," I cry, burying my face in the crook of his neck.

"Listen, I don't wanna rush you, but there are things that have to happen tonight. Look at me," he says, cradling my face between his two hands. "We have to take care of club business, you and me. I know you don't understand what that means, but I need you to trust me. What happens here tonight, stays here tonight. Ward is trusting you... I am trusting you."

His eyes frantically dart back and forth between mine. I don't have a clue what he is talking about, but I trust him, so I nod.

"Just do what I tell you. Okay?" He pulls his hands away from me so that he can stand up. He reaches them back out and I go to him without question.

I try my best to pull down my skirt, and tug at my

sweater to cover myself. I only have one shoe and no panties. He places his arm securely around my waist, guiding me out the door. We happen to pass by a mirror on the way out. I shudder at my reflection. My face is swollen on both sides, the bruises already turning a nasty shade of purple. I look horrible.

As we walk into the hallway, I look around and take a guess that we are on the second floor of the clubhouse where the bedrooms are. Some are for guys who live here, but most are for members to use when they don't want to go home. My dad used to stay here a lot. We walk down a flight of stairs, side by side. Hold never lets me go. I do trust him and lean my head against his shoulder.

We walk into a larger area. I have never been in here, but I know immediately this is the main gathering room. There is a large bar on one side and pool tables and videogames on the other. On the left is a large pair of doors, with axes hanging across them. My dad once told me that was the club's inner domain, their meeting room. All decisions are made behind those closed doors.

I glance around to see members of the Hell's Highwaymen Motorcycle Club stoically lining the walls or sitting at tables and chairs placed around the room. Everyone has a cut—only club members are here. Nobody says a word as they stare directly at us. The silence surrounding these larger-than-life men is a horror in itself. The doors to the meeting room fly open and Ward steps out, followed by his second-in-command, Sandman. His eyes search the room until he finds Hold, standing with me.

"Come to me, Hels," he says, motioning his hand toward me.

I glance up at Hold and he nods. I carefully take a step, and then another, until I am directly in front of Ward. This whole thing is like an out-of-body experience. I can't help but notice all eyes are cast on me. Spine-tingling chills rack my body, but I don't retreat.

"Your dad was our brother and by family you are part of this club. We believe that your future position to the MC, and the situation tonight, warrant us to make an exception and give you something that no one besides the club's married females have. It will be a mark meant to declare you as one of ours. No one will touch what we Hell's Highwaymen have claimed," Ward says loudly for the room to hear.

The sound of cheering voices rings loudly through the room. My head is fuzzy. I cannot hear what else Ward is saying—I only get about every other word. I look over at Hold and he nods. He won't let anyone hurt me. I close my eyes for only a second, before opening them. My face hurts, the swelling feels like it is getting worse by the minute.

"Do you understand, Helen?" Ward looks down at me, waiting for an answer.

I nod, not sure what I am agreeing to.

"First, retribution is in order. Judgment has been made

and Hell's justice will be served," he says raising his voice.

I first hear the muffled sound of someone screaming for help before I see him. It is my attacker. One of the prospects brings him to the center of the room before throwing him down on his knees. He is gagged with his hands tied behind his back, his face bloody and bruised from the beating Hold and whoever else gave him.

He searches the crowd, desperately looking for anyone to help him. I watch him weep, the terror on his face funny to me. Everything within me wants him to pay for what he did. When the police come for him, I will watch, laughing, as they take him away. I hope he rots in jail.

"Do you want to dole out the punishment?" Ward glances down at me again.

I have never hit another person in my life and meant it. Sure, I've given Hold plenty of playful arm slaps, but nothing that was done in hate. Before I think about what I am doing, I walk over to look him square in his eyes. I see that he is scared and I am glad. Happy. A fury that I can almost taste rises within me. I rear my foot back, slamming it into his crotch. I actually hear a crunching sound seconds before he falls to the floor, groaning. The sound of men's laughter reminds me that I am not alone. I do not walk back to Ward, but straight for Hold. He opens his arms and I walk directly into them. I bury my face in his chest, my body trembling uncontrollably. Ward is saying something, but I block his words out.

"While that may be entertaining, that is not the punishment that was agreed on. Holden Dawson, do you protect what is yours with club honor?"

My head pops up at Hold's name. I glance in the direction of his face. He looks down at mine, his eyes appearing to be laden with sadness.

"Yes," he answers, his gaze never wavers from mine. He leans down to gently kiss my cheek. "Close your eyes and don't look. D' ya hear me, Hels? Do not look," he whispers into my ear.

His arms let me go, leaving me bereft as he walks away. I do what he tells me to do, not only because it's Hold, but because my head is killing me. I'm nauseous and the banging in my skull sounds like there is a marching band taking over my brain. I am sure he is going to beat the hell out of him again for touching me. Something inside of me relates to the term bloodthirsty, and I completely understand it now.

I stand still, not hearing anyone speak. Minutes later, my entire body jumps at the sound of two muffled pops. I spin around to see Hold standing there with a gun that has a funny looking barrel on the end. My eyes follow to see where everyone else is staring. My rapist lies in a puddle of blood, red rapidly growing beneath him. His vacant eyes stare out at the room. I hear someone screaming, not realizing that the sound is coming from me. Hold rushes to my side, wrapping me in his arms so he can hold my shaking body against him. I do not want him touching me, not with those hands. I try and push him away, not sure what is happening around me. I cringe, wanting to crawl into myself.

"Get her a drink," Ward says. "It won't hurt for her to be drunk. Do you understand, boy?"

My eyes travel frantically toward Ward. I don't miss the proud smirk he wears, obviously over Hold's actions. He likes this, being the judge and juror over the MC. I see the darkness he wears like a shroud and the evil he proudly wears upon his head as a crown. This is what this life will gift to Hold.

"Yes, sir," Hold says, picking me up to take me somewhere. "Get me a bottle of Crown and a couple of sodas," he orders someone.

He sits down, gently placing me on his lap. I keep my face tightly against his chest as I cry. What just happened? How could he... how could he do this? Did he just kill someone? He strokes my back and my mind wars over whether to let him or try to get away. Everything is happening so fast. Did Hold mean to do that? Did he know? Did Ward want me to kill that guy? Murder?

"It had to be done, Hels. Do you understand?" His voice pleads in my ear.

I shake my head no, never raising my face from his shoulder.

"His daddy is some big-shot judge. That was the only reason he was a friend-of-the-club. He would have gotten him off. I couldn't stand the thought that you had to be scared because that piece of shit was walking around. We will just forget it ever happened. Okay?" He leans down to cover my head in kisses. I can feel his lips and every single touch of his mouth revolts me.

I don't say anything. What is there to say? Eventually, my sobs quiet as my body drains of any emotion.

"Here, drink this, Hels," Hold says, pushing me to sit up.

I try to stand, to get away, but he wraps his arms around my waist. He holds me tightly, sitting in place. Some guy pours the dark liquid into the soda. He swirls the cup around. I watch him place a straw in it before handing it to Hold.

"Hold your nose and drink all of this."

I do as he asks. The sugary, bitter taste almost makes me gag, but I force myself to drink it all. It seems that as soon as I finish, my body warms me from the inside out. My toes tingle, and the pounding in my head calms. Everyone is talking around me, but I don't care. Suddenly, everything seems hilariously funny. Surely, it was all a dream. It had to be. I am all hot and fuzzy inside.

"Hels, are you okay?"

I hear Hold's voice and turn in that direction. There he is, right under me where I left him.

"S'kay." The words leave my mouth, brushing against my lips as they depart. For some reason, I find this hysterical. "More," I say.

"No," Hold says.

My mind is foggy, but I still know when my Hold is sad. I look at the top of his shaved hair. He bows his head in silence. I place my hand underneath his chin, slowly I push up, needing to see his eyes. The watery blue shreds what is left of my heart.

"Why?" I can't keep the emotion out of my voice as everything comes back into focus. "Why, Hold?"

"We take care of our own. You are mine. You've always been mine."

"Not like this, not ever like this. I belong to no one. I am no one's."

"Mine," he insists, placing his head against my chest.

I feel his body shudder underneath me. I know he regrets what he did. He has to.

"Do you regret it, Hold?" I have to hear him say it. I need him to tell me that it was an accident. That Ward made him do it. Something… anything.

He makes a garbled sound—I am not sure if it's a laugh or a cry—and raises his fevered eyes to mine.

"Yeah, I regret it. I regret not killing that bastard with my bare hands. That is what I fuckin' regret, Hels. Anyone, anyone who ever fuckin' touches you will die," he says, his voice raising with every word. "Goddamn it, you're only fourteen. I need so much more from you than what you're ready to give me."

I don't understand what he is saying. I don't understand anything anymore. My mind is entirely too full with everything that has happened and my thoughts are hazy. I shut my eyes tightly, trying my best to wish it all away. I have tried praying only once in my life… the night my sister died, but, God, if you are real, if you are listening, please make all this be a nightmare. Please don't let Hold be a killer. Don't let me be almost raped. Make it all disappear and I will be good. I won't hate you for takin' my little sister no more. I won't hate you for takin' my momma, either.

"Hold, it's time," Mikey says. I look up to see Mikey talking from the doorway.

"Is it time to go home, Hold?" I turn to ask Hold. His eyes lower before he shakes his head no.

"Not yet, Hels."

He tries to help me stand, but my feet won't stay on the ground. I find it hilarious, but for some crazy reason, I cry instead of laugh. He hoists me up in his arms and the world spins overhead. I close my eyes tightly. My stomach rebels, the vomit only stopped by my sheer will. I hate to puke.

My eyes flutter open, then shut again. I float freely through the air, until I come to a sudden stop. Hold lays me down on... where am I? Out of the corner of my eye, I see green underneath me. Outside? On the grass? I look up to see the club's ceiling, so I know I'm indoors. I feel the soft felt material beneath my fingertips. Wait... a pool table? Yeah, I look over to see the pockets and the eight ball resting on the corner of the table. I giggle. Maybe Hold is going to play some pool before we go home. His voice sounds loud; he's somewhere near me.

"I am fuckin' covering her. Any of you bastards who peek are getting their eyes fuckin' cut out. Got it?"

He stands over me, tucking me in with a white sheet.

"You sure are cussing a lot t'night. You never cuss s'around me," I say, my words slurring once again. My tongue feels thick in my mouth. I click it against the roof of my mouth to feel it tickle. Is that me laughing?

"Well, it's been one hell of a night. Hels, I need you to look at me," he says, patting my cheek.

It doesn't hurt, but it gets my attention. I try to focus on his words.

"I need you to do one more thing for me. Okay?"

"Not for the club." I don't want to do anything else for the stupid killing club.

"No, this is for me."

"S'kay," I tell him.

My eyes keep shutting, but I try to make them stay open to look at Hold. He nods at someone over me. Ward comes to stand just above me. I don't like him. I don't like him at all.

"It will be official. Welcome, my daughter," he says, leaning down to kiss my forehead.

I shiver with hatred for this man. I almost start screaming for him to move away, but then I hear the sound of buzzing. What is that? It seems to get louder. Ward steps back to grasp my arm. I feel other hands tightly grab my legs, my other arm, and shoulders to pin me in place. An overwhelming sense of fear swallows my soul. I glance around to see that I am surrounded by Hell's Highwaymen. They circle the pool table, pressing my body unwillingly against it.

Oh my God! What is happening? Hurt me? Rape me? Not again! Please, not again!

"HOLD!" I scream his name at the top of my lungs. I try to move my body, but they won't let me.

"I'm right here, baby," he says, his face leaning down to mine. His hands cradle my cheeks. "Hush. It's okay. I'm not going anywhere. Remember, Ward talked about this in the meeting. Badger is going to ink you so that everyone will know who you belong to."

"Ink me?"

"He's going to tattoo you."

"With your name?"

He looks away from me. I watch his nose flare in and out.

"No." It sounds like the word is forced from him.

Suddenly, my mind clears. I am all too aware of my surroundings. It's like a light switched on somewhere inside of me. Someone's hand is placed low on my abdomen, too close to my privates. What is happening?

The feel of something sharp pokes my stomach. It digs into my skin, stinging painfully. I scream. What are they doing? It doesn't stop.

"Hold, help me. Please help me," I cry. Glancing up to look at his blue eyes, I beg him. "Please. It hurts so bad, Hold. Save me." I try to wiggle away but the hands hold me securely in place. I start to shake all over as I sob.

"Goddamn it to hell!" He yells, looking up at the ceiling. When he looks back down, fat tears fall from his eyes to splatter hotly onto my face. "I love you, Hels. Please don't cry. I love you. This is to protect you."

The stabbing pain doesn't get better, but worse. It's like they're trying to kill me now. Maybe because I saw what happened and I'm not a member?

"Stop! Stop! It hurts." I chant over and over, knowing no one will ever save me. Not even the one person I trusted always would. I glare up at him, letting him see the hatred that I feel. For *him*.

"Stop. Ward, tell him to just fuckin' stop," Hold says, bawling like a baby above me.

"Son, this is for her own good and the club's. She is yours. Man up, Hold. Take care of what is yours. That means marking her as ours."

"She's just a kid," he whispers, not looking at me now.

"No, she's your woman. Soon to be your old lady," Ward says. "Sage will spend the next couple of years preparing her for this life. For you. She was meant for it, born into it, whether she wants it or not. The same as you. Tonight she was forged in blood to the club. You understand what that means for the few it applies to in our inner circle. It falls to you to make sure she understands the beauty of it. Blood in and blood out."

"Blood in and blood out," voices echo around me.

I close my eyes, wishing I could shut my ears as easily. I don't understand what he is saying. I don't care. I don't care about anything or anyone, me included. Kill me now. Get it over with. Isn't that what he means by blood in and blood out? If I die, at least I might get to be with my mom and Tara.

Time passes slowly. My entire body trembles from the constant torment, when finally the buzzing stops. My lower abdomen aches, but I don't feel the press of something sharp anymore. Are they finished or is my torture only paused for the moment? I open my eyes to see that one by one, each of the men who held me down, releases me. I gently sit up on the pool table. They walk by, patting me on the shoulder and each one says, "Well done, little sister." I see that some even have red eyes, almost like they have been crying. Mikey walks by muttering something. His eyes even have tears in them. I am left alone with only Ward and Hold.

"Sage is here and will drive her home. Her Expedition is waiting downstairs. Carry her down there, then come back in for some club business," Ward says, before stepping toward me.

He reaches his hands out to grasp both of my shoulders. His face leans in to cover my cheeks with quick kisses. My body now shudders from the touch of this man. I can barely contain the revulsion I feel for Ward. Some internal warning prevents me from saying anything, keeping my mouth firmly shut. I steel myself, but I can't hide the hatred that burns inside of me. I watch him see it in my eyes, and he laughs.

"You keep that, my daughter. Hate makes us survivors. It makes us strong. Just be very careful that you don't hate the wrong person. That could only make us stupid." He turns to walk out.

I don't look at Hold. I can't. It's like I have opened my eyes and seen the truth. The monster. The one I already knew existed, but thought I could keep him far away from it. I thought I could save Hold from its clutches. My eyes close when I think of all I lost tonight. Pain once again threatens to break me, but this time it's from within. I am alone. I have no one.

"Hels," he whispers my name, "I'm sorry. I am so sorry. You have to forgive me—I did it for you."

I hear him, but I don't. Not anymore. His voice lies. He is a lie. My Hold is gone. I open my eyes, but still I don't look at him. I slide carefully off the table, hissing from the pain. I don't look to see what they have done to me beneath my skirt. I survived. Just like I survived almost getting raped. Just like I survived watching a man die. Just like I survived the betrayal of the only person I had left in this world.

"Let me carry you," he chokes out.

His cries even sound like lies. I shake my head and walk away from him. My legs barely hold me up to get me outside, but I make it. I open the car door to climb in. Sage turns toward me, her eyes red and puffy.

"Baby girl." She reaches over to pull me toward her, hugging me. "It will be okay. Our boys took care of that."

I don't say anything. Let her believe their lies, because I have seen the ugly truth. No one is ever safe from these people. No one. Not her, not Hold, and certainly not me. I will not cry for them ever again. I will not cry for me. It made me sick to see Holden crying.

She lets go of me so that she can drive us away from here. I silently hope that I never have to return.

SEVEN

March 2008

"Are you seriously going to tell me that he wanted his balls pierced with bells?"

"Yes, it was awesome!" Billy smiles while regaling me with what happened last night at the shop. "Every time he walked, you could hear a tiny ding from his tiny dong."

I bust out laughing, the mental image smacking me upside the head.

"Dude, you should have been here. It was epic for a Tuesday night," she says, turning to clean her work area.

"Are you serious? I have been working nonstop for weeks. This coming weekend will be the first entire one I have had off in months. And I am not answering my cell phone for anyone," I loudly say, looking straight at Malik.

"It's your job," he says, while tatting his latest customer.

I know he is just kidding. I hope. Right? I look at him waiting for a punchline that I think is never going to come, until he raises his head to wink at me.

I turn back to my station, shaking my head. I have no idea what I am going to do with my off time. Not cleaning, that's for sure. Ginger is working all weekend so I'm on my own. Not that it is any different than normal, but it would be nice to spend some girl time together that we have been lacking these last several weeks. Seems that Mr. Bartender finally got his act together and they've been spending every waking minute with each other, which is great, but leaves me by myself. Alone. As always.

"Penny for your thoughts."

I shut my eyes and turn my face toward the ceiling.

"Honestly, I'd pay more than that. Possibly even a dollar."

"Stalk much?" I ask, glancing over at him.

"Only on my off days. But actually today I am a customer," Vin says, swaggering over to sit in my chair. He stretches his legs out, crossing them at the ankle.

"I should have warned you that tattoos could become addicting," I say, clicking my tongue. "I also forgot to tell you that the second one you get is artist choice. And in your case, I am going to give you a tramp stamp that says, "Come and Get It." My quip earns a chuckle from him.

"Are you always this customer-friendly or is it just me who gets the special treatment?"

"Roll over, Romeo, and let's dance," I say playfully, picking up my machine and pushing the pedal for a little buzzing action.

He laughs first and I follow. Why, oh, why can I not get him out of my head? It's been two whole weeks since he walked away from me and it feels like forever. Literally, forever. I have never had this problem getting a guy out of my head. Usually, it's, like, forget him, Keller. And I do. No problem. But not Vin. I spent an entire day sketching that mental image I had of him. Personally, I had thought I'd drawn him a little too handsome, until he strolled in today and I now realize that I was right on the mark.

"Why are you really here, Vin?"

"That day at the coffee shop, before I noticed you, I saw the girl who works up front here with the funky hairdo. She asked how my tattoo was and I said fine, but that I was concerned that a part looked lighter than the rest. She told me that I could come by here to have it checked out or go talk to you that morning. That is what led me to your table. And you know the rest. I never got around to asking about the tattoo and I've been too busy to come by the shop until today."

"So you called to make an appointment with me," I say, shaking my head at myself for letting him get under my skin.

"Yep. I called her a couple of days ago. That Ginger is a wealth of information, unlike some people that I know. She is definitely not missing a certain gene, if you know what I am saying," he says, clicking his tongue at me.

"Yeah, yeah, yeah." I tell him. "At least you wore a shirt this time and you're not the total douche I initially thought you were. Alright, wise guy, unbutton it, please," I say, indicating the navy button-up he has on today.

"Usually a girl at least buys me dinner before getting me naked. Are you always this forward?"

"You wish," I say. "Let's take a look at your tattoo. Sometimes different skin types have problems with holding ink. Most of the time it's the color saturation and the shading is what I have to touch up."

While he undoes each button, I place my gloves on. I pull back his shirt where his tattoo is located. At first glance, it looks fine to me—no touch-up needed. I run my fingers lightly over his chest, making sure there isn't any scarring. Even through the latex, I feel the warmth of his skin.

"Go to dinner with me?" His voice whispers against my ear.

I start to shake my head when his fingertip lightly traces the birdcage tattoo on my arm. My eyes shut at the sensation. His touch.

"I dream about you almost every night."

Join the club, buddy, I want to tell him. I dream about me every night, too… well, until I met him. Now I dream too damn much about him.

"Just one date and I will leave you alone if you never want to see me again. Deal?"

I open my eyes to gaze into his. There are too many things happening at once. Everything within me says to tell him no. Nothing good can come of this. I know what I have to tell him.

"Dinner, not a date," I say, looking him square in the eyes. Holy hell! *What did you just do, Keller?* Really? Seriously?

He grins, not hiding his happiness at my words. I step away, allowing him time to button his shirt up.

"Dinner then dessert, and, Keller, it will definitely be a date," he says, standing up. He reaches for my cell phone lying on top of my workbox.

I am stunned into silence at his words. My mind searches for a quick comeback, which doesn't easily come. I think he has made me stupid. I watch him replace my phone.

"My number is programmed into your phone. Text me your address and I'll pick you up around seven o'clock Friday night," he says, before leaving.

"Wait," I say, regaining my senses. He turns toward me. "How do you know that I don't have to work?"

"I already asked Ginger. Like I said, a wealth of information, that one. She says you love Italian food. I found a great place a couple of blocks over. I'll see you Friday," he says.

My eyes are glued to his backside as he walks out. What the hell just happened? Do I have a date? Like a real date? A high-pitch shrill breaks into my thoughts. I am going to kill Ginger.

"Hot damn, girlfriend," Billy says. "Did you just get yourself a date?"

"I think so," I tell her, still stunned.

"Good for you."

I nod, realizing that every employee and customer must have heard the last of our conversation. My gaze falls to Malik to see him smiling at me. He looks down to finish working on his client. My world is a mess. Why am I breaking the rules? Rule number one—do not complicate my already crazy life. Maybe it's time to move on. Too many people are becoming entangled with my life. I don't need the stress, but for the first time, I have no desire to uproot everything I have built.

"Keller, your next client is up," Billy yells.

This is mine. These people. This place. This life. Just for a little while longer.

I keep myself busy for the rest of the week. Friday looms like a bad omen, but I am drawn like a zombie to flesh. Ginger goes with me shopping and we find the perfect little black dress. It has been too long since I have decked myself out for a date and I have never had a female friend to share in the excitement.

I take several deep breaths. I am a mess and not even a hot one. Screw him, if he's ashamed of me. Something deep inside tells me that Vin wouldn't be, but what do I really know about him? I shouldn't be going out with him or with anyone. I am not looking for sex—I have a vibrator that takes care of that.

Turning toward the clock, I see that it reads 6:35 p.m. Way too late to cancel. I blow out a loud breath. I can do this. No matter what he said, it's just dinner. I rush to finish getting ready.

My heart stutters at the sound of him knocking on my door. This is it. I can do this. I go ahead and slide my coat on. I have no plans for him to enter inside this apartment, before or after dinner. I reach for my purse before turning to open the door. He is in mid-knock when it swings open.

"Whoa," he says, standing back to look at me. His eyes travel my entire silhouette.

My hair falls in big, soft curls. I actually took the time to apply makeup tonight, accenting my features. Black heels give me enough height so that I don't have to stare at his neck, but his face. And may I say what a nice face it is? He is so alien to what I am usually attracted to. So clean cut. My last date had a tribal face tattoo that I honestly thought was the greatest thing since sliced bread. That is, until he passed out halfway through the date from whatever drug he was on at the concert we were attending. I had to find my own way home. That was two years ago.

"You look great." He steps backward, so that I can close the door.

"Thanks. You too." I feel my cheeks heating.

We walk down the steps and I take extra caution not to slip in these shoes. Once we reach the bottom, he guides me to a newer model white Ford F-150 truck.

"Nice," I say.

"It gets the job done. Watch your step," he says, helping me into the cab.

Once Vin is in the truck, he glances over at me with a grin on his face. "I had convinced myself that you would call to cancel."

"It was too late by the time I decided to." I tell him honestly.

He laughs before backing the truck out into the road. I watch him turn the heat up.

"You warm enough?"

"Yeah, I'm good."

"We have reservations at Little Italy. Have you eaten there?"

I nod. "Ginger and I have been a couple of times. It's really good. You?"

"Are you kidding, I love me some pasta. I found it the first week I arrived. That is my game plan whenever I am sent somewhere new to work. I scout out the Italian and Mexican joints before even finding a grocery store. I exist on take-out most days."

I laugh. "Typical male. So how long does it usually take to renovate a house?"

"That depends on the client. Most of the ones we deal with are, nicely put, wealthy. They don't necessarily rush our creativity, but if they require a certain time frame we bring in a bigger crew. This particular project is for a couple moving back here to teach in the fall. I have two of our guys coming out next week to work on some of the

118

big stuff, but I am the only one who stays here full time for now. I am hoping to have my job wrapped up by June or July at the latest. You know, we do have at least one thing in common," he says, glancing over at me while driving.

"What?" I am truly curious for his answer. I shift my body so that I am facing him.

"Art," he simply says.

"Art?"

"Yes, art. What do you think it is that I do all day? I see the beauty in the ruins, bringing it to life with my bare hands, molding and shaping it. When you look at a building, you probably don't see the art within the structure. The same way I imagine that most people don't look at a tattoo and see the sophisticated beauty in the design. I look at your tattoos and see moving, breathing art. There is an intricate story, carefully and artfully designed on your gorgeous skin," he says, reaching for my hand that lies on the seat between us.

I am mesmerized by his words... and totally stunned by his actions as he brings my hand to his mouth, brushing a soft kiss against it. He doesn't let go and for some odd reason, I don't retract it. He captures it tightly within his, resting them both back on the seat.

I clear my throat, finally finding my words. "Maybe I haphazardly threw some ink on my body."

"No, you thought them out. I bet every single one has some meaning behind it," he says. "I can't imagine someone going through that amount of pain to have something randomly etched on their skin."

"Oh, believe me. I see it all the time. These college kids come in to have some of the most moronic ideas tatted on them. But honestly, grown men are the worst. I have seen some sick and depraved…" I pause, realizing I am talking about another time, another life.

"Kids? C'mon, you have to be about the same age as those college 'kids,'" Vin says, oblivious to my distress.

It's too easy to talk to him. I have to stay on my toes to make sure that I don't reveal something that I shouldn't, something that could place him or me in danger. I glance over to see him waiting for an answer.

"I'm twenty-one."

"Whoa, you're barely legal. At least I don't have to slip you wine at dinner," he says, smiling.

"I don't drink," I answer.

"Well, that makes two of us," he says, squeezing my hand that he still holds tightly. "I may have a glass of wine on special occasions, but I learned at a young age that alcohol wasn't for me."

"Overindulge in college?"

"No, my old man was an alcoholic. That is why I was raised by my grandparents."

"Oh," I say to his honesty. I know a thing or two about that, but, of course, it is something I don't share. I have to change the subject. "So how old are you?"

"Twenty-six. You know they say with age comes experience. I just want to throw that out there."

"So what are you saying? That you have a lot of

experience." I emphasize *a lot*. "Is that equal to calling yourself a man-whore?"

He gives a loud whoop. "Damn, you really know how to sufficiently put me in my place. You certainly keep me jumping. But to answer you, I really don't have tons of that particular experience. I am by no means a monk—I've done my share of playing the field. Now I am old enough to know the difference. I'm not saying I am looking for happily-ever-after, but I'm not looking for a one-night-stand either."

I snort, not knowing if I entirely trust him. I don't have tons of experience with players, as Ginger would call them, but I'm certainly not naïve enough to believe everything that a man says.

"You know with my witty sense of humor and your quick sarcastic wit, we are almost dangerous together."

"I don't know about that," I say, pulling my hand away from his. Something about his words throws a red flag up in my mind. Dangerous is right, but not for the reasons he believes.

"Here we are," he says, luckily finding a parking space in front of the restaurant.

He turns off the truck and opens his door to get out. I don't wait for him to come around to open mine.

"Whoa, hold it right there," he says, approaching the passenger door.

I am still sitting on the seat, turned so that I can get out. As he comes near me, I am nauseous at the thought of him blocking my exit. Memories assault my mind: hands that pinch and the smell of sour breath. "Don't touch me," I whisper, holding my hands out to keep him away. My breathing rushes in and out in rough gasps of air. Out of the corner of my eye, I watch him step slowly away from me.

"Whatever it is, it's okay," he says, his voice lowering as he talks to me. "Just tell me what you want me to do. You are in charge. Do you hear what I am saying, Keller?"

I hear him and nod. He isn't my rapist. This is now. I am Keller. I draw in a deep breath, slowing my racing heart that threatens to explode out of my chest. This isn't the first time something has jarred a memory that pulverizes me, but it's the first time I have been around someone else when it happened.

"I'm okay." I have to make up a lie to tell him something. "Sorry, I get these dizzy spells," I say, smiling. I slip to the ground, straightening my dress so that I don't have to see the questions in his eyes. As I glance up, I see that he looks suspicious. I compose myself the best way I know how. If I were to ask him to take me home now, it would only give him cause to think there is something different about me.

"Are you positive that you are alright?" He quietly asks, as he stands with his hands in his pants pockets, staring sadly at me.

I nod and smile. I start walking toward the entrance, his footsteps sounding on the pavement behind me. When I reach the door, he leans in to open it for me. The smell of garlic wafts sharply in the air, sharpening my senses. I take a deep breath, my mouth watering at the yummy scent.

"Man, that smells good," Vin comments, before turning to talk to the hostess.

Within minutes we are sitting at a small booth toward the back. A deep baritone voice sings softly in Italian over the speakers. A waiter comes by to ask if we would like wine, which both of us decline, ordering sodas instead.

"What do you normally order when you eat here?" He looks over his menu at me.

"The eggplant parmesan is really great," I say, realizing this is the first time I have seen him without some type of hat. He's classically handsome, but he has this boyish charm that softens him, especially when he smiles.

"Vegetarian?" He gives me the stink eye.

"No, I eat meat sometimes," I say. I can't help smiling at his exaggerated expression of relief.

"Thank God. I was hoping I didn't have to break up with you on our first date. That would totally suck. I'd lose my girlfriend and my tattoo artist in one fell swoop."

"So that's what it takes? I have been trying to get rid of you for weeks. If only I knew. Can I change my answer?" I jokingly kid along with him. It's fun. He's fun.

We spend the next hour talking about him. I can tell that he has learned to play my game of "let's don't ask Keller any personal questions." He tells me about growing up on the bayou and helping his grandfather restore houses from the time he was little, igniting his passion for the same. The stories he tells of his college escapades have me almost rolling on the floor laughing. He has traveled all over the world and I intently listen to him describing places I will never get the chance to visit.

After dinner has cleared, I turn down dessert, but request a cup of coffee. Vin does the same.

"You know, you are breathtakingly beautiful when you laugh," he says, catching me off-guard.

I shyly smile in answer. It has been one of the most enjoyable nights of my life. In so many ways, I don't want it to end. Our coffee arrives, saving me. I take a small sip of the strong, hot liquid.

"I have a great idea. Come see what I do tomorrow—you can see my work, my art." He leans back, a grin tugging at the corners of his mouth.

This evening, the entire time he spoke of his work, I could see the pride and love he has for what he does. It piqued my interest to see for myself the art he speaks of. The question is—can I take this chance? I don't know how much deeper I can delve and still keep my solitary existence intact. In all honesty, it's already falling apart at the seams. Everything in my life is screaming at me to run, but yet a part of me wants to stay and build a life for myself, be a young woman for once, one who goes on dates to see where a hello might lead.

"Why not?" I answer. I can go see what he does for a living. Nothing more.

"Yeah?" He scoots forward in his seat, giving me that big, goofy smile of his.

"Yeah," I say, laughing at him.

"Well, alright. It's a second date."

"It's not a date. It's simple curiosity about your art. Don't go getting ahead of yourself."

"When it comes to you, Keller, I'll take what I can get," he says, winking at me.

EIGHT

June 2002

The sky shades many different colors of burnt orange as the sun rises above the water. It's early morning, but the humidity is already sticky. I wrap my arms securely around my knees, laying my head on top of them. I watch two Northern Mockingbirds play tag across the inlet in front of me. I walk out here every morning to get away, so I can be by myself. Otherwise, I have to pretend to sleep, letting everyone finish their morning routine so they can leave and I don't have to see their faces.

Now that summer has arrived once more, I have no idea how I will fill my days. So much has changed, but still so much stays the same. I turned a year older, but it didn't alter my situation. My life irrevocably shifted that October day. After that horrific night—the official end of my miserable childhood—the next morning I stood looking in the mirror and promised myself that I would get out of here—alive or dead. They may have tattooed their brand on me, but I don't belong to them. I can play their game until I find my chance to be free.

"Hey, kiddo," Sage says behind me.

"Hey," I say, glancing back at her.

"Mind if I join you?"

I shake my head. She comes to sit beside me with her cup of coffee.

"I love it out here in the early mornings; it's peaceful."

"Yeah." I really want to add that it was very peaceful until she invaded my space.

"I wanted to talk to you about having Hold over for dinner tonight. Now that he lives at the clubhouse, I miss cooking for him. You okay with that?"

"Why wouldn't I be?" I ask, shrugging my shoulders while looking out over the water.

"Why wouldn't you be?" She asks with a hint of sarcasm in her voice. "Well, where should I start? You didn't talk to him for months until he moved out and since then you haven't even seen him. Doll, shit went down that night and I get that you both needed some space to work it out. Hold received the brunt of your anger. I believed you would eventually stop blaming him and get your head out of your ass, but that doesn't seem to be happening. Did you even call to wish him a happy eighteenth birthday? I'm going to take a shot in the dark and say no."

She would definitely be right about that, but she has no

idea what it was like losing him. I didn't care about the little bit of childhood I had left—I lost most of it long before the fire. I mourned the loss of Hold. It was painful and I wanted to die. I didn't sleep for months because of the nightmares that I couldn't escape. Every single time he tried to talk to me, I couldn't stand to hear his voice. It reminded me of that night, over and over. When I refused to talk to him, he started disappearing.

One day, Sage told me that he decided to move to the clubhouse. I felt a sweet relief at not having to see him every day. I had not attended school for a month. Sage's doctor had been writing me excuses, saying that I had mono. When I did return after Christmas, I began riding the school bus, cutting Hold completely out of my life. And I didn't see him again.

"I'll stay in my room," I say.

"Damn it, Hels! You certainly will not. I've had it with your shit. In this life we live, sometimes you have to take the bad with the good. There isn't always black and white here. There are shades of gray that you have to deal with. You accept what you can't change and roll with the punches." Sage glances away from me, out over the calm water. "You know, your momma and me had some rough history, but I decided when Hold took a liking to you to let all that go. The good of the club always comes first."

My mind races with questions about what she is talking about, but I don't have the energy to get into it with her.

"Listen to me, kiddo: you are dealing with me now, but if you don't change your attitude, you'll have to deal with

Ward. He's had it with your behavior," she says, her eyes narrowing on me.

I stay out of Ward's sight. In fact, I go weeks without even seeing him. The time hasn't come to leave yet. I am broke as a joke and have nowhere to go.

Sage lays her hand firmly upon my shoulder, turning me to completely face her. "I know how much you loved my son. Somewhere inside of you that love still lives. He didn't betray you, so get over it. He handled a situation, protecting you the only way he knew how, the way his family expected him to. Do you understand me?"

I nod, because I do. It doesn't mean I have to like it.

"Hold is going through some shit. He's lost, baby girl. You have always been his reason, so it's time to put your big-girl panties on and be that for him. The club doesn't need Hold hitting the bottle and weed hard right now. Ride this out with him. That is what he needs. He blames himself enough for the both of you. Can you please forgive him before he does something incredibly stupid?"

I glance up into her eyes to see a worried expression. "Hold wouldn't do anything stupid," I say.

"He's not the same Holden that you and I knew, Hels. He's getting mixed up in stuff that could be bad for the club. You are going to have to nail him down. Nail him to the fuckin' wall if you have to. That is what a good old lady does. You need to put my son first, as he always has you, baby girl."

I look back over at the water where I spent the only happy moments I had as a child. This woman was more of a mother to me than Paula ever was. She has always been kind to me. Hold loved me. He didn't have to tell me that night, because I always knew that he did. What I wouldn't give to redo everything. It was all my fault. I am the reason that guy died.

I know that I blame Hold for things that Ward ordered. No one stands up to him and lives to tell about it. My head tells me this, but my heart knows that Hold was never going to be the same after what he did. My Holden was gone long before he moved out. If it didn't happen that night, it would have happened some other way. He had already decided to give his life over to the Hell's Highwaymen. He chose his path when he quit school. I know now that he already knew what that included and had accepted that responsibility.

The question I ask myself is whether or not I am going to hate him forever? If I too am stuck in this life, never to escape, will I hate him every day of it? I don't want to. I especially don't want him to go do something stupid and never have the chance to tell him that I forgive him. *Do* I forgive him?

"I would die if something happened to him," I say, looking at her with tears falling down my face.

She wraps me in her arms. "I know, kiddo. You just needed someone to remind you of that. Let's you and I go in to town to pick up his favorite meal for tonight. What do you say?"

"Yeah," I say, pulling back from her.

We both stand up to walk back to the house. I climb

into the SUV to wait while she goes in to get her keys. In only minutes, she returns and we head to town. Sage makes small talk, but I only nod to let her think that I am listening. What is Hold doing drinking and smoking pot? He is going to get an earful from me, after I apologize for acting the way I did. I still blame him, but I also know that he had as much of a choice as I did, which was none at all.

Sage stops on Main Street in front of the florist shop.

"I am going to grab some fresh flowers for our dinner. You want to come in with me?"

I shake my head no.

"Well, then make yourself useful. Go into Hard Ink and give this to Badger. He owns the place. If he isn't available, give it to his old lady, Diamond." She hands me a sealed envelope.

I start to give it back and tell her that I don't want to, when she gives me that look. The one that says do it or die. I have never been on the receiving end of that look, just witnessed it with Hold.

"You are going to get over what happened. It wasn't Badger's fault that you were tattooed either. He does as he is told. Every old lady has the same motorcycle surrounded in flames on their lower abdomen. Don't think you were special or anything because he saw your cooch. He's been tattooing for the club since he was fifteen and has seen everyone's, including mine."

"I don't," I say, rolling my eyes at her. I don't point out how young I was and the fact that I wasn't anyone's old lady, because I can't stand to hear her mouth anymore.

"Get your scrawny ass out of my car, and go," she says, pointing out of the SUV.

I jerk the door open and hop out. My feet almost trip over the lines of the sidewalk as I march to the tattoo shop. I can see through the windows that it's not really busy. The sound of music, blasting from inside, escapes as I open the door to walk in. My dad's favorite band, Motley Crue, blares over the large speakers placed in the corner of the room. Memories of hearing this same song playing from his bedroom bring him clearly to my mind.

"I'll be with you in a second," a scratchy female voice calls from the back of the shop.

The buzzing sound of a tattoo machine threatens to collapse my knees. I place my trembling hand against my stomach when it flips at the sound. A million emotions swamp me. I cried for days over that tattoo. In my mind, it represented something that I couldn't get away from, like always being stuck in this town. I thought about trying to shave the skin off, but when I dug the razor in, it hurt worse than getting the tattoo. I was also scared that even if I managed to get it off, Ward would just order someone to tattoo another one back on.

When I'm in my bathroom and I look in the mirror, the black ink motorcycle with matching flames kills me. It's ugly. Why would people do this to their bodies on purpose? There is no beauty in it. One day, I looked on the computer at school and saw where people could pay big money to have them removed.

My eyes dart to the left and right, checking out the

décor. Several old couches sit off to the right, but their condition looks too iffy to sit down on. Attached to the walls are these large poster boards covered in art. Some of the designs are beautiful. I step closer to see a drawing of an angel that looks a lot like my mom. I blink back the tears at the thought. I don't have any pictures left of my family, but it looks just as I remember her.

My mom's family died when she was young. She was raised by an elderly aunt who had long passed away by the time my mom married and had kids. I once remember her saying that my dad's family was all degenerates who eventually end up in prison to die out. So I have no pictures of any of them, except some of Dad in the MC's clubhouse.

I stare at that angel, my heart yearning for something like that to remember my mom. I wonder why people draw these incredible pictures to hang in a tattoo shop?

"Hey there, sugar. What can I do you for?"

A woman with bleached-white, spikey hair smiles at me. She can't weigh more than a hundred pounds soaking wet, except for her exceptionally large breasts. She has on a black cutoff tank top and tight—super tight—jeans. I am mesmerized when I see that her body is covered in tattoos, beautiful color tattoos covering her arms and neck. I gasp when I notice different real-looking birds painted exquisitely on her skin. I read different quotes and dates. I want to ask her about every single one. Her body looks like a storyboard.

"Earth to Mars," she says, snapping her fingers in my face.

"I am so sorry. They're beautiful," I say, still staring at her tattoos.

She smiles. "Well, thank you. I think so."

I remember why I am here and glance over to her. "Um, is Badger here?"

"Who's asking?" Her look turns leery now.

"Sage Dawson wanted me to drop this off to him or Diamond," I say, showing her the envelope.

"Who are you?"

"Oh. I'm Helen."

I watch her eyes go sad at the mention of my name. In fact, her entire face frowns.

"Aw, kid. Come here and let Diamond give you a big, old hug," she says, not waiting for me to move. She smothers me against her balloon-size chest. "Badger told me about what happened. I was spitting mad. Don't get me wrong—I'm all about what the club wants—but they could have been more sensitive. At your age, they should have brought me in. I've been with Badger for about five years, and I know he is the only one that does the old lady tats, including mine. But they could have made an exception."

I am blown away by her words, by the compassion she seems to have for me when she speaks them. I slip out of her arms.

"I saw you looking at the tattoos on the boards. You thinking about getting another one? Tattoos are addicting, honey-pie," she says, smiling at me.

"That is a tattoo?" I point to the angel on the wall.

"Sure it is. That is one of Badger's designs. I've been tattooing for over twenty years and I am better than all these boys that think it's a man's world. Even Badger said that I am the best artist he has ever seen. I'm faster with my gun than Annie Oakley ever was with hers."

I am amazed. "You can tattoo it exactly like that on skin?"

"I sure can. I can tattoo anything you like. Almost all the boys have my tats on them."

"I like to draw, too," I say, my mind racing with what she is telling me. "I didn't know that you could tattoo beautiful designs like that."

"Did you think it was all black flames and motorcycles?" She laughs at her own question, until she sees my face. "Aw, honey. Of course you probably did."

I take a deep breath, my mind made up. "I want you to tattoo that angel on me. It looks like my momma."

"Slow down, little sister. How old are you?"

I look at her, determined to get this tattoo. "Your husband has already tattooed me with something I didn't choose. Something ugly. Now, I want this one. Something beautiful. I want it…" I say, pausing to think where I can put it. "I want it on my back. Can you please do this for me?"

"Do you have any money? That tattoo will be pretty expensive."

"No," I say sadly, but then think of something. "But I

could work it off this summer for you. I could sweep floors and dust. Do whatever you need."

At the sound of the front door opening, we both turn to look. Sage walks in, sliding her sunglasses to rest on top of her head.

"Hey, Big D. What's taking so long, kiddo?"

I square myself off to look at Sage. "I want to work here all summer in exchange for a tattoo," I say. "Please?"

She raises her eyebrow at my answer. "What type of tattoo?"

"She thinks the angel on the wall looks like her momma," Diamond says, pointing to the picture.

"Mmm, I guess it does," Sage says, glancing curiously at the art. "Where do you want it?"

"On my back."

She looks at me for a second. "I tell you what. I have to talk to Ward about it, but if he says it's okay, then I am fine with it. Deal?"

"Deal," I say quickly.

"Well, slap me pink and call me Miss Piggy. I think I'll love having you around. You just come on by when you can. See you Saturday night, Sage." Diamond hugs us both before taking the envelope and walking to the back.

We walk out, heading straight for the SUV. When we get to the Expedition, Sage reaches for my arm before I can open the passenger door.

"One more thing, Hels. I want Hold to come home," she says, surprising me. "You, and only you, can make that happen. I want us to all be a family again. If you want that tattoo bad enough, I can make Ward say yes. You scratch my back and I'll tattoo yours. That's the deal."

"How can I make him come home?" I plan on talking to him and telling him I am sorry, but what would make him move out of the clubhouse?

She moves in closer to me, patting my blonde hair that has grown overly long. "You are a young woman now. A beautiful young woman, I might add. My boy loves you. I'm sure you can think of something. I have always known that you would be my daughter-in-law someday. Now or later is fine with me." She smiles and walks over to the driver's side.

Her *what?* Has she lost her mind? I only turned fifteen in January. My mind is blown. Is she crazy? I don't love Hold like that. I never have. I numbly open the door and climb in.

"Sage," I whisper. She has to know that I don't have feelings for him like that. "I love Hold like a brother. I have never loved him any other way."

She leans toward me over the center console, her eyes narrowing directly at mine. "Well, then you better learn to."

I don't miss the look in her eyes. She is dead serious about this. I nod, scared not to acknowledge her. I sit back in my chair as she cranks up the SUV to leave. It seems to take forever to get home as we stop by the grocery store on the way. Sage acts like nothing has happened and all is good. Of course, I have always known that she is first and foremost about the club. Hasn't she been drilling that into my head for the last four years? I even remember Ward saying she was grooming me for this life, whatever that means. Now it all makes sense. They always knew I would end up with him, one way or another. Was that the only reason they took me in as a child?

When we arrive home, I mindlessly help her unload the groceries. Afterward, she tells me to go ahead and run upstairs to get dressed. My body feels as if it's on autopilot. I shower, wash my hair, and towel-dry off. I return to my bedroom to find a new sundress lain neatly across my bed. I hold it up to me while looking in the mirror. It's a little more daring than I am used to, but incredibly beautiful. It is a pale pink with a large white dandelion hand stitched on the front. I touch the little seeds that look as if they are being blown across the bodice. It is sleeveless and short... shorter than any of my previous miniskirts. It will barely reach mid-thigh.

I lay it back on the bed so that I can finish getting dressed. I blow my hair out in soft waves. The summer sun has already given it that sun-kissed look. Last year, Hold gave me my favorite sweet-smelling cotton-candy lotion and body spray that we both found while shopping at a drugstore. We couldn't get over how much it smelled like the real thing. I rub my body down in it, before spritzing the body spray all over. I want to remind him of the good times we had together.

The weight of what Sage said to me this afternoon hits me like a ton of bricks. I sit down on my bed. She can't be serious. Hold doesn't think about me like that... does he?

And if he does, could I love him like a boyfriend? The thought doesn't excite me in the least.

I slide the dress on before slipping into my white sandals. I add a little black eyeliner that Sage bought me months ago and some pink lipgloss. I don't want to go downstairs until Hold gets here, so I sit at my desk to draw. I have been working on some portraits of Sage for her birthday coming up. I start shading in my latest sketch, resisting the urge to add two horns and pointed tail.

After about thirty minutes, I stand to go downstairs. I can do this. I've thought about it… and Hold did what he was told. I can't blame him for that. I know what this life does to you, what they expect of you. This afternoon proved that all too much.

I hear Ward and Sage talking to Hold before I walk into the kitchen. I pause to eavesdrop on their conversation.

"Boy, you got to lay off the weed and booze," Ward tells him. "Hey, I remember what it's like being on your own for the first time, but when you start endangering yourself, you're endangering the club."

"I also heard you've been messin' with that stupid junkie hooker over in Gainesville." Sage says to him.

"Ma," Hold says, "that's none of your business."

My heart stops when I hear his voice: he sounds older somehow… he doesn't sound like my Hold. I realize now that I haven't seen him in almost six months. How could it have been that long?

"Sage," Ward says, his voice sounding like a warning.

"That is none of our concern."

"It is when I don't want him near a crack whore." Sage says.

Hold laughs and even that doesn't sound the same. They all start speaking at the same time. I take a deep breath before deciding to go through the door.

"Here she is," Sage says, when she spots me.

I don't look at her, but directly at him. Oh, God. Before me stands a man. A. Man. He's taller and his shoulders seem wider than before. He has on standard club attire with his "Prospect" cut, white t-shirt, and jeans. His face is covered in dark stubble that makes him look much older than eighteen. His hair is growing out. But it's his eyes that break my heart. They look tired, so incredibly tired and red. I recall my father's bloodshot eyes and his looked exactly the same.

Those blue orbs follow me from head to toe—or toe to head. I watch them start at my shoes and travel up, before moving back down. Over his head, I see Ward look at me, then at Sage. She gives him a smile and a wink. I don't want to talk to Hold with them standing here. I personally don't even want to be in the same room as Ward, but I have to pretend that everything is okay.

"Hey, Hold," I say. "Can we go outside to talk?"

He nods wordlessly and walks with me out the backdoor. I head straight for the water.

"You've grown up, Hels," he says, following behind me.

"So have you. Has it really been six months?" I glance

over my shoulder to catch him staring at my behind. "Hold," I say, trying to get his attention.

"What? Yeah, I guess it has." His face turns crimson.

There he is. My Hold. I finally catch a glimpse of the boy I once knew. A gentle breeze blows the ends of my hair away from my shoulders. I stop so he can walk beside me. We stroll along the bank until we reach the boat dock. The sun is starting to set, its last rays casting light out on the water.

"I am so sorry, Hold," I whisper, not knowing exactly where to begin. "I blamed you for things that you couldn't control."

"Shut up, Hels."

The sound of his angry voice shocks me.

"I take full responsibility for what happened that night. I shoulda never brought you out to the club. It wasn't my place to do that and it sure as hell wasn't somewhere you should have been."

"Hold," I say, stopping when he throws his hand up.

"Listen to me for one damn minute. I need to get this off my chest. I wish I could do it all over. You shouldn'ta been exposed to any of that shit. It's hard enough bein' in my head. I thought I could choose the club and still keep you. Everyone told me to let you grow up first and then things would change. But they didn't know you like I did. You've wanted to get outta this place since you were a kid. That hasn't changed, has it, Hels?"

I know what he's asking, and I start to answer him honestly when I hear Sage's voice in my head about convincing him. She wants him away from the drugs and booze as much as I do. I don't want him found dead somewhere. And I especially don't want him picking up bad habits from a junkie whore.

"Yes, it has," I answer, glancing shyly up at him.

His face changes before my very eyes. I see how my words surprise him. He straightens his back, not looking so broken any more, and his eyes seem to be much clearer.

"How? How has it changed?" His voice sounds raspy, like he is getting sick.

I know what he wants to hear; I know what Sage wants me to say. "I grew up." My heart feels like it might just bounce right out of my chest. Was I ever a child? Because I don't remember ever being one.

Within seconds, his arms surround me, trapping me against his hard body. "Don't you fuckin' mess with me, Hels," he says, directly into my ear. "I can't take it. Not again. I have been going ape-shit crazy thinking I'll never get to talk to you. I just wanna be near you. Please don't offer me my dreams and then take them away."

"I missed you, Hold," I say, giving him the truth.

"God, Hels, I missed you so much. So damn much," he says, holding me tight.

I feel his lips moving against my neck, small, innocent kisses, one after another. It doesn't repulse me, but I'm also not begging for more. I stand here, waiting to see what he does next. The feel of him getting closer toward my lips, creates this intense gnawing in the pit of my stomach. It's not totally uncomfortable. Finally, his lips brush softly against mine.

At first, it's like he is sampling how I taste. His tongue slips through his lips, wetting mine. I close my eyes, not wanting to watch all of this up close. My tongue mimics his. He moans against my mouth, the sound vibrating my lips. He reaches his hand up to gently hold the side of my face, angling my head so that his entire mouth can cover mine. Our tongues touch. I am shocked and slightly lightheaded at the intensity of this kiss. I definitely feel it all the way down to my toes.

He breaks the kiss, pulling his lips back only inches. "Tell me what you want and I'll give it to you. Anything. Every single thing. All you have to do is just name it." He sounds out of breath.

Wow, this is pretty easy. Way to go, Hels—you just whored yourself out for a tattoo. I shake my head at my own thoughts. No, I am doing this to save Hold. Not for Sage and definitely not for Ward.

"No more booze and weed. What were you thinking?" I point my finger directly in his chest.

"Ah, there's my bossy girl," he says, smiling at me.

He still holds me tightly in his arms. For a warm night, he shivers uncontrollably. I glance to see that his teeth seem to chatter. He leans his forehead down to touch mine, his nose brushing against my nose, our breath blending together.

"I need you. I can't do it without you, Hels. Blood in and blood out." His voice breaks when he says that.

I see a tear leak out of his eye, trailing down his cheek. My heart stutters when I hear and feel the rumble of his moan. I watch his mouth repeat silently, "Mine."

A little voice in my head whispers to run, to hurry, and leave before it's too late. What have I done? What am I doing? I turn my head away from him to look out over the water, knowing the choice is already made for me.

NINE

March 2008

My feet hurry along the walkway to the massive house that sprawls out in front of me. Vin said that I could come by any time after 2:00 p.m. for a tour. I would never admit it to him, but I am excited to see what he does. He really did catch my interest last night at dinner when he talked about his work. The artist in me loves that type of enthusiasm. My creativity actually feeds off of it.

My eyes travel the exterior of the house. I can see why he loves it, with its large turret and ornamental brackets. It's very romantic looking and I'm not even a romance kind of girl.

"What do you think? She's a beaut," he says, standing in the doorway, watching me.

I nod my head. "I never noticed this house before

today. Not that I come down this street very much, but yeah, she's an eye-catcher." I climb the steps to the wraparound porch.

"Well, let me give you the full tour," he says, offering me his bent arm.

I smile, knowing now that this is part of his charm. After he drove me home last night, we argued in the car for five minutes straight about him walking me to my apartment. I said I was fine and he said he was a gentleman. I finally opened the door and tried to make a run for it, which didn't work very well in heels. He easily caught up to me, walking me straight to my door before saying good night and leaving. That was it. Not that I wanted him to kiss me, or anything, but I thought I would at least get the pleasure of turning him down.

My sleep was severely affected by constant tossing and turning. I blame him for my not getting a decent night's rest. So many times this morning I hovered between coming and canceling my trip, but my curiosity won out. I had to see this art.

He leads me into this huge foyer with a combination of low and vaulted ceilings. A large, rectangular, multi-colored stained-glass window highlights the entire area. My breath catches. Sunlight shines through it, illuminating the brightly hued glass. It has flowers depicted in each panel with over fifty different kinds. Words fail at describing the sight of each ethereal frame. I see a hyacinth, lilacs, sunflower, tulips, rose, peony—so many that I have no idea what they are. Vin tugs my arm, breaking into my reverence of the beauty surrounding us.

"As you can see, I am restoring the main staircase now, but if you look at the four large posts, you can view some of my finished work. I only need to stain them."

I let go of his arm to walk to one of the posts. If I tried to hug it, my arms wouldn't even reach around its width. I rub my hands over the smooth wood, noticing the detail of each design that is hand-carved into it. It's amazing. I can already imagine the time and effort it must have taken him.

"C'mon, let me show you more." He smiles at me while offering his hand this time.

I don't hesitate, reaching for him. We walk the entire house. He points out everything from the different types of wood used throughout, to the floor layout that he plans to modify next week, giving the master bedroom more available space. Our hands remain interlocked the entire time. He finally leads me to a large open kitchen area where he grabs me a bottle of water, finally releasing me. I sit down on one of the high-back chairs at the kitchen bar.

"Hit me with it. What do you think?" He takes a large swig of his water.

"I think it's wonderful. I can truly see the art that you spoke about and even felt it when I touched the wood. You have really done an amazing job, Vin," I say, raising my water bottle to him.

"Thank you. Thank you very much," he says, doing a bad Elvis imitation.

I laugh. He makes me laugh and I haven't done that

with any other person of the opposite sex in years. He's an incredibly handsome, intelligent, charming, sometimes bull-headed Southern gentleman.

"So you do all this work and then you have to walk away from it. I get it. I know how heartbreaking it truly is. I spend countless hours working on most tattoos, making sure that every single line is perfect for my customer and most of the time they walk out never to return. I spend months, years even, thinking about the people who might have previewed my work or the places it gets to visit that I never will," I say, picking at the label on my water bottle.

"Why can't you visit those places? The world is your oyster. Treat it as such." He walks over to throw his empty bottle in the trash, returning to stand next to me. He leans on the counter top, resting on his elbows, while waiting for my answer.

"I really don't have the time to travel," I say, lying through my teeth. The truth is that I don't have a real license or passport to be able to travel anywhere, not to mention funds. "I once had this customer tell me she was going to visit Machu Picchu the following week. All I could think about for months is how this tattoo of mine made it there."

"That is really a sad story," he says, acting like he's crying.

I playfully hit his arm. "No, it's not. It's supposed to be a happy story of how my art travels to all these different places."

"That you think you will never get to visit. Is that it?"

"Yes. I mean, no," I say, pissed that he is misconstruing my words.

"Well, is it a yes or is it a no? I can't explain myself, I'm afraid, sir," he says, obviously referring to Lewis Carroll's beloved character and one of my all-time favorites.

I laugh at his attempt at levity, which must work. "And he quotes Alice's Adventures in Wonderland to me. Are you purposely trying to drive me crazy?" My eyes roll of their own accord.

"Madder than the Hatter," he says, wiggling his eyebrows. He leans up. "Stay and let me cook you dinner tonight. I microwave a mean can of soup."

An unwilling smile shapes my mouth. "Sorry, I need to get home," I say, standing. He follows me as I walk toward the front door.

"C'mon. Now that we have all the pleasantries down, such as you know everything about me while I still know very little about you, we can chill like old pals. It gets lonely around here. Boards don't talk back."

My lips purse together when he makes the comment about him knowing very little about me. When I reach for the door handle, I turn back to him.

"Keller, you don't have to talk to me about anything if you don't want to," he says, sounding serious. "But I really enjoy spending time with you. I find it generally easy to talk to you. And believe it or not, you may think I'm this outgoing, charming guy, but that's not always the case."

"I actually have plans," I say, not really lying to him. Ginger is getting off early to come by my apartment tonight. Mr. Bartender has to work, and she wants to hear everything about my date.

"Oh," he says, looking embarrassed.

Ah, he thinks I have a date. "My girlfriend is coming over because her guy is working tonight," I hurriedly explain.

He smiles at me. "Well that wasn't awkward or anything," he says jokingly.

Before I think it through, I open my mouth. "I could take a rain check for tomorrow. If you aren't too busy."

"Tomorrow is great. Tomorrow is good," he says.

He opens the front door for me and I step outside. "Same time?" I ask.

"Yeah," he says, leaning against the doorjamb.

I turn to climb down the stairs.

"Keller?"

"Yes," I say, glancing back at him.

"You like monopoly?"

What? "Uh, I haven't played it since I was a kid."

"Well, bring your game-face tomorrow," he says, backing into the house before shutting the door.

In the middle of the sidewalk, I die laughing. He is so random. I walk to my car with the cheesiest grin on my face.

The next several weeks fly by in a whirlwind of Vin. I see him almost three or four times a week. Sometimes we meet at the café for coffee before I go into work and other times he takes me out to dinner. What really shocks the hell out of me is that the nut likes to play board games. We have spent hours at the house hanging out, playing his favorites. And that is all we do—hang out.

I have spent many restless nights wondering why he hasn't even attempted to kiss me. Not even a hug. Not that I want him to. It's usually just a have-a-good-night buddy tap to my arm. I am trying not to get offended that he sees me like a guy pal, but after years of not allowing people into my life and finally letting one of the male species get a little closer to me, it backfires.

Ginger thinks he's gay because he hasn't tried to sleep with me yet, which is great if he is and would be just my luck. But, as I have told her twenty million times, I don't get that vibe. No, he is most definitely straight. There is an attraction that I felt in the beginning between us, a connectional pull. Sometimes, when I spend time with him, I get this feeling that he is holding back from me, which is ironic, considering how much I am keeping from him. Maybe that is it: he doesn't feel like he can let go with someone who is so emotionally closed off.

Since we are having an early spring day, he is planning to show me the gardens at the back of the house. I haven't had a chance to really check them out. I arrive later than our arranged time, making it barely before the sun sets. When I spoke to him on the phone an hour ago, he told me to follow the path around the house and he would meet me there.

When I first arrive, all I notice is how dense and overgrown the shrubbery is by the entrance, but once you clear it, the beauty reveals itself. A small stone path winds its way to an ornate white metal gazebo that sits beside a small pond. Vin is standing inside, waiting for me. I take my time walking down to him, spinning around to enjoy the extraordinary view. The sun setting within this scenery is unimaginably gorgeous. And the weather is almost perfect. It's still warm enough that even though I need a jacket, I pull the sleeves up a bit.

"Wow, Vin. This is awesome," I tell him, watching the sun completely disappear from the horizon. The night now surrounds us.

"Wait for it," he says, bending over to plug something in.

Hundreds of tiny white lights burst into life, twinkling throughout the gazebo. It is absolutely stunning and the magical beauty steals my breath. A tinkle of laughter escapes me at the rareness of the moment, sounding nothing like me. I turn in a complete circle, speechless at the vision before me.

"When I first came out here after meeting you, I would visualize your face when I showed you this place. I knew the artist in you would love it. But never could I have envisioned the transformation that I just witnessed."

I look warily at him. "What are you talking about?"

"Whatever haunts you, Keller, whatever made you *you*,

completely faded away as if it never happened. You let your guard down to experience life instead of looking at it from a distance. It was beguiling."

"You don't know me," I say, my anger rising within. "You don't get to make those types of observations about me." I say, pointing at him, ruining this moment for us both.

He charges toward me, pointing his index finger right back at me. "You're damn right I do. What do you think has been going on this last month, Keller? You think you get to corner the market on pain? You think I don't look at all of your tattoos and see that you might not talk about your past, but you plainly put it out there for the world to see. The funny thing is… you never get close enough to anyone for them to figure out that your entire life story is as clear as the pictures tattooed on your body."

"You don't have a clue about what you're saying."

"I don't have a clue, huh?" He shakes his head. Before I can move, he grasps my wrist, pulling my jacket sleeve higher up to show my tattoos. "I would bet all the money that I have that there is nothing on your body that doesn't have some significant meaning to you. You weren't some wild-child teenager who wanted to piss off mommy or daddy with some tats. No, I would bet that your life story is etched painfully on your skin."

I stare at him, both of us breathing heavily. I jerk my arm away from him and turn to stumble out of the gazebo.

"You have no idea…" I say, stopping only when he forcefully spins my body around.

"You're right. I don't have any idea because you don't share a goddamn thing about yourself. You expect too damn much from me, Keller," he yells at me.

"I don't expect any damn thing from you, Vin," I yell back at him.

"Well you should." His loud voice echoes in the night sky. "You deserve respect and love and everything your heart desires," he whispers. "You need to live your life instead of watching it pass you by."

I am suddenly tired of battling him. I am worn thin from this constant emotional yo-yoing. "Why do you care?"

"Because you're you," he simply says.

Before I have time to think about his words, he kisses me. His lips seduce mine as he brushes them softly against my mouth. He nips at my bottom lip, soothing the sting with his tongue. Time seems not to matter to him. His arms surround me, pulling me tightly against him. He trails kisses down my neck, sucking on the right spot so that my knees weaken. When he pulls back, I feel the loss immediately. My moan of protest surprises me the most.

He gives a quick laugh, before devouring my mouth. This kiss I feel with every fiber of my being. Every young woman dreams of experiencing this depth of excitement at least once in her life. His tongue strokes mine, setting fire to every nerve I possess. I feel it from the roots of my hair down to my toes. It is the single most sensual moment of my life.

I push away from him, breaking our physical contact.

What are you doing, Keller? Are you crazy? Did you forget who you are? Do you want to get him killed? I shake my head to clear all these questions that I don't have answers to.

"Keller," he says, reaching his hand out toward me.

I step back, not wanting him to touch me. My hands flatten out in front of me in warning. "Can we please just be friends?" I beg. I have no clue how to give him what he needs emotionally.

"I thought we already were," he answers, placing his hands in his jean pockets before turning to walk away from me, up to the house.

Chapter
TEN

August 2002

"Hey sugar, can you make sure to sterilize Badger's equipment first?"

"Sure, Diamond," I say, capping all the ink bottles that the men constantly leave out.

Diamond, better known as Big D to most of the club's men, is the only tattoo artist at Hard Ink who doesn't leave an absolute mess every single time she tattoos. All the other ones, who happen to be males, are filthy animals—including their clients. I dread sterilizing their needles because

God knows what type of disease I could pick up just from accidentally sticking myself. I have spent the entire summer cleaning, sterilizing, and picking up lunch every day for the entire shop.

I know more about a tattoo machine than half the artists working here. Diamond taught me how to take one apart to clean and put it back together, and I could do it in my sleep. I have learned all there is to possibly know about the equipment and art. Every day, I continue to watch Diamond with her line work and shading, listening to everything she teaches me.

The entire summer I arrived before Diamond or Badger opened up and stayed until they kicked me out. How was I to know that when Sage sent me in here two months ago, it would be my salvation? All because Diamond showed me the beauty that lies within the art of tattooing. If you respect the magic, appreciate the art, and forge yourself in the blood, a piece of your soul lives on with another. That is what she told me. She also said that when you choose to mark your body to make it count. Each piece should be something that pierces your heart and soul in pain or joy. Either will help you harness the passage of time, reminding you of where you came from and where you should be going.

One late July afternoon, Diamond lovingly inked my angel onto my back. I remember lying there knowing that this was my choice. The entire four hours, I didn't move an inch. The pain of the needle was like a promise of having my guardian angel residing on me, with me, forever. My mother. When she was finished, she held my hand as I looked into the mirror. I broke down in tears, seeing my angel in beautiful blues and yellow, outlined in bold black. Diamond held me, and right then and there, we bonded.

After seeing my own drawings, she was impressed with my talent and offered me an apprenticeship. She even volunteered to be my first skin. Yesterday, I completed that tattoo—a sexy biker pin-up girl on her leg that I designed just for her. Diamond squealed with delight when I finished, swearing that it was some of the best work she has ever witnessed. I have been on cloud nine since, and for the first time in months I feel alive.

Alive. What really does it mean? I wake up every morning, I eat, I sleep, and do it all again. I thought that this would be it forever. And I knew that I couldn't survive this life for much longer being alive like this. Tattooing changed it all. It brought a level of realness that my personal life had lacked, a reason to live.

"Fuck," Sandman says, as Badger tattoos something on his side.

His colorful language catches my attention. It's only four o'clock and he already has a pint of whiskey, halfway empty, tightly gripped in his hand. I walk closer to see that he is getting a pistol tattooed directly on his ribcage. The handle is lightly shaded with dark lines marking each kill that he has made. I heard him request that little added design. I once dared to ask Diamond what Sandman did for the club. Her answer was that he was the grim-fuckin'-reaper and never to ask that question to anyone else ever again.

"Goddamn, I love this song," he says, closing his eyes,

singing the first line to Enter Sandman by Metallica.

The rock music pours loudly out of the speakers. I start to turn away when I notice him looking directly at me.

"Well, if it isn't Hell's little queen herself," he says over the sound of the machine and music.

I stare back at him, waiting for his next words. Sandman darkly fascinates me. He's of average height, but built as solid as a bull with his thick barrel chest. Old scars crisscross his bald head and bisect his once handsome face. Now that I am Hold's girlfriend, he brings me to all the club's functions. Most of the men are generally nice, especially Sandman. At the last cookout he shared stories of my dad with me. I never knew the fun-loving, happy man who he described. I was enthralled with the tales he told, wanting to know more about this stranger who was evidently my father.

"You did a great job on Big D's tattoo. I've been wanting a sexy biker chick ridin' my leg. I think I'll let you tat me up." He smiles at me.

"I think everyone was impressed with her work," Badger says, looking up from his shading. "The detailing on the face was right on."

"Well, draw something up and if I like it, I'll be your first paying customer," he says, closing his eyes to hum the music.

I start to turn away, when I hear him call me.

"Little queen, just so you know, I like big tits and ass. Get it right and we'll do business."

I smile to myself, because I might have found the possibility of financial freedom.

"Hey, sweetie. Tall, dark, and sexy just walked in to pick you up," Diamond says, walking into the storeroom in the back.

I have been making a list of the items that she or Badger needs to pick up for the shop. At her words, I take a deep breath. Every night is a struggle for me. I have become a great actress. That night I forgave Hold and put everything to the side, things dramatically changed. Not in the ways that I hoped, though. He still drinks, and I have smelled pot on him a time or two, and he wouldn't move back home. But who could blame him for that? I have become what I never knew he wanted. His.

He proudly displays me as his girl. He picks me up every morning to bring me to the tattoo shop and returns every night when he finishes at the garage. He eats dinner with Sage and I when he takes me home. Sometimes Ward joins us and, for the first time, that man even looks happy. We sit around the table, my secret hatred for most of them magically concealed. I smile, I laugh, I even talk, but it is all fake. Let them think I am happy.

Sage was pissed at first that he wouldn't come home to live. I overheard him telling her that it was because of me. He explained that it would look bad to the kids at school for my boyfriend to be living here and he couldn't do that to us. She was content with his story after that, happy to at least see him coming around more.

Hold has always been the one person who knew me inside and out. When we were little, he would know something was wrong even before I told him. We always had a special bond, but that night shattered our connection. Suddenly, he is blind to what I am feeling or maybe he couldn't care less to know. When I smile at him, it's like he ignores the sadness. When his lips touch mine, he doesn't feel the confusion that unravels me.

I know my body sings to his—we can't control the mutual response. I feel the rock hardness when it is pressed up against my stomach. It always prompts a heat that spreads deep inside of me. My body aches for something, but my mind says not with Hold. I know the moment is coming when he will expect more. And soon.

"I could stay later to help out tonight," I say, acting like I am busy shelving. My heart races with hope. I don't know how many more times I can sit at the dinner table without losing my mind.

"You know, every night I watch you leave through the doors, sadder than when you came in that morning," she says, crossing her arms across her ample chest. "And, girlfriend, I can't imagine why. Any other girl would skip out the door with that good-looking son of a bitch. Now, we've had many talks and not one time have you mentioned Hold. You want to talk about him?"

I swallow the extra saliva in my mouth before shaking my head no.

"Sugar, look at me."

My hands shake with nervousness. I turn slowly to look at Diamond.

"Does he make you do something you don't want to? You act and look so much older than fifteen. I sometimes forget myself that you're not an adult. I guess this life makes you grow up faster than most."

"No, he hasn't done anything to me," I say, before changing my mind. "Diamond, can I really trust you?"

I see the surprise on her face at my words. And also the grimace she gives, but I need someone to talk to about me and Hold.

"Well, honey, that is a loaded question. You can trust me to a certain point. Badger is afraid that you might know things that I don't need to know about the club because of where you live and who you date. So, let me say that I am here if you need to talk about your love life. I promise that information will not go further than you and me."

Yes, there are things I know that I shouldn't have knowledge of, and I have learned to keep my mouth shut. When I asked Hold last week who the Russian men were who called on his cell phone, he went ballistic. He told me to never mention a Russian connection to the MC. Ever. To anyone.

"Does sex feel the same if you don't love the person?" My face warms. I can't believe I just asked that question out loud.

I see her trying not to laugh at me. My eyes close so I can hide my embarrassment.

"Ah, sugar. I am sorry. Look at me," she says, grasping my shoulders in her small hands. "You don't love Hold?"

I look into her kind eyes. "No." I'm not even sure I love him as a friend anymore, but I don't tell her that.

She looks shocked. "Hels, that boy worships the ground you walk on. He can't take his eyes off of you. It's like you're the center of his world. Not to mention, Sage already has her grandchildren's names picked out." She lets go of my arms and steps back. Her eyes search mine. "Do you think you have to sleep with him?"

"Yes. Eventually," I tell her.

"Because you live with Sage and Ward? Did they tell you that you don't have a choice?" She whispers like the walls have ears.

"No," I say, only partly lying.

"Are you a virgin?"

I nod my head yes.

Her mouth drops open. She reaches behind her to shut the door. "Do you want to sleep with him?"

"I don't love him," I say, answering her question.

"Honey, women fuck men every day that they don't love. Most of the time it's their own husband. It's a tale as old as time. And, personally, love or not, I don't see how you have resisted temptation this long. I would have jumped on that stallion and rode him a long time ago. Are you at least attracted to him?"

"I have eyes, Diamond. He's cute. He's really only

kissed me, but my body wants more," I say, nervous about my admission. "And my heart and head don't feel the same way." I don't add, like it does when I get near Jake Carrity at school.

"Close your eyes and picture someone else, but for the love of all things holy, never, ever tell him that." She walks up to me, hugging me quickly before pulling back. "This is a shit-storm waiting to happen. You are in for life and he's never going to let anyone else have you."

"I know," I say, knowing the truth before she speaks it.

"No, you don't. And to answer your first question, the best sex I ever had is where I fucked my brains out and it had nothing to do with love. If you don't love him, then get what you can from it. Sex can be a substitute for the shitty situation you find yourself in, especially when he looks like a damn god," she says laughing. She stops to glance at me. "You have any questions about the process?"

"Uh, no. I got that." I quickly tell her. "Thanks, Diamond."

"I wish there was another piece of advice I could give you, but there isn't. It could get us both in trouble. You think you could come to care for him?"

"I guess I could," I say, shrugging my shoulders.

"Let's hope you do. Take your time and see where it goes. Okay, let's get out of here." She gives me a one-arm hug before turning to open the door to leave.

I walk behind her. When we reach the front, I see Hold talking to Badger. He glances up, as if sensing my presence, and smiles.

"Hey, babe," he says, standing.

I watch him walk toward me, thinking about what Diamond just said. She got the looks part right. Hold is blessed beyond belief in that department. That's why it's so hard to hate him, not because of his handsomeness, but because I see the boy who I loved as a child.

Some days I think to myself, if I wouldn't have witnessed the murder or him not helping me escape from the tattoo, could I have come to love him naturally in that way? I'll never know because that chance was taken from me. I've tried to love him these past couple of months to no avail. What I haven't tried is only feeling when we touch, instead of worrying about emotions.

"Hey," I say as he reaches me. He leans down to kiss my mouth, but I turn at the last second. His lips softly catch the corner of mine as I awkwardly pull away.

"Diamond, you sure you don't need me anymore tonight?" I give her one more chance to change her mind.

"No sweetie, I'm good," she answers, getting ready for her next client.

I nod before walking over to grab my backpack to walk out with Hold. He leads me to his motorcycle, stopping before getting on.

He stares down at me. "What's the deal, Hels?"

"What are you talking about?" I ask, slinging my backpack on. I place my thumbs under the straps and glance up at him.

"You wanna stay here? You don't have to go with me."

"I don't know what you're talking about."

"It's obvious. You look like you're walking the plank when you leave with me every night," he says, reaching for his helmet.

"It's not that." What do I say? I can see the pain in his eyes.

"What is it then?" He doesn't look at me as he picks at his chin strap.

Think, Helen. "It's just that we never go out like a regular couple. We have dinner at the house with Sage or attend stuff at the club. We've been to the movies a couple of times, but I was the one who asked you."

"Is that it?" he says, looking down at me. A frown pulls at the corner of his mouth. "Things have been so different with us. You don't talk to me anymore." His eyes glance away from mine. "When I kiss you, you zone out."

So he does notice.

"I have been trying to take things slow and build back what we used to have, but deeper. I know I hurt you. I know that I lost your trust. I didn't want to rush this with you and lose you completely, but damn if it doesn't feel like I did anyway." He continues to avoid eye contact.

"Hold," I say.

"Do you have any idea how much I love you, Hels?" Hold finally looks at me, his stark need visible. "I can't breathe until I see your face every morning. I wonder what you're doin' while I'm at work. My mind focuses on nothin' but you. I fuckin' ache to touch you, but I make myself wait until you are ready. It's like I've spent my life waitin' for you: waitin' for you to grow up, waitin' for you to feel the same, and goddamn it, but I hate waitin'." He gives a bitter laugh. "You stole my entire world and I'm not sure how to live in it anymore."

If my heart beats any harder or faster in my chest, it will explode. His confession opens something inside of me, something I thought was closed off forever to him. I do love Hold and I hate to see him hurting. If I am forced to live in this world, I can take advantage of it so that I don't feel as lonely.

I let go of the straps of my backpack and step closer to him. My eyes travel up the center of his throat, to the stubble of his beard, over his mouth until I reach his eyes. I place my hand directly against the black leather that covers his heart. My body slowly rises to the tips of my toes so that my mouth is level with his. I feel the hem of my short blue-jean skirt lift against my bare thighs.

"Kiss me," I whisper, initiating the action for the first time.

His eyes search for answers only seconds before his mouth devours mine. The touch of our lips is different. I can tell he loves that I am the one wanting this. My eyes close. I will my mind to stop and allow myself to only feel. My hands grip at his cut as his tongue and mine go to war with each other. My breasts tingle and my privates clench, needing something I have never experienced. I can't help the high-pitch moan that escapes me.

He is the first to pull back, our bodies both trembling. I should be scared... anything but curious and excited.

"I don't want to go home," I say, knowing exactly what I am asking for.

His lips brush mine. Once. Twice. His eyes glaze over. He steps back and gracefully mounts his motorcycle, before helping me to sit behind him.

I reach for my helmet as he slides his on. Within minutes, my arms are securely wrapped around his waist and we are on our way. The motorcycle vibrates between my legs, heightening this weird throbbing sensation there, and the wind whipping against my skin sends currents of burning need to parts of me I didn't realize existed. I cradle his body with my naked thighs, gripping him tightly around every curve and bend. My chest rubs achingly against his back.

He drives fast—faster than the speed limit allows. Does he fear my decision? Or does he sense what is happening inside of me right now? Thank God he can't read my thoughts. A shiver travels my entire frame just thinking about doing the things I have read about in Sage's wicked romance novels.

When he stops at the gate in front of the garage, my heart stutters for a second, interrupting the pleasure I am experiencing for the first time. I've been here several times since that night and it always triggers unwanted memories. I close my eyes and force back everything, except what I am feeling. What I want for me.

He drives us straight to the front door, parking the motorcycle literally in front of it. I slip off the seat behind him, my hand shaking as I try to undo the strap of my helmet. We stand gazing at each other. My breath quickens as the tension climbs higher by the second, before he grabs my hand to lead me inside.

I avoid seeing the other guys who loiter around the clubhouse, keeping my eyes downcast. They say their hellos to Hold. At first we walk, but then his pace hurries us up the stairs to end in his bedroom. He slams the door shut, turning to stare at me. The look in his eyes scares and excites me. The flush of color in his cheeks must match the heat rising in mine. I am in unfamiliar territory.

The ticking of a clock somewhere in the room clicks away the last seconds of my virginity. I'm in too deep to stop this now. He licks his pale pink lips, hungrily staring at my body. I lower my eyes, taking a step back to slide my backpack off. Do I have the guts to go through with this?

"Don't be scared," he whispers, brushing a strand of hair away from my face. "You want this, right?"

I nod, still looking down at the stained carpet below me.

"Look at me, Hels."

My eyes lift to his blue orbs. Deep inside, unknown feelings churn. More than half of me wants to experience sex and a small part screams that this is Hold. This is my decision, even if my life is seeming to dictate it as a foregone conclusion for Hold and me. If I am going to go through with this, with sex, at least it is with Hold. I know how much he loves me and I guess that's more than some girls get for their first time.

I attack his mouth with mine, clearing my mind of

everything but how this feels inside of me and it works like a charm. I kiss him like tomorrow doesn't matter as my body presses intimately into his. I have no clue what I am doing, but he obviously enjoys it. We don't close our eyes as our lips taste each other. His gaze burns into mine, his breathing erratic, and his body literally hums. I feel it beneath my fingertips as they caress his neck.

The intense pleasure building inside of me incinerates any doubts left about what we are doing. My skin feels electric, sizzling every strand of my hair. His hands roam freely over my body. They trail down my back, grasping the cheeks of my butt, hard. I gasp, surprised that his tight grip feels strangely... hot. He drags my aching body against him, both of our moans clashing into the silence. I can't get enough of his kiss. It's like the next one is better than the first. Why haven't I allowed myself to only feel before now? It's amazing. It's everything.

I lace my fingers behind his head, needing more of his mouth. He seems to want the same, his tongue licking the inside of mine. He lifts me upwards and my thighs open to him. My short skirt rides completely up. I wrap my trembling legs around his waist, scissoring them behind him. He licks my lips, before trailing hot, wet kisses across my throat.

"Hels," he cries, his teeth biting down on my shoulder. "I didn't think I'd be able to wait much longer for you. You're my everything." His warm breath washes over my skin.

There is something strange happening to me: it's like a

tiny fire is sparking inside. It flames with every touch, every kiss. When he slips his hand under my t-shirt to touch the lace covering my breasts, my nipples painfully harden. Is this normal? I swallow hard as this inferno burns higher. Nothing can stop it. I see it mirrored in his eyes, raging uncontrollably inside of him. When he rocks his groin into mine, it threatens to undo us.

"Ahh," I yell, throwing my head back. This experience is more than I imagined. I'm not sure what comes next and I am not afraid. I just want to hurry toward it. His mouth sucks at the frantic pulse in my neck. I shiver at the feel of his tongue licking its way up to whisper in my ear.

"I fuckin' need you. I can't wait," he says, moving his face so that I witness the longing in his eyes. "I'm sorry, Hels. I tried. You are the only thing I have ever wanted."

I whimper, wanting him, too.

He takes a couple of steps before we are tumbling down on his bed. My leg is pinched beneath his, but I don't feel the pain. The need is too great. He moves, shifting us.

"Unbutton my jeans," his raspy voice begs.

My hands shake as I try to do as he asks. It takes several tries until I am successful. He pushes them down, along with his boxers. I watch as he leans awkwardly over me to remove his shirt, leaving him completely nude above me. A tingle of unease shivers down my spine and I feel overly warm.

His hands reach for my shirt, and my arms rise above me so that he strips it over my head. I shut my eyes tightly, not wanting to see what is happening.

"You are so beautiful," he whispers, clumsily removing my bra.

For several seconds, he doesn't move. The sound of his heaving breaths above me spikes my curiosity so I open my eyes to find him staring at my bare breasts. Then lowering his head, he slowly kisses the tip of one. I cry out as my abdomen painfully clenches. The sound of his groan only intensifies whatever is happening inside of me.

His body covers the length of mine, taking back control of my lips. My hands slide around his back, my nails trailing downwards. I can't help it. Something inside of me urges me to dig them into his skin and mark him.

"More," I say, not knowing what I am asking for. My body writhes wildly underneath his, begging for what only he can give me. I whimper when he moves away, feeling the loss deeply. My eyes keep shut, not wanting to spoil what I am experiencing.

Hold's hand moves between us. It softly tickles my flat abdomen, enticing a nervous giggle. As his fingers drift downward, they brush my highly sensitive skin, setting off smaller fires. One finger slides from the top of my mound, to my center. He touches me through the thin cotton of my panties that he hasn't removed. *Oh, God!* That feels too incredible for words. I let these new emotions increase until I am almost bursting from them.

"You are mine," he simply states.

I feel him push the crotch of my panties to the side so that he can touch me. He has to notice the wetness that gathers there. His fingertip gently enters inside, and I can't help it when my body grinds down on him, inserting it further in. At first he goes slow, giving me time to get used to him. I know the instant he adds another finger, stretching me. A touch of discomfort flashes through me for a second, before the pleasure returns twofold.

His constant motion starts something within, building higher until it breaks through. Everything inside of me releases and I cry out. My body quivers from the aftermath and I continue to rock against his hand already wanting more.

"Shit! One second," he says.

I groan, but I don't open my eyes. The sound of paper tearing alerts me to him grabbing a condom. Within seconds, I feel his body sliding to cover my sensitive skin. His full weight on top doesn't smother, but consumes.

"Hels, look at me," he says, interrupting the pleasure I am experiencing for the first time ever.

My eyes open to his, the burning love very apparent for me to see in them. I long to shut mine again, not wanting anything to interfere with what is happening to me. The thought of acknowledging who is giving me this immense satisfaction may ruin everything. He expects too much from me.

I lean up to capture his mouth with mine. He moves over me, his hand pushing my panties and skirt down toward my ankles. His groin grinds against mine, and once more these flammable emotions set me on fire. I can feel him between my thighs, seeking entrance and all the sensations that burst free seconds ago, come rushing back.

At first, he pushes slowly into me before driving himself deep. A streak of pain halts my breath, paralyzing my pleasure. Hold groans above me before letting several curse words fly. My vagina feels full with him entirely too big inside. He doesn't move as his body shakes so badly that I am afraid he might be having some type of seizure.

"Are you okay," I barely breathe out, this pain unlike any other I have ever experienced.

"No. Not yet," he says, panting.

His lips touch mine as his eyes try to convey more than I want. I shut mine tightly, keeping him out emotionally. He doesn't move, letting our bodies adjust to one another. The touch of his hands caressing my arms should be sensual instead of loving. His invasion doesn't hurt the inside of me like it did before. I can feel my body clenching down on him, testing my limits.

"Stop," he yells, shaking harder. "Don't do that, Hels. You're killing me."

I lift my body to slide back, then toward him. His length brushes against my inner walls and we both groan. The fire ignites once again.

"I can't last for much longer," he says, pumping in and out several times before freezing on top of me. His yell of completion sends chills down my spine.

My eyes open to look up at him. His gaze never leaves mine as he continues to drive himself into me. Something feels so incomplete. My body yearns for something more. I can't look at him as I move underneath him, needing to

---

---

reach something out of my grasp. But all too quickly, he removes himself from me.

"No," I cry, my eyes finding his.

"Babe, I'm sorry. Just give me a couple of minutes," he says, moving away from me.

I watch as he climbs from the bed. He stands before me, the first naked male body I have ever seen. My eyes roam freely, committing his body to memory. He reaches for the condom he is wearing to dispose of it.

"Hels," he says, stepping closer to his bed. He reaches his hand out to tentatively touch my cheek. His fingers fan out to run through my hair, combing it back from my face.

I watch his face lean down toward mine as he tugs the back of my head to meet his lips. Our mouths mesh together, tongues sliding against one another. He pulls back from me, his breathing harsh in the silence.

"I love you."

I know what he wants to hear in return. I see his eyes searching my face for the only answer he requires from me. My eyes stare back into his, silently begging him not to force this.

My emotions are all over the place, this all-consuming need beating a shallow rhythm underneath my skin. I understand now what I have read in my books. It all makes sense, including why women will lie, steal, and cheat for this one pleasure. I lust for him, but I know that I don't love him. I want him to fuck me—just thinking the word sends a thrill through my system—but that is it.

He can have my body, but my heart screams it can never be his.

"I know," I say, closing my eyes.

ELEVEN

April 2008

Days pass in a constant hurry. My time with Vin seems to be rushing to an ultimate destination, one that my body slowly hungers for. He has proven to be a friend in deeds rather than words. Over the past month he stopped nagging for information from me and concentrated on helping me live in the moment. He hasn't tried to touch or kiss me since that night, being the friend I requested. Ugh.

I never knew how much I was missing out on life. Of course I have heard of the saying, stop to smell the roses, but living it is another matter. My entire existence changed overnight, but I can't tell him how much. I have given myself a reprieve for just a fraction of time to step out of my self-made prison.

He is unbelievably amazing. I spend hours watching

him work on the house. The love for what he does is evident in his craftsmanship. It in turn creates a greater passion for my job. When he has time and the days are warm, he reads to me as we sit in the gazebo. We both find that we have a joint love for humorous poetry and, subsequently, dirty limericks. When I sometimes get introspective, anxiously thinking about the past or future, it's like he knows what I am doing and brings me out of myself. And the board games he loves to play, well, they surprisingly charm me instead of annoy.

"Your turn," he says, yelling from the living room of the house.

"Just a minute," I reply, pouring the last of the cherry soda in my cup.

I return to find him lying on the floor, resting on his stomach, the atmosphere cozy with the fire burning in the large hearth and music playing almost as an afterthought in the background. I sit down across from him, cross-legged, a checkerboard between us. He counts the black pieces he has accumulated from me, a superior gleam in his eyes. There are way more red pieces left on the board than black. *Damn it!*

"Did you cheat while I was gone?" I raise my eyebrow at him.

"Are you questioning my integrity?"

"Yes."

"I'm offended that you think I have to cheat. You're way too easy to beat at checkers."

"Is that so?" I narrow my eyes.

He lowers his head, but not before I catch the smile on his face. When he looks at me, he is serious once again. "No offense, but I pretty much kick your ass at everything. Is there any game that you are good at?"

I think for a second. Sadly, there isn't, but I'm not saying that to him—two can play this game. I glance back at him. "Well, I am really good at poker," I say, nonchalantly.

"Poker, huh?"

"Yeah, you know the strip kind," I say, innocently biting my bottom lip.

His eyes widen, and his mouth drops open. He jumps up from his prone position on the floor and runs down the hallway. I am shocked. What is he doing? Where is that idiot going? He comes running back, his socks sliding across the hardwood floor before stopping, and dropping back down in front of me. His smile can't possibly get any wider.

"I'm in," he says, dropping something between us.

I glance down to see a deck of playing cards. The laugh that bursts from me echoes throughout the house as his joins mine. I can't stop the rolling laughter that consumes me, my abdomen literally aching from the muscles tightening.

"You did not just do that," I finally stop long enough to say.

"I never joke about strip poker. Ever," he says, shaking his head at me.

"Not going to happen," I tell him.

"One game," he counters, his eyes daring me.

"No," I say, shaking my head.

"C'mon. One game. That's it," he says, stopping me from saying anything else. "You can't throw down that challenge and not come through. Tease."

His words don't offend me because I know that he is joking, but they still sting a bit—enough that I actually give in.

"One game," I say.

"Oh, yeah!" He pumps his fist in the air. "Alright, ante in," he says, rubbing his hands together.

What have I gotten myself into? I glance down, realizing that I don't have much going for me in the extra clothing options. No socks to start with. I have my jeans, a tank top, and a pullover, not counting my lace panties. The tank is more of a comfy bra, so... nipple city. I look to see him staring at me.

"You first." I tell him.

"I am not scared," he says playfully. He stupidly tries to be sexy as he slowly rolls his sock down before removing it, throwing it between us. "Thank God for cold feet."

"Really?" I roll my eyes at him. "Wimp." Actually, I am jealous. I took my socks off earlier because I love the feel of the cold hardwood floor beneath my feet. Alright. Man-up. I reach for the edges of my pullover, making sure to separate it from my tank top before pulling it up and over my head. The static electricity makes my hair rise unattractively in the process. I ceremonially toss my pullover in with his sock.

I watch the laughter leave his eyes and something else replaces it. *Need.* His gaze switches from my eyes to my chest. My nipples hardening have nothing to do with the cold. I'll give him credit, though. He is really trying to keep his eyes on my face.

"Vin?" I snap my fingers to get his attention.

"Uh... yeah. What?" His confusion is endearing and sexy as hell.

"Deal the cards," I remind him.

He snaps out of his daze, laughing to himself. He reaches for the deck, getting them ready.

"Okay, this is what we're playing for: if I win, you have to keep your shirt off and let me ask you about your tattoos."

I start to interrupt him, but he shakes his head.

"Hear me out. You don't have to tell me exactly why you got them, just something about them. And if there is one you don't want to talk about, you can say," he says, pausing, "just say... next. Now if you win, you get to keep my stinky sock. Deal?"

"Vin," I start to say. "I don't..."

"Wait. You are the professed strip-poker goddess. What do you have to lose?"

"I'm not."

"Keller, shut up and look at your cards."

I look down to see he has already dealt them. I know how to play... I'm just not that good at cards. Just like board games. Me and my big mouth.

"Nothing wild. Five-card poker. Sound good?"

I nod. "One game. Let's do this."

Within minutes he has kicked my butt.

"You lied," he says, accusingly.

"Yeah, lucky for you." I throw my cards at him and turn to grab a large pillow off the couch. I place it on the floor in front of the fire while he places the cards back in the pack. My eyes follow his hands. He has the sexiest, long, elegant fingers. *What are you doing?* I fall back on the pillow, resting my head.

"Do you want something else to drink?" he asks, stoking the fireplace behind us before sitting.

"No," I tell him.

He turns to position himself so that he is lying next to my body. He props his head on his hand, looking down at me.

"Why the teacup?" He points on the underside of my arm.

"You don't waste any time," I tell him.

"Time with you, Keller, is a precious commodity."

Something about his words sounds almost desperate. I look up at him, trying to figure it out. When I can't, I decide to answer him.

I raise my arm, pointing to the teacup. "My absolute love for coffee. I didn't want a manly mug, so this is the next best thing." The heat from the fire overly warms my bare arm, so I lower it.

I watch him raise his hand so that his finger can trace over the different art pieces decorating my arm. His touch surpasses my skin, reaching deep down inside of me, stealing my breath away. I try to stay unaffected by his movements to no avail. He finally comes to a slow stop on another tattoo.

"What about this? What do these numbers mean?" He points to a date inside an intricate design all in black ink. I almost say next, but it really isn't something that has anything to do with the club—which is what I can't divulge.

I take a deep breath. "It's the date my sister and father died."

"I'm sorry," he says, his hand reaches for mine, gently squeezing it.

"It feels like a lifetime ago," I answer honestly.

"What about the sexy reaper?" He points to a female grim reaper I have on my forearm in the style of a pin-up.

"Next," I say, not hesitating. This one I got for Sandman, in honor of him sharing stories of my dad with me. He loved it, getting the exact replica on his calf. I don't want to explain how I know someone named Sandman or that he is exactly as his name suggests—the MC's man at arms. A foot soldier. A known killer.

He takes a slow breath before moving his finger to another tat. "What about the pair of blue eyes on your arm?"

"Next," I say again. We are not going there. He has to notice that they're a pair of men's eyes. Well, of course he does. Duh.

"Okay, this one," he says, placing his fingertip gently on top of my left breast. "I think it's pretty self-

183

explanatory, but I am going to ask anyway."

He points intimately to an anatomically correct red heart with blue veins and chambers inked on my breast. No sissy valentine heart here. It has a black chain wrapped around it with a lock in front. Self-explanatory, my ass.

"Next."

"Are you kidding me?" He stares down at me.

"Next," I say, returning his stare.

He falls back to the floor, his head next to mine on the pillow. I look over to see him gazing at the ceiling, a tic pulsing in his jaw. In most men, I've learned that usually means they are frustrated. I watch him close his eyes and I do the same.

We lie here, listening to the crackle of the fire and the music softly playing. I hear the deep baritone of his voice and open my eyes. His head is turned toward mine. He watches me as he sings the lyrics to the current song. Our faces are only inches from each other.

"Don't know what I'm gonna do... about these feelings inside," he sings, humming the rest. His fingers rub against my cheek.

I can't turn away from him. His eyes move down to my lips, hungrily staring at them. He turns on his side to inch closer to me and my body mirrors his. We lie facing each other, not saying a word, our eyes saying everything we can't. I'm not sure who moves first, but enough is enough.

Our lips touch, taste, tell the story that is locked inside. It isn't just a kiss, but a song. A poem. The touch of his mouth wakes my very existence, every cell of it. I'm drowning in desire, my body becoming alive for him. What is it about him that has this effect on my self-control?

His arms lock around me, rolling me to my back. I grasp his shoulders holding him close to me. I never want this to end: his lips devouring mine… his tongue stroking mine… his body covering mine. It feels right. I can't deny I long for more, much more.

A phone rings somewhere in the house.

"Shit," he says, pulling back from me to sit up.

My lips chase his with a whimper. I capture them, linking us once again. His tongue dances with mine, kissing me back with as much vigor. But he still continues to move away from me.

"I have to answer that," he says, staring at me. His arms hold mine in place. "Fuck it." He brings his mouth back to my lips.

This kiss is one of ownership and I'm entirely unsure who wants to own whom. His mouth moves aggressively against mine. I feel his hands everywhere: running though my hair, down my body, over the crotch of my jeans. It all would be perfect if the damn phone would stop ringing. One minute it's his cell phone and the next the home phone rings. When he doesn't answer one, the other starts again.

"What the hell is that?" I ask, looking around, desperate to shut it up.

His lips follow mine, capturing my mouth again. We reach for each other, with him half pulling me into his lap. I can feel exactly how much I am wanted underneath me.

"Goddamn it!" He stops, pressing his forehead against mine.

We both breathe heavily.

"Stay here. Don't you dare move, Keller," he pleads with his eyes. He sits me down beside him, before standing up.

I look up, immediately noticing the bulge in his jeans.

"Nice," I say cheekily. My smile threatens to crack my face.

"Give me two seconds and I'll show you nice," he says, looking down at me, smiling himself.

He turns to jog over to his cell phone. "This is… Vin," he answers, looking at the screen to see who is calling. "And it better be damn good."

My body is still burning, not because of the roaring fire beside me, but the one in me. I squeeze my thighs tightly together to try and stifle it. I can't help but hear his side of the conversation.

"What? When? Well, how long? Fuck! Can you? No, I understand. Tonight?" He turns to glance at me, before looking away. "Shit. If I have to. No, I understand. Yes, sir. I'll be there by twenty-two hundred hours."

I watch him press the end key, rubbing his hand over his face, before turning back to me.

"Problem?" I curiously ask.

"Work. My grandfather needs me on another job."

"Your grandfather ex-military?"

"What?" He looks confused.

"You gave him military time." Is he lying to me?

"Sorry. Yeah, he is." He walks toward me.

"Whatever," I say, standing while yanking my pullover back on.

"Keller, don't," he says, reaching his hand out.

I shrug away from him. Something tells me he isn't being forthcoming with his story.

"What? Do you think I am lying to you?"

"I don't know, Vin. Are you?"

"No. Do you want me to get him back on the phone, because I will?"

"I really don't care," I say, sliding on one of my canvas tennis shoes. I reach under the chair to grab the other one, when I feel him close behind me.

He places his hands on my arms, spinning me around. "Stop it," he says, his eyes search mine. "Don't ruin tonight. Just talk to me."

"Was that really your grandfather?" I glare at him.

"Yes. Who do you think it was?" He pauses, before shaking his head. "It wasn't another woman if that is what you are thinking."

"No," I say, unconvincingly. "Not another woman, but maybe a friend warning you about someone back home."

"First off, I swear it isn't about another woman. There are certain things that we don't know about each other. And second, those who live in glass houses shouldn't throw stones," he says, stepping away from me. "I really hate beyond belief having to end this day earlier than expected. But now I have to get out of here. I'll call you tomorrow. Okay?"

Is he dismissing me? I suddenly remember the shoe in my hand and launch it toward his face. My aim is precise, hitting him square in the nose. I haven't been this angry in a long time. Well, since…

"You did not just hit me in the face with your shoe," he says, his voice low and angry. He reaches over to pick it up off the ground beside him, while rubbing his nose.

"You better be glad I didn't wear my shit-kickers tonight," I say, bowing my chest out. I walk straight up to him and grab the shoe away. He doesn't say a word as I slide it on. "Nice knowing you," I tell him, turning to walk away.

I only make it two steps before he grabs me from behind. He picks me up over his shoulder and carries me back to the couch, dropping me on top of the soft cushions.

"You can't do that," I yell, moments before his body and mouth cover mine. I lose myself for about a minute, before he once again pulls back.

"This isn't easy for me either. My plate is full with getting this house done and other things, but you are important to me. Got it?"

I start to shake my head, when he kisses the daylights out of me one more time. His lips become gentler, sweeter almost, before he pulls back.

"Got it?" He whispers, looking down at me.

"I got it," I say, lost in his eyes.

"Oh, my. That is so romantic," Ginger says, dreamily looking outside the tattoo shop's window.

"I can't believe you hit the bastard between the eyes and he came back for more. That is my kind of date," Billy says, sitting on the corner of the counter, digging for every last kernel of caramel popcorn at the bottom of her Cracker Jack box.

I was discussing last night's date privately with Ginger when Billy rudely interrupted and stayed to listen to the entire story. Well, except the part about glass houses.

"Yeah, but I haven't heard from him. Should I be worried?" I can't believe that I am telling them all of this like a girl would. This is so out of the norm for me.

"No, not yet. I think his wanting to know about your tattoos is extremely sweet," Ginger says.

"I don't know about sweet," I tell her.

"Oh, come on, Keller. Your secret past just about kills me and we aren't even dating. Poor guy. You need to cut him some slack," she says, shaking her head.

We all turn toward the front door when it opens and a large bouquet of hot pink, blue, and yellow Gerbera daisies arrives. The flowers are so out of place in the tattoo parlor.

"Any of you ladies named Keller?" The delivery guy scans the three of us and asks, shifting the flowers in the vase to the other arm.

My mouth drops open, and anticipation overloads my internal circuits. I have to physically restrain myself from jerking the small white envelope off the flowers. I nod, and he hands me a clipboard to sign.

"Have a nice day," he says, transferring the flower arrangement to me before walking out the door.

"Holy hell! Would you look at that?" Ginger jumps up and down, clapping her hands.

Billy snags the card, before I can.

"Hey!" I yell, sitting the vase down on the counter. "That is mine," I say, grabbing the envelope back. I tear it open. It has a small printed card inside.

"Read it out loud. Please," Ginger begs.

I loudly clear my throat. "There are so many things that I want to say to you and can't. You've changed my life. Made colors more vibrant. I don't look at anything the same way I used to. You make me happy. Let me do the same for you." I can't hide my cheesy grin.

"Slick bastard, isn't he?" Billy leans over to smell the flowers.

"Shut up," Ginger says, playfully slapping her arm. "This is Keller's first real boyfriend since she moved here."

"Whoa. He is not my boyfriend," I say, turning to look at the flowers.

A group of girls comes through the door, thankfully interrupting us.

"Ginger, I'll leave these up here with you today." My station doesn't have the space for them, but I instantly regret not making room.

"Yay me," she says, turning from me to the client.

I walk down the steps to my area, glancing over to see Malik staring at me.

"Pretty flowers," he says, closing his laptop.

"They are." I stop to answer him.

"Are they from the guy you've been seeing? The same one you tattooed that day?" He stands to walk forward.

"Yeah," I say, putting my hands in my back pockets.

"Can I ask you a personal question?" Malik stops directly in front of me.

"Sure."

"You move here and you don't know a soul. It takes months for you to even warm up to Ginger, much less me. And over the last year you've opened up a lot, but nothing like the last three months since he has magically arrived. I'm just curious what the change was?"

His words shock the hell out of me. What is this about and why does he even care? I am stunned.

"Listen, don't be mad. I am not stupid, Keller. I know you weren't a hundred percent honest with me when you moved here. Yeah, you were running, but not from who you told me," he says, lowering his voice.

"Who do you think I'm running from?" I ask quietly. My heart seizes in my chest. I look around suspiciously, not wanting anyone to hear our conversation.

"I don't know. What I do know is that you drove into town with your piece of shit car, one suitcase, and your tattoo equipment. That is an act of desperation that speaks louder than words. It says you are running from people who don't make idle threats. Don't get complacent. That will make you stupid. When people who are running get sloppy, they make dumb mistakes, like trusting the wrong people," he says, leaning down to speak into my ear. "I worry about you and I sure as hell don't trust him."

"You don't know him," I say, resenting his words.

"And you do?" He looks down at me and I stare back defiantly.

When I don't answer, he shakes his head before turning away from me. I move to my station, swallowing back the tears. He doesn't know what he is saying. But the truth is, neither do I. Vin obviously has his own secrets and I have mine, and for now, that is the way it has to stay.

Chapter TWELVE

January 2003

"Let the clutch out slowly. Slowly," Hold yells, as I once again pop the gear, stalling the car.

"Sorry," I say, grinning at him.

"What are you smiling about? You are never gonna be able to drive this car I bought you," he says, throwing his hands in the air and hitting the car's ceiling.

My sixteenth birthday gift was a complete surprise. I had gotten my learner's permit last summer, so I still have a while to go before I can get my actual driver's license. My main goal has been to save the money I make tattooing to buy a car. When I found out that Hold bought the bright blue Volkswagen Beetle, I about died. I offered to give him all my savings toward it, but he wouldn't let me. I have learned to take what I can, when

I can. That is what this life is teaching me.

The only negative is the five-speed manual transmission. It is taking me forever to get the hang of it, but I have to admit, I am having fun learning. And Hold will not say it, but it's the only activity other than sex that we enjoy doing together lately.

"Okay. Okay. I am serious now," I say, turning the ignition again. It doesn't take me long to be back in the same position with a dead car. Ugh.

"That's it for today," he says, frustrated. He gets out of the car to come around and open the door.

I step out, pouting. The wind whips my hair around. It's a cool fifty degrees, cold for us Floridians. I look around at the empty school parking lot where we are practicing. It's early for a Saturday morning.

"Do you want to come back to my room?" he asks, leaning against the open car door. His eyes plead for me to say yes.

Ever since the first night I spent with him, things have turned even more awkward with our… relationship. When we have sex, everything is fine between us. In fact, it is perfect, but that doesn't mean we have a lot of it. Just because I gave it up that first time doesn't mean we *do it* all the time. I am still conflicted about my feelings.

I don't love him, but I absolutely love what we do together. *Love it.* I love the way it makes me feel, like I am in control when in reality I have none. My touch makes him completely helpless. The pleasure we both experience is too immense for words, but I have to deal with all of his questions afterward. Why can't you love me? What is wrong with me?

"I don't know, Hold," I say, kicking at the concrete ground.

My body reacts to the closeness of his. A lot of the kids at school smoke, some drink, and more everyday become addicted to some drug. I hear them talking about it, craving their next sip or hit, and I immediately understand. At night, I dream of being with Hold and all during the day, my mind constantly drifts to memories of his touch. His kiss. My desire for his body scares me, and I am terrified of myself. Am I a whore because I hunger for his body and not his love? I start feeling dirty and it's easier just to stay away from him.

It's been over a month since we had sex, the last time ending in a huge fight where I didn't speak to him until my birthday two weeks ago. Plus, between school and working nights including weekends at Hard Ink, I barely have time for anything else. And I like it. When school started up after summer and kids found out about my part-time job, I became popular overnight. Half of the senior class—at least the ones over eighteen—has become my clientele. It's crazy cool and much better than tattooing the roughnecks who frequent the shop who want all naked girls and devils tattooed on them.

"I'd better get to the shop. I have several tattoos scheduled for today." I watch him clench his jaw, his anger evident.

"Tell me what I am doing wrong. Please, Hels. I can't

change if I don't know what it is that you want."

Here we go again. Usually, I just let him ask these questions, ignoring the answers screaming inside of me, and sleep with him. Diamond's advice from long ago reminds me to take my pleasure and use him. Let him have my body and enjoy the perks of it. That is what I have been doing, but I am losing myself in the process. I can't bide my time here like this, because eventually I am going to corner myself in it, one way or another.

"What I want? Is that what you need to know, Hold?" The calm inside of me snaps. This façade falls away. I slam my hands against his chest, pushing him back against the car. "You know what I have always wanted. To leave here. To forget this life," I yell in his face. "Can you give me that?"

"Anything but that," he whispers, looking at the ground.

"Look at me," I scream at him, but he continues to stare at his feet. "Look at me! See what you are doing to me, what this life is doing to me." I step back, stripping my sweatshirt off, leaving only my plain white bra. My body overloads with the anger consuming me. It is hard for me to fill my lungs with air when my chest is crushing me from the inside out.

His eyes lift slowly, running over my exposed skin. My arms and chest are covered in colorful ink. I know what he sees, tattoos beginning to cover a good part of my flesh: intricate pictures, quotes that speak to me, and actual dates that have defined my existence. I know without asking that he doesn't see the story, carefully and lovingly tattooed on my body that I can never speak of: my life history that is slowly eating me up on the inside, killing me quietly.

"I don't understand, Hels," he says, his eyes finding mine. "Are you saying it's my fault that you tattoo dandelion seeds across your chest or fireworks scenes? You're the one that keeps puttin' more shit on your skin."

"No. No, I now decide what is inked on my body, not like your mark on me!" I step back, screaming at him.

"You want me to pay to have it removed? Is that what you want, Hels?" He moves away from the car, coming closer to me.

"No! You are not listening to me. I wouldn't have it removed for anything now. It's an everyday reminder of what this life is capable of and things I can't talk about."

"If you need to talk about things, then talk to me," he says, reaching for me.

"No," I say, stepping away from him. "I hide what is in my heart!" My hand slaps my naked chest, the sting lingers on my skin. "You know what I want and do nothing about it. You refuse to see how the MC is killing me."

"You know the rules," he says, shaking his head.

The thought of asking for the unthinkable crosses my mind. Can I take a chance to ask and sacrifice even more of myself for a chance of a life outside the MC? I take a deep breath before opening my mouth.

"Let's go. Right now. Let's get in the car and drive away. We can get married and you can have all of me," I say, moving to stand before him. I slide my arms around his neck, my fingers grasping his warm skin. My body shivers, the cold finally penetrating my naked flesh. I close my eyes as his hands glide around my waist, pulling me against his body heat. My eyes open to silently beg him.

"We can't. The MC is our life. You and I were born to rule it. I will give you everything you want, Hels. Anything," he says, bringing his mouth to mine, brushing over it. "But not that. This is our family. And there is no escape."

I lean to press my own lips to touch his before pulling back all together from his arms. "And this is the reason you will never own my heart." My arms tremble as I place my sweatshirt back on. I don't look at him again. The wind catches my tears as I turn to walk away.

His cursing gets louder the farther I walk. The sound of him kicking the car and calling my name doesn't slow my steps. I hear the sound of the car engine, not knowing what I'll do or say when he comes for me. The sound of it getting farther away instead of closer surprises me. I glance back to see the blue bug turn onto the main road and disappear around the corner.

With every step I take, the tears fall freely. I silently cry. The thought occurs to me that I could go directly to the bus station. I have almost three grand saved from tattooing. It blows my mind how much people will pay. The way Hard Ink works is that I have to turn over a percentage for use of my chair to Badger and then because it is considered a club business, the MC gets its own cut.

It's not even a choice to try and run now. I have

nowhere to go, no one to run to. To be surrounded by family, as Hold calls them, I am utterly alone. Diamond is the only person I can really talk to, and the truth is that I can't. I am smart enough to realize that the information I know can get people killed.

I stop to sit on some bleachers that overlook the practice football field. This conversation had to happen between Hold and I. All of the lies between us can't continue. It is driving us both crazy. If I am honest, I hate the thought of him with someone else, but I can't keep him for all the wrong reasons. He has to let me go as well.

"You okay?"

My stomach flips at the sound of the voice behind me. I turn to see Jake Carrity standing with a football in his hand, his blonde hair shining in the sunlight. Great. Really? He has to see me looking like this?

"Yeah," I say, sniffing my nose while wiping my eyes with the back of my hand.

"I couldn't help notice what just happened in the parking lot," he says, looking embarrassed. He tosses the ball between his hands.

My cheeks have to match my red eyes. Kill me now. I bury my face in my hands.

"He didn't hurt you or anything? Did he?"

"No," I answer, not looking up. My voice is muffled by my hands. I plan on hiding in plain sight until he goes away.

"Can I ask you a question?"

The sound of the bleachers creaking, alerts me to him

stepping up to sit down. I glance up to confirm that he is next to me.

"What?" I ask, baffled by his actions.

"Did getting all those tattoos hurt?" Now his face turns a slight pink. "Wow, sorry. I should be honest and say that I also saw the part where you took your shirt off. I guess the gentlemanly thing would have been to turn away, but I was concerned that you were in danger."

I shake my head at his confession. "Um, yes. They hurt like hell."

He laughs. "Yeah, I thought so. You keep them covered at school. I've heard some of the seniors say that you tattooed them at that place downtown and you are a really good artist."

I shrug my shoulders.

"I plan on getting one when I turn eighteen. My parents aren't cool with tats so I have to wait until then. Maybe you can hook me up with one," he says, smiling at me.

"Maybe," I answer. I wrap my arms around myself as the wind continues to steadily blow.

"Are you cold? Here," he says, taking off his jacket to place around my shoulders.

"Thanks," I answer.

"So I guess he is your boyfriend."

"Who?" I glance over at him. He tosses the football while staring out at the field.

"Hold Dawson," he says, giving a funny laugh. "I don't want to get my ass kicked. You know I have been warned since you were little to not even look your way."

"By Hold?"

"Nah, he didn't have to. Everyone. Guys." He glances over at me. "I've heard you live with him."

"I live with his parents. They took me in when my dad died because I don't have any other family. Hold doesn't live there now."

"But he is your boyfriend, right?"

"No," I say, reaching to pull his jacket off. "But it doesn't matter." I hand it back to him. "Thanks. I should get going." The roaring sound of an approaching motorcycle catches my attention. I watch it ride around the school, the rider looking for something or someone.

"Looks like your ride is here," he says.

I don't say anything as I start walking toward the sidewalk.

"Hey, Helen."

I turn to see him standing behind me.

"I don't think you should cover them."

"Cover what?" What is he talking about?

"Your tattoos," he says, tilting his head to the side. "I think they're beautiful. Like you." He grins at me.

Oh my God! This is Jake freaking Carrity. Did he just say that I was beautiful? He is my biggest crush ever. I am at a loss for words as we stare at each other. He is so cute.

The rumble behind me tells me that the motorcycle and its rider has found me. I turn to see that it isn't Hold, but Mikey. So, he sent his lackey. He stops behind me, killing the engine before removing his helmet. Mikey has filled out in size like Hold. I swear they get bigger every time that I see them. Mikey stepping off of the motorcycle is an imposing sight. I glance over to see Jake standing his ground. Now would be a good time for him to walk away. I make my legs move toward the motorcycle.

"What the fuck are you doing?"

Mikey's menacing voice gives me a slight scare. I start to answer when I notice that he isn't even looking at me.

"Playing some ball." Jake nonchalantly throws the football in the air.

My head volleys between both guys. They are similar in build: tall, wide shoulders, blonde hair, but it ends there. If you were betting on a fight, you wouldn't hesitate to put your money on Mikey. No doubt he is clearly the badass he thinks he is. And he is all about being a Hell's Highwaymen. The MC is his life. He wears it with pride by his clothes, on his skin, and in his fuck-you attitude.

"Playing ball, huh? I think you need to take your balls and go play somewhere else, man. Do you know who she fuckin' belongs to?" Mikey steps forward, while cracking the knuckles of both his hands.

"I don't know, man. Herself?"

"You think you're being funny, pretty boy? I can be funny, too," he says, charging toward him.

I slide to stand in front of him before he can pass by me. My hands push against his chest in a feeble attempt to stop him. It's like trying to halt a raging bull.

"Stop it!" I yell in Mikey's face.

"You don't fuckin' get near her," Mikey yells over my shoulder. He points his finger at Jake. "You don't fuckin' look at her. And you sure as shit don't talk to her. She is marked as a Hell's old lady. You got me?"

Jake laughs like it's funny. Does he have a death wish? I can tell Mikey is trying not to hurt me, but he wants to get by me to likely beat the holy hell out of Jake.

"Whatever, dude. Helen, I'll see you at school," Jake says, smiling at me before turning to walk away.

"I'm going to kill that fucktard," Mikey says, trying to push me to the side.

"Mikey, don't. Don't!" I scream in his face. "He was being nice."

"I don't give two shits, Hels. What the hell were you doing talking to him?" He finally stops moving to look at me.

"Hold left me stranded. Jake was making sure I was okay. I don't have a cell phone and it's Saturday so the school is closed. How was I supposed to get home?"

"Why do you think I'm here? You should have known that Hold would take care of you, even though you pissed him off. What the fuck did you do?"

"Where is he at?"

"Damn if I know. He calls me and tells me to get my ass over here to pick you up. The next thing I know, I'm talking to my fuckin' self. Let's go," he says, grabbing my hand to pull me toward his motorcycle.

Mikey drives me to Hard Ink and drops me off. I can tell that Diamond is dying to ask why I rolled up with

Mikey today, but doesn't. I prep everyone's station, including mine, but I am a million miles away. My mind is occupied with this morning's events. I could never have dreamed of the conversation that I had with Jake. And he called me beautiful. Did I imagine that?

As much as I want to dwell on Jake, I begin to get busy. I take tattooing very seriously. My total concentration is needed with as much detail as I put into my designs. Hound, one of the original Hell's Highwaymen, is having me tattoo an actual portrait of his mom on his arm. It's supposed to be this big deal that he's letting me do it considering Badger is the only person to ever tattoo anything on him. Badger showed him my portraits and really pitched me to do it.

"That is amazing, Helen. Your dad would be proud," Hound says, looking down at the tattoo of his mom.

These guys speak of my dad with reverence. Sometimes I wonder if it's only because he's dead. My own memories never come close to the legend that they have built him up to be.

"Thanks," I reply, wrapping it for him. I am glad he is my last one of the day. It is almost 11:00 p.m. and I am really tired. My eyes keep glancing over at the door, wondering where Hold could possibly be. He never has been this late picking me up.

We all turn toward the windows at the sound of tires screeching in front of the shop. Sage gets out of her Expedition and runs inside. When I see her eyes, I know something is wrong.

"Get your shit. Let's go," she says, looking directly at me.

I nod, and walk swiftly toward her.

"Sage, what is going on?" Diamond runs to catch up with us as we leave.

"Hold. He's got himself into some trouble."

Sage doesn't say anything else until we both are in the SUV and driving down the road.

"He gets one phone call and he calls me to make sure someone is picking you up. Did he call a lawyer? No, it was about you," she says, reaching into her purse for a cigarette. She pushes the lighter in and waits seconds for it to warm, before using it.

I watch her take several drags. "What happened?"

"I don't know the full story yet. From our guy at the police station, I gather they charged him with causing an affray, destruction of property, resisting arrest, and assaulting a police officer. Separately, they are misdemeanors, but together they are a clusterfuck of epic proportions. And considering Hold's history and connection to the MC, they are gunnin' for him," she says, puffing away.

The hand with her smoke in it trembles slightly, revealing how upset she is. History?

"What history?" I ask, not understanding what she means.

"Hold has been in trouble a couple of times with the law this past year. There have been a few where he had to appear in court and was lucky enough to get off with a warning. He didn't want you to know, kiddo. Lord forbid you think that he is only human."

"Trust me, Sage, I know all too well how human he is," I say, tired of her attitude when it comes to Hold and I. My heart hurts that he thought he couldn't tell me, but then again, we aren't the same as we used to be.

"Well, the pretty kitten has claws. Who knew?" She glances over at me while she drives.

I look out the window to see us pulling into the driveway of the house.

"Shouldn't we go to the police station?"

"And do what? Hang out with all our cop buddies? No, our lawyer will handle it."

Ward's and Sandman's motorcycles are parked outside the house. Sage jumps out and heads into the house, so I follow.

"Hey, baby. Have you heard anything?" She rushes over to Ward and into his open arms.

"The lawyer is trying to bond him out. It's bad, though. He's going to have to do a little time for this," Ward says, glancing over Sage's head at me.

"C'mon, little queen, let's you and me have a chat in the kitchen," Sandman says, walking in front of me as I follow. "Sit down." He points to the kitchen chair.

I do as he says. "What happened?" I ask, placing my hands flat on the table.

"See, I'm hoping you could fill me in on that part. Mikey is the only other soul that knows and he ain't talkin' at Hold's request." Sandman's presence seems to completely fill the room.

"I don't know," I say, shaking my head. "How did he end up in jail?"

"Well, he and Mikey, the stupid bastards, evidently decided to go to the Shack and beat the hell out of a bunch of kids, inciting a ruckus. Then they smash in a couple of windows at the joint just for the fun of it and when the cops come to arrest them, they decide that they are having such a good time, they decline their offer. But the kicker is that when a cop insists, Hold punches him in the goddamn face. Now can you believe that? I couldn't. Not our sweet Holden," he says sarcastically. Sandman walks around the kitchen while he speaks to me. "You see, Ward and me, we think there is more to the story. A heck of a lot more."

I drown in a sea of worry. There is only one group of teenagers that hangs out at the Shack that Holden can't stand. And there is only one reason that I can think of, that would send him over the edge to do what Sandman said. Damn, Mikey. He must have told him about today. *Oh my God!* Jake!

"I can see in your face, little queen, that you know what I am talking about. Tell old Uncle Sandman about what happened."

Quietly, I relay everything to Sandman that happened this morning, except my demands of leaving town. Hold has repeatedly warned me to never say anything to anyone about that. I only tell him that we fought about our relationship and then how he left me at the school. As we talk, I watch him listening to me, and I see closely he pays attention. I stress to him how innocent my discussion with Jake was, definitely leaving out the beautiful comment, before detailing everything about when Mikey arrived to pick me up.

After I finish, Sandman doesn't say anything for several minutes. At some point he must have grabbed a soda and I watch him take a drink of it.

"Are the guys they beat up okay?" The curiosity is killing me. I have to know if Jake is in the hospital.

"Mmm," he says, looking wearily at me. "You mean is Hold okay? Right? That is your first priority, but just so you know, everyone is okay. My understanding is all of them are a little banged up, but considering it was, like, two against ten, our boys kicked ass."

"Do you think Hold will go to prison?" My stomach literally falls through the floor at the thought.

"I have a feeling our boy will spend some time up in county." He walks to my side, placing the can of soda on the table next to me. Sandman slowly leans down until we are face to face, and I stare at the mangled mess that mars his handsomeness. His entire demeanor changes in front of me.

"Do you know who I am?"

He is so close that the smell of cigarettes on his breath curdles my stomach. My body shudders from the hate emanating from him.

"Yes… y-yes, sir," I say, stuttering my words.

"Do you know what I do for the club?"

The feel of his hands running upwards through my hair sends chills down my spine. I nod my head.

"You see, little queen, I take care of unnecessary problems. The shit that just doesn't need to be an issue for the MC. We have enough on our plate without other personal distractions," he says, his fingers wrapping strands of my hair around his hand.

I whimper not from pain, but from the all-consuming fear swallowing me whole. Tears gather in the corner of my eyes and one by one, they drop to the table. I have always known who he is, what he does. Every single person in my life wears an invisible mask, hiding the evil that lives down deep, losing his or her humanity for the Hell's Highwaymen Motorcycle Club. This life destroys the good inside. As I stare into the black abyss of Sandman's eyes, I know he would kill me without another thought if he wanted to. If Ward ordered it.

"Ahh," I cry as he jerks me by my hair to stand. The excruciating pain almost brings me to my knees. It feels like my scalp is detaching from my head. He pulls me around the kitchen so fast that my feet drag on the linoleum. I clumsily try to regain my footing. The front of my body slams against the wall, jarring my bones. He painfully presses my face close against the wood.

"Hold will one day be my prez," he whispers into my ear behind me. "That doesn't mean you will necessarily live to be the prez's old lady, which is a sacred title. I don't think I have to remind you that we take that little tat of yours seriously. Any man caught messing with you receives an automatic death sentence. And who do you think will carry that out, little queen?"

"You," I say, my chest heaving from the sobs locked tightly within.

"Me," he answers. "I suggest that from this day forward, your one and only goal in this life that you have been blessed into, should be to make Hold so damn happy that he smiles like a shit-eater, twenty-four-seven. Happy Holden—happy me. You feel me?"

I nod, my cheek scratching against the wood grain of the wall as I move.

"Good. Now, we never tell Hold about this and you and I will be right as rain," he says, letting me go.

I close my eyes, not moving a muscle until I hear him exit the kitchen. My knees buckle from underneath me, sending me falling to the floor. The sobs that I held tightly in minutes before burst forth. I want out from this life. The painful reality is that I have no one, not a single soul who cares what I want. I am their puppet, their whore. I lie down on the cold linoleum, wishing that I died in the fire all those years ago. I can't live like this.

Chapter THIRTEEN

April 2008

The sound of someone knocking startles me. It is barely eight o'clock in the morning and I am in the process of getting out of the shower. Fear overloads my system. I hurriedly dry my body before grabbing the little jersey skirt that I slept in. The matching t-shirt rests on the floor beside it and is better than only this towel.

I reach for it, sliding it on as I hesitantly walk toward my front door. Another soft knock comes from the other side. It stops me in my tracks. My wet hair drips down, soaking my shoulders and the back of my shirt. The beat of my heart goes into overdrive with the worry of who is on the other side. Old fears resurrect themselves, threatening every shred of my sanity. Get it together, Keller. This isn't the MC's style. They would have already busted up in here, destroying everything in their path, as usual.

I take a deep breath to calm my frail nerves and walk over to the door. My eye hovers over the peephole to see that it is Vin. My relief is instantaneous. He stands on the other side, looking at the rain that falls in a torrential downpour outside. A smile claims my mouth the way he is beginning to do the same with my heart. My hands tremble at the thought.

"Hey," I say, as I open the door. He turns around, his jacket dripping wet from the rain.

"Hey," he replies, his eyes only for me.

"So you're back." I raise my voice slightly over the sound of the storm in the background.

"Yeah, I couldn't stay away."

"Thanks for the pretty flowers last week. It would have been nice to have a phone call or a text to go along with them," I say, crossing my arms while leaning against the doorjamb.

I watch him place his hands in his jean pockets and shrug his shoulders. "I thought the card said it all."

"Oh, it was sweet, too… it just didn't say that you would be gone for over a week. I didn't know if you died or if you weren't coming back. Or weren't interested anymore." I internally blanch. I didn't mean to add that last part. It came out on its own.

He takes a step forward and I take one back, we repeat the same actions until he is in my apartment, shutting the door behind him. At first he doesn't say anything. We stand facing one another. His eyes seem to burn holes into me, the intensity strong enough to touch places deep within. I watch him struggle with the same feelings that consume me.

"I needed time," he says, sliding off his wet jacket before tossing it onto the chair.

"For what?" My voice comes out in a breathy tone. Oh, shit, I have gone all Marilyn on him.

His eyes flash with a hunger that hints of starvation. I know because mine no doubt mirror his.

"To get you out of my system, or at least slow down these feelings I have for you."

"It work?"

"Hell, no," he says, reaching to hold me against him. "I don't have control over whatever this is between us and I don't have a fucking right to take it further. What am I supposed to do when you are the only reason that matters anymore?" He sounds upset.

I can feel my skin humming from his proximity. Every single inch of me responds to him, this *between us* confusing and exciting me. He is waiting for me to answer him, but I don't have any answers when everything inside of me feels the same way.

He kisses me. No, that's not even close. His mouth makes sweet love to mine. My hands grip his arms, holding him to me, swearing to myself that I won't let him go. He is mine and I am his. He pulls back, breathing hard against me.

"I can't. I just can't," he says, stepping back from me.

"I have to leave soon." The words sound torn from him.

"And I can't let you go now," I say, closing the distance between us. He leans his forehead down to rest against mine. I feel him internally struggling to keep himself from me.

Our eyes lock, his brown capturing mine. I am uncertain as to why he is pushing me away, fighting this thing between us. My lips feel the hot air that he releases from his quick breaths. My hands tightly grasp his, imprisoning them at our sides. A hunger for more than I have ever experienced burns me from the top of my head to the tips of my toes.

"Vin."

A look of sorrow crosses his face at the sound of his name. "No," he says, closing his eyes and clenching his jaw. "No."

No? He doesn't want me? I tremble from the overwhelming fire of lust. My nipples hurt, aching for his touch, and only his. I have never experienced such a devastating need. It threatens to rob me of my senses, my secrets. And I don't care.

"Why," I cry desperately. I tilt my hips forward, gasping when I feel the hardness waiting for me. I don't miss his hungry expression, or the trembling that rocks his body against mine—I know instantly that he wants me. Why is he trying to restrain himself from me?

"You don't know…" he says, stopping when my lips hush his words.

I move my mouth merely inches away from his. "I

don't care." I have no idea where this sheer bravado comes from, but I am thankful for it. Something is building, threatening to burst deep inside of me. The time for waiting is over.

He grimaces, his jaw flexing with some type of emotion. We are so close that every time he swallows, I feel the strain he feels from physically withholding himself from me. I want him to be my lover, my first in years.

I watch him, calculating my odds on how this ends. I bring my lips back to his, licking and nipping. My mouth begs his for entrance, for acceptance. When he doesn't grant it, my lips follow the lines of his jaw. The stubble of his unshaven face scrapes against my sensitive cheeks.

"I have feelings for you," he whispers into my ear, the warm air gently caresses the outer lobe. "Real feelings." His fingers interlock with mine, finally holding me to him. He brings his face back so that we are staring at one another. "This will be the only thing between us that isn't filled with lies. When we are together like this, you will be mine—body and soul. Agreed, Keller?"

I can give him my body without giving him my heart. That is nothing new for me. Let him have it, Keller, a voice cries within me.

"Say it. I need to hear you tell me. This is fucking killing me," he growls, seconds before his mouth ravages mine.

His lips steal the words from me. He kisses me like he would die without my taste. My body quivers from the touch of his tongue stroking mine. His kiss speaks of experience, of a knowledge as old as time. He imparts it to me, teaching me with every touch, every nuance of his body language. The groan that he emits makes my nipples harden to tiny points. His hands release mine, sliding them around to my rounded rear, bare beneath my skirt. I feel his fingers dig in, gripping me, as he guides me backward.

Small moans escape me between kisses. He is drowning me with these incredible sensations. I reach my arms up and around his neck for support, my knees weak with this overwhelming passion. He is wrapping me in a cocoon of need from which I never want to emerge.

My body hits the wall behind me, halting our movements. He breathes roughly against me. Whatever I am feeling is obviously mirrored in him. A dull ache of lust burns in my pelvis, spreading like a wildfire. I have waited anxiously for this, for him. Years have come down to this single moment in time.

I feel his hand gripping my butt, my raging pent-up lust waiting specifically for my next move. This is my Vin. He makes me think I am guiding us, but in all reality, it's him subtly maneuvering me. He braces my body against the wall, giving the illusion that I could be free from him if I chose, but we both know the truth.

My hands slide down, reaching for the hem of my shirt. I draw it up and over my head. He gasps when he sees I am wearing no bra. I had zero amount of time to put on any undies in the bathroom earlier, not having a clue that this moment would come. His orange-tinted brown eyes glide over my chest and my nipples painfully tighten harder beneath his gaze. A sensual cry escapes me.

"You are so beautiful," he says, his voice raspy. "I have never wanted anyone or anything more in my life." He grinds his groin upwards against mine, fitting himself snugly between my thighs.

My abdomen clenches at the sound of his husky voice. His words threaten to tear down my defenses, releasing me of my lies. He is right. This moment between us can be real. He knows I hide my past and is willing to let me, but not here, not behind my touch. Not from his caress.

His hand hovers over my breast only moments before his fingers lightly touch me, tracing the tattoos down my chest before creating invisible circles around my nipple. A tension grips the walls of my vagina. I can't contain the moan that passes through my lips at the touch of his mouth, replacing his fingers. His tongue laps at my nipple before sucking it deep in his mouth. Heat spears downward, threatening to release the mounting tension.

I feel his other hand now stretching the band at the top of my skirt. He gently pushes it down my legs, letting it fall to the ground around my ankles. I step out, nudging it away with my toes. He swiftly lifts me in his arms, cradling me against his chest. My arms wrap tightly around his neck while his mouth swoops down to capture mine.

He carries me several steps before gently laying me on my bed. I lean up on my elbows to watch him remove his t-shirt and jeans. He grins at me as he lowers his boxers, freeing his erection. I glance at the thick, veined shaft that seems to twitch under my stare. I swallow hard, closing my eyes against the emotions that swamp me. I feel the bed dip as he climbs onto it. He moves over me. I know without opening my eyes because the heat pours off of his body, searing mine.

"Look at me, Keller. Watch me touch you," he says.

My eyes flutter open to see his fingers drift lazily down my stomach. The tip of his finger brushes over my Hell's tattoo, momentarily causing me to panic. But he doesn't stop as he goes lower, sifting through the curls that cover my entrance. I forget the past. I can't help myself from spreading my legs for him. He dips one finger into my wetness, pulling out to massage my outer folds. He repeats his movements while gently adding an additional finger. His motions stretch me wider than my vibrator, stroking places it could never seem to reach. The rhythmic in and out increases the pleasurable ache in my center, threatening to uncoil me.

"Let me have you," he says, gazing down at me with unbridled passion.

"Yes." I barely get the word out.

He leans back to stand, reaching for something in his pant pockets. A condom appears in his hand. I watch him tear it with his mouth before rolling it down on himself. The feel of his body once again covering me, elicits a deep moan, and he touches his lips back to mine, sending ripples throughout my body. My eyes start to close, but I force them open. I want to watch his as he enters me. We gaze at each other, everything in this moment open between us.

I feel the rounded head of him against me as he places himself at my entrance. He gently pushes inside. With a quick thrust, he completely fills me, stretching me farther than ever before. My muscles clench down at the invasion and he hisses as if in pain.

"Does it feel okay?" I ask. It has been too long. He is only the second person I have ever been with. My heartbeat skips at the thought of something he doesn't like about me.

"Yeah," he says, panting for air. "More than okay."

I feel him throbbing inside. Nothing in this world matches what I am experiencing right now. He trembles above me, looking at me with a primal hunger. My body arches underneath his and I throw my head back from this intense pleasure. I ache for him. My thighs capture his hips, grinding him impossibly deeper.

"Keller." He growls my name, seizing my lips while thrusting his hips. "You feel like wet silk," he says, surging in and out.

My body moves of its own accord. I writhe underneath his body that plunges harder and faster into mine. I respond to his hunger. It controls me. His grunts of satisfaction spiral me higher, building me toward an orgasm that almost scares me in its intensity. How far can I fall before getting hurt?

His hands grip both of my hips, guiding me, instructing me. The edge is closer than I imagined. My entire body centers before imploding. I hear his guttural cry of release, but it doesn't matter. Nothing does. I float aimlessly, content for the first time in my existence. I don't fear the fall. I don't fear the future.

I wake to the pitter-patter of rain against the windowsill. Lying still, I listen to the rhythmic drops that fall, until I hear something else. Somewhere in the distance music plays softly, something about the wicked games people play. I can't help the knowing smile that lifts my lips. I really missed this type of wicked game.

"Is that smile for me?"

I lift my head to see him standing next to the window. My hand grips the thin sheet that barely covers my nakedness. He leans causally back against the wall, his arms crossed over his bare chest. My mouth actually waters at the sight of his V muscle, highlighted by the button he's left undone on his jeans. He has sexy bed hair, locks sticking out everywhere. I notice red marks on his chest and arms, obviously scored by my nails.

I can't help the rosy blush that covers my body at the thought of everything we did in this bed today. I turn to bury my face into the pillow. The smell of him prompts another wave of lust in the pit of my stomach. My body is hypersensitive to the smallest touch—even rubbing against the sheets sparks an electrical current underneath my skin. I clamp my legs together, trying to quiet everything that is pooling there.

When he doesn't say anything else, I raise my head again to see him staring out the window. My eyes outline the contours of his face. I am entirely out of my league. He is out of my league. Girls like me never get guys like him. I bet in his school he was like my Jake Carrity. At the thought of Jake, All-American nice boy, my heart tightens in sharp pain. There must have been a girl like me, loving Vin from a distance, never dreaming big enough that one day she could be in his bed, in his life.

He turns his head, catching my perusal of him. We stare at each other. I wonder if he is thinking the same thing about me. He turns his head back to watch the rain.

"Keller, I..." he says, then stops before turning to glance at me. "I have a past, too. Things I can't talk about. They didn't matter before when we were just friends, but now things are different."

His words settle into my brain. So many things that he said before we made love make sense now. I thought he was mainly referring to me, but I guess not. I can't press him for answers when I am not willing to give my own, so I nod toward him. That doesn't stop my mind from going into hyper-speed. He must have a girlfriend. Someone back at home, maybe more than a girlfriend. *Holy shit!* A wife?

I sit up in the bed, trying my best to wrap the sheet around me.

"Look at me, Keller," he says, and I do. "You can't press me for answers if you are not willing to give your own." He reads my mind.

"I'm not an adulterer," I say, the words turning sour in my mouth.

He gives a bitter laugh. "And you think I am? I am a lot of things, but an adulterer is not one of them. That I will tell you and it is the living truth. No wife. No girlfriend. Any other answers are going to cost you."

I hear the sincerity in his voice and I believe him. I take a deep breath to calm my racing nerves and steady my shaking hands.

"Tit for tat, Keller. Anyone special you aren't being forthcoming about? Should I be worried about a jealous boyfriend?"

His words burn me because they are the truth. Just like that, the haze of lust is evaporated by my life. Reality wallops me upside the head—I can never keep it away for too long. I try to slide to the side of the bed, but the sheet makes it difficult as my long legs tangle in it.

"So is there someone going to cut off my hands for touching you?"

My eyes rise worriedly to his.

He pushes away from the wall, stalking toward the bed. His eyes narrow solely on me. I scoot my butt back to the center of the mattress.

"Is that it? Who is going to kill me for touching you, Keller? For being deep inside of you," he says, his legs brushing the side of the bed.

"No one," I whisper. I can't look away from him. I am mesmerized by the intensity in which he stares at me.

"No one is going to kill me? Because I would. After being inside you, the thought of anyone else touching you enrages me," he says, his hands reaching for his jeans riding low on his hips. He grabs for the zipper, slowly tugging it down.

"No one," I say, repeating myself. My mouth is dry as all the liquid in my body heads south again.

"No one *what?*" He leans over to push his jeans down his legs.

I watch him step out of them before placing his hands on the edge of the bed. I lick my lips. His hands gather the ends of my sheet and with a quick pull, he jerks it away from me, leaving me exposed to him. I gasp at the loss. My hands cover my breasts while I cross my sore thighs. He crawls toward me on the bed, stopping on his knees before me. I try to keep my eyes on his, but they keep slipping to his hard erection bobbing up and down, reminding me of something I have never done before. I've read enough books and watched plenty of movies to know how to give a blowjob. I even practiced on a carrot once and it didn't complain.

Before he can stop me, before I can stop myself, I lean forward to lick the top of the slick head. Surprisingly he tastes salty. Thick, blue veins trace the top side of his penis. My tongue follows each one. I hear his gasp of surprise and I continue. Once he is entirely wet with my saliva, I place my lips securely around him, sucking him completely to the back of my throat.

"Stop," he says, grasping my shoulders painfully to push me back against the mattress. He follows me down, lying on his side.

"Did I do something wrong?" I blink up at him.

"Hell, yes! You are killing me," he says, quietly yelling at me. I watch his heavy breathing.

"Oh."

"And she says, 'Oh.'" He shakes his head. "We were talking and you ambushed me."

"You don't want me to do that?"

"Yes, I want you to do that. As much and as often as you want to do that, but I need an answer," he says, staring down at me. He lifts his hand to brush his knuckles against my tender cheek. "What previous lovers of yours are coming after me, Keller?"

"There is no plural," I say quietly, staring up at him. "There was only one other before you."

"One?" He looks perplexed.

"You are really ruining my first BJ experience," I say, trying to change the subject. I tug my bottom lip between my teeth. "Well, except for that carrot, but you just showed me that there is a huge difference. Gigantic," I say, smiling up at him.

He glances away from me, his eyes searching for something around the room. I watch his mouth moving silently. When he finally looks back down, I see the truth finally dawn on him.

"Are you telling me what I think you are telling me?"

"It's no big deal," I say, my eyes locking onto his

tattoo. I trace the numbers with my fingertip across his chest.

"Look at me, Keller. Being only the second person you've ever been with is a fucking big deal. I know what trust means to you and knowing you trust me…" His lips quickly find mine.

They devour me; his tongue licks at mine, our teeth clash. His reaction is visceral in nature. My hand presses against his heart and I can feel the frenetic beating pumping against my palm.

"It's a big deal to me," he says, in between moments of the war he has waged on my mouth.

His body covers mine. My own heart beats a crazed rhythm, in perfect tandem with his. I don't close my eyes so that I can watch him staring at me. His usual grin hinders his next kiss.

He pulls back slightly. "Gigantic, huh?" We both laugh before he lowers his mouth again.

Chapter

FOURTEEN

October 2003

"My world burns from tiny cinders of lies, setting me aflame. My skin blackens from the blood boiling underneath. But I stand still, willing the orange and red to hurry. Burn, burn, burn. Death is not my destination, but my salvation. So hurry fire and burn." I finish reading the poem I wrote, in front of my peers, before sitting back down in my chair.

"Interesting, Helen," the teacher says, walking in front of the classroom. "Dark, but very deep. Okay, who is next?" She is interrupted by the sound of the bell ringing.

I grab my backpack up, sliding my notebook inside. The sound of everyone rushing from the room, signals the end of another day. I hear them talking about going to the big football game scheduled tonight, a normalcy I have never known. I wait, giving them time to clear out before leaving myself.

Things haven't changed much since Hold has been locked up. I live in a house with two complete strangers, pretending that we are family. It's my own personal prison. Hold has forbidden any of us from visiting, especially me. Of course, Sage silently blames me for her not being able to see her son. His lawyer thinks he may be out before Christmas for good behavior.

I spend every waking minute when I am not at school at Hard Ink. Diamond and Badger have become more of a mother and father figure than Sage and Ward. Many nights I stay with Diamond, but we both know that Sage wouldn't allow me to move out. I am Hold's.

The sound of someone calling my name stops me before I reach where I am going.

"Hey, beautiful."

Jake is leaning casually against my locker, his hands resting in the pockets of his letterman jacket.

"Jake, what are you doing?" I glance to make sure none of the other MC'ers are around. The halls are mostly empty.

"I am trying to ask the prettiest girl in school to come watch me play football tonight," he says, shrugging his shoulder.

"Do you have a death wish? Move," I say, waiting for him to step away so I can open my locker and throw my books inside.

"What have I been telling you? I don't care about them. They don't scare me."

"They should. They should scare you to death. You have already had the shit beat out of you because of me. That was your warning. I have told you that this entire time. Stay away from me," I say, slamming my locker before turning to walk away.

"Hey, wait one minute," he says, running to catch up with me. "Talk to me, Hels."

I turn on my heel, stopping to point my finger in his face. "Don't call me that. You don't know that girl. You don't want to."

"Okay, Helen. But I do. I want to know everything about you."

Someone walking down the hallway toward us makes me jump. I glance around, noticing the girls' bathroom. I grab his hand, pulling him inside. The first thing I do is check the stalls to make sure they are empty. Next, I place the trashcan in front of the door. He leans against a sink, watching me.

"I am getting a college scholarship and going away to school," he says, looking at me.

I give a bitter laugh. "You won't if you're dead."

"Let me finish. I have been thinking about it, and you could come with me. Get out of this town and away from them. When you turn eighteen, you can move out. They aren't your parents. You shouldn't have to stay there anyway."

"And go where, Jake? It doesn't work like that for me.

I'm never getting out of this town away from them. There are rules that you don't understand... my world is different than yours." My heart hurts hearing him speak of everything I dream about but can't have.

"Well, run away. You can hide out in my basement if you want to. My parents never go down there. At least, until we figure something else out," he says, pushing away and walking toward me. "I have someone who I can ask about this if you want me to. He can tell me how you can get away."

I freeze, my body paralyzed by what is happening. Jake hasn't left me alone since January when he got his ass kicked. I dreaded that first day of school after it happened, so I faked being sick for several weeks until Sage said that I had to return. I begged to quit like Hold, but evidently my getting my diploma is a must, where college is out of the question. When I did return, Jake acted like it was his mission in life to save me. Why, I don't know. I have tried to warn him away, but he doesn't take my dire predictions seriously, which terrifies me.

"Stop it," I hiss at him. My mind and stomach churn with the turmoil his words generate inside of me. "They will kill you if they even hear we are together. Do you understand me?"

"They aren't going to kill anyone. I am sure they're just scaring you away from me," he says, standing in front of me.

Something between a laugh and a sob escapes me. "Yeah, they will," I cry. "He will."

Jake's arms surround me, pulling me closely to him. I am tired of fighting him—it wears me emotionally to the bone. My head lay on his chest and I quietly cry.

"Shh, it's going to be fine. I can protect you," he whispers into my ear.

I close my eyes, knowing this boy before me doesn't have a clue. He lives in a world where cops are always good and the bad guys aren't really bad, just scary on the outside. He can't even begin to contemplate the inner workings of a demon. I can, because I am one of them.

The sound of somebody trying to open the door rattles the trashcan. A voice sounds on the other side. I physically push him into a stall and he shuts the door. I rush to turn the water on to seem as if I am washing my hands when the door swings open. The trashcan hits the wall behind it. The janitor peeks his head inside.

"Everything okay in here?"

"Sorry," I say. "How did that happen?" I start to walk past him. "Um, I would wait a little while to clean it. It sounds like somebody is sick in one of the stalls. I think it's a teacher. She said she is fine, but I would give her a little while longer."

He nods. "Thanks," he says, before turning to walk down the hallway.

I run out of the school by myself, not stopping until I get into my car. What is Jake thinking? He can't possibly understand the ramifications of being near me. I don't breathe a sigh of relief until I am parking my car in front of Hard Ink. A knock on my window startles me. Mikey stands on the other side, smoking a cigarette.

"What do you want?" I ask, getting out of my car and locking it behind me.

"We need to talk," he says, flicking the ashes to the ground.

"What about?" There is no way he knows this soon about Jake.

"Hold."

My hand reaches for his. "Is he okay?"

"Yeah, he's fine for a man who's spent the last nine months in jail. I spoke to the lawyer today and he's pretty sure he can get him out in the next thirty days. That means you and I have business to attend to." He shakes my hand free.

"What is it, Mikey," I say, leaning against the car.

"I don't know where his head is going to be when he gets out, but he has got to lay low. That means he gets no shit from you. I'm praying that the poor bastard has wised up and realized that there is prettier pussy in the world, but I have feeling that won't be the case," he says, throwing his cigarette butt down on the ground.

What is he trying to say?

"Do you know your place, Hels? If you can't be a good little future wifey, then we need to seek other alternatives—one that cuts you out of the picture completely. You read me?"

Is he offering me the death I secretly wish for? I wonder what he would say if I ask him to put a bullet in my head, ending this life of misery. Would he have that same smug smile on his face? It doesn't matter. As much as I think about death, I can't seem to follow through—something keeps me going.

"Yeah," I say, nodding my head. I walk past him, brushing his shoulder with mine as I go by.

The tattoo shop is slow when I walk in. Badger is the only artist currently tattooing what looks like a rose on some man's neck. Diamond is out of town visiting her mother who just found out she had cancer. She asked if I wanted to go, but Sage wouldn't allow it. All the other artists, except for me, are MC guys who are attending a party at the garage tonight. I begin to clean the shop, doing the work that the men refuse to.

Hours pass and before I know it, night falls. It's a Friday night so you can expect late-night tats and drunk customers. Badger is busy working on a skin. I just finished my last one and clean my area.

"Hels, can you grab the next customer coming in?" Badger yells over to me.

"Sure," I say, turning to walk to the front. My stomach rebels at the person standing there. Jake.

"You missed my game," he says, still wearing his number-seven football jersey.

I don't stop walking as I grab his arm, hauling him back out the door. The thought of what Badger just saw scares me to death. Badger likes me, he may even care for me, but he is an MC man through and through, one of the original seven members of the club. We stop at Jake's car.

"If you are curious who won, we did. I had the game-winning touchdown. Hey, ouch!" He rubs the spot where I just pinched his arm.

"I am going to hyperventilate," I say, putting my hand to my chest. It is almost impossible to try and slow my breathing down.

"Just quit acting crazy. What are they going to do? Shoot me in a public place?"

"No, first they are going tie you up and gag you. Next they will drive you somewhere, and then they will shoot you."

"You watch way too much television."

"I don't watch any TV," I say, shaking my head at his stupidity. "I have to get back inside. Now."

"Helen, you are killing me," he says, acting like he is holding his heart.

"Now you get it. I am, Jake. I really am." I turn to go back inside when he grabs my hand, spinning me back around. His lips roughly land on mine. Instinct takes over, and my palm connects with his cheek, hard. "Don't ever do that again," I hiss. His eyes convey a world of hurt. He doesn't realize that I am saving him as much as me.

I look up to see Badger standing in the doorway.

"Time to come back in, Hels," he says, talking to me, but looking at Jake.

"Stay away from me," I whisper over to Jake. "Please."

My feet move, swiftly carrying me through the door of the tattoo shop.

"Do I need to make a phone call?"

I close my eyes at the sound of Badger's voice. "Please don't. I handled it."

He nods. "Go ahead and lock up," he says, returning to his customer.

In less than an hour he is finished. I wait while he gets the money ready. We both walk toward our vehicles.

"You got trouble. I have to alert Ward, Hels. That boy has some nerve to walk into your place of business that is a known MC spot. It only tells me he has a death wish. You want this shit to blow back on you?"

"Please don't. He doesn't listen to me when I tell him to leave me alone. I don't know what else to do. He's a good kid, Badger. He doesn't deserve to die because he doesn't see the danger. It will be all my fault."

"This has to be finished before Hold comes home. He's one of those kids Hold beat up, isn't he?"

I nod.

"The main one?"

I nod again.

"Shit. Stupid fucker," he says, shaking his head. "Get in your car and go straight home. Do you hear me?"

"Badger, please. Don't do this," I say, begging him.

"Get in your car and go home, girl. Now!"

I turn and run to my car. This can't be happening. I don't have a clue where Jake lives. The only place I can even think to look is the Shack.

It takes me less than ten minutes before I drive up to the front door. Several of my classmates glance over at me as I run in, but I ignore them, looking fervently for Jake. I see a booth full of football players in the back. But not him. However, they might have his cell number.

The entire group of them looks up to see me walking their way. Some glance down, pretending I don't even exist as I stop right in front of them.

"Do any of you guys know Jake's phone number?"

"I have it in my cell phone," one guys says, pulling out his phone.

"Dude, do you know who she is?" Another guy punches his shoulder, looking at the owner of the phone like he is an idiot.

"Can you call him for me? Please," I say. My hands shake uncontrollably. I have mere minutes before I have to head home. No one can know what I am doing. These guys have no clue that I am risking my life right now. And that if I don't get on the phone with Jake soon, his too.

"Hey man, that MC chick from school wanted me to call you," he says, speaking into his cell phone.

I reach for his phone, taking it from him. "Where are you?"

"I am home."

"I'll be right back," I say, speaking to the owner of the phone. I turn to see the girl's bathroom and breathe a sigh of relief that it is empty, locking it behind me.

"Helen, what's wrong?"

"Listen to me: I only have seconds. Do not leave your house this weekend. If you have family you can go visit, go. You did a very stupid thing tonight. They will be looking for you. Stay away from me. You will get us both killed."

"I don't understand."

"I know you don't," I say, leaning my head back against the bathroom door. "Just listen to what I am saying."

"They aren't going to shoot me, Helen. Those guys aren't stupid enough to get near me after the fight last January or they will end up in jail like Hold. You act like they are gods or something. They have, like, this Jedi mind control over you. Let me take care of us and quit worrying so much."

For some odd reason the saying, 'guns don't kill people... people kill people,' runs through my mind. "There are other weapons besides guns in the world," I whisper.

"Quit worrying about me. Did they threaten you? If so, come to my house right now. You don't have to go home."

"Stay safe, Jake," I say, looking at my watch to see that time has run out.

I flip the phone closed to end the call. The internal voice in my head says to go to him. I'll either be free or dead, but then another part of me knows that I can't involve him or his family deeper in this, and going to him will only ensure that.

The owner of the phone is waiting for me when I come out of the bathroom. "Thanks," I tell him, handing it back. I literally run out the door and jump into my car.

My foot floors the gas pedal the entire way home. I

lose control of the car several times, but thankfully I am able to make it there safely. Sage meets me at the door.

"Well, look what the cat dragged in," she says, moving back so that I can enter. "Ward called and said to make sure that you made it home. Would you mind telling me what is going on now?"

"Stupid stuff," I tell her. "But I am home, like I was told to be." My eyes meet hers.

"You know, Hels, I never told you, but my mother was a lot like yours."

Her words hold me in place. "How so?"

Sage moves until she is directly in front of me. She tilts her face downward to meet mine and I don't miss the gleam of malice that shines brightly in them. "They both were town whores, using pussy to get what they want. I've always felt a kinship toward you that you didn't fall into that same trap. It really would be a shame, baby girl, to find out otherwise."

My first thought is to deny what she is saying about my mother, but then unwanted memories remind me of times better left forgotten, so many nights of my daddy complaining about her not coming home. My mother crying, trying to explain she couldn't help it. I remember my dad destroying every picture of her after she died and using the word whore over and over. The sound of Sage's bitter laugh reminds me that I am still standing here with her.

"'Night then," she nods, clearly dismissing me.

As I climb the stairs, I push thoughts of my mother away, returning to worry about Jake's safety. I can only hope that he listens to me. Otherwise, we both will pay the price.

Monday morning rolls by without Jake saying anything to me at school, thank goodness. He obviously didn't go out of town to visit relatives, but he at least is keeping his distance. I worked all weekend at the shop without one misstep. Badger didn't elaborate on what Ward said, only for me not to worry about it. I am hoping they realize that he is just a dumb kid and not a threat to the MC.

After school, I arrive at work to see that a lot of the Hell's Highwaymen are sitting around the shop hanging out. It's not an unusual scene, but something about today sets off warning bells in my head. Mikey especially is giving me the creeps. He meanders around the shop, glancing at me the entire day.

Sandman walks in around 8:00 p.m. I watch him stroll around, talking and joking with the guys, his eyes seeming to always find mine. I pay no attention, concentrating slowly on the skin I am tattooing. One of the prospects wanted a Celtic cross on his arm.

"Move it, Prospect," Sandman says, standing over us.

I pull my machine back from my customer, while taking my foot off the pedal. The prospect stands up without question and walks away. Sandman sits down in his place.

"Well, hello, little queen. Long time no see," he says, looking directly at me.

To say that I am scared would be an understatement. I am petrified. The last time I spoke with Sandman was the night at Ward's. We aren't buddies anymore. I would like nothing better than the earth to open up at this moment. Terror threatens to cause me to meltdown, here in front of everyone. I don't move as he continues to stare.

"You know what time it is?" He smiles at me.

I shake my head no.

"Answer me when I talk to you," he says, leaning forward. "Do you know what fuckin' time it is?"

"No, sir."

"That's better," he says, a knowing smile bends the scars lining his face. "I will tell you what time it is. It is tattoo time. Do you know what kind of tat I am getting today?"

I don't have a clue. "No, sir."

"Well, it's more of adding on to an existing one, but I think you are just the person for the job. Why don't you clean everything up to get ready for me?"

What is he talking about? It doesn't make... *Oh, no. Oh, God! NO!* My equipment drops from my hands, clanging loudly against the floor. I stand quickly. The stool beneath me rolls away. It can't be possible.

"No. No," I chant, shaking my head back and forth. I step away from him, my body forcefully trembling.

The world seems to shrink. The sound of Sandman laughing enrages me. I look over to see him, laid back in my chair.

"What have you done?" I scream at him, choking back a sob at the same time.

"What had to be done," a voice states behind me.

I whirl around to see Ward standing there, surrounded by his murdering posse.

"No. No. He was at school today. I saw him," I say, confused. I know I saw him. Jake can't be dead. They are only being cruel to me.

"It was really a sad story," Sandman says. "One of the guys only heard about it an hour ago. The kid finished football practice and on the way home something went horribly wrong with his car. He lost control of it and crashed. Evidently, the damn thing burst into flames. What a shame. Such a waste of a young life."

Oh, God. My world crumbles around me. Am I next? I glance around at the faces of my so-called family. A calm covers me. I'm not afraid to die. It's not the worst fate imaginable. Living amongst the monsters is a fate worse than death.

"Helen, you will listen to me."

I slowly spin around to see that Ward is speaking to me.

"It is finished. You are not held accountable for others' actions. It will be ruled an accident, and that is exactly what it is. Do you understand?"

I don't hide the hate I have for him. The thought of

agreeing with him makes me want to vomit. I straighten taller to glare back at him.

"I talked to Sage today and we agree that maybe homeschooling will be the right choice for you. That will give you more time to work here. She will withdraw you tomorrow. And it's probably not a good idea for you to drive, since you are understandably upset, so Mikey will drive you for the next several weeks and stay with you. We wouldn't want you to be alone in your current mental state," Ward says, barely hiding the smile on his face.

"Your world is going to burn with you in it and it won't be me who lights the match," I say, not sure where my words are coming from.

Ward delivers a slap across my cheek, rocking me backward. The bone aches from the impact. My hand automatically covers it, but I don't stop glaring at him. I stand before him and his entire crew, not giving him or them another tear. They have had my last one.

"Why don't you do us all a favor and put a gun in your mouth, little queen," Sandman says.

I refuse to let them break me, and I'll be damned before I will give them the satisfaction of my death. They will have to take it from me.

"But you're so good at it, Sandman. Why would I deny you the pleasure of another notch on your gun?" The words spout from my mouth before I can stop them. I have no clue who this brave Helen is, but she needs to stick around.

"Sandman, that's enough," Ward says. "Hels, that isn't

what we want. Emotions are running high. We all need to sleep on it. Mikcy, get her out of here." Mikey doesn't move at first. "Mikey, get her the fuck out of here and don't leave her side!" Ward yells, finally losing his cool façade.

I don't stop Mikey when he grabs my arm, jerking me to his side. We both walk out of the shop.

"Where are your car keys?" He looks almost sick and his hands shake as he tries to light a cigarette.

I reach into my pocket for them, handing them over to him. He unlocks the car doors and motions for me to get in. We both seem in a hurry to get away. He actually squeals the tires out of the parking space.

"Oh, shit. Hold is going to having a fuckin' heart attack. He is going to kill Ward if he ever finds out he hit you. Father be damned. Club be damned. He won't give one fuck. Shit!" Mikey hits the steering wheel repeatedly, ashes falling everywhere from the smoke in his hand.

At first, I don't say anything as I look out the window. My tears fall freely, my heart crushed from my loss. I want to kill them all—every single one. I can't go to the police—the MC would find out that I ratted and I wouldn't know whom to trust anyway. I'd probably get one of the cops on their payroll. Plus, it won't bring back Jake. Nothing will.

Mikey's cursing finally snaps something inside of me. I swiftly turn, facing him in the car.

'Why!?!" The sound of my screams catch him off-guard. I swing at his arm, not caring that he is driving. He drops his lit cigarette in his lap.

"Crazy fuckin' bitch," he says, swatting the crotch of his jeans with the hand that is not on the steering wheel.

"Yes, I am! I'm the crazy bitch you've all made me," I yell, attacking Mikey, blaming him. "Why Jake? He was just a kid. He had football and college. But here you still are, you lowdown piece of shit." He tries to fend me off with one hand. "Why!?!" The feel of his flesh underneath my punches gives me a modicum of peace, so I hit harder, using both hands.

"You're goin' to kill us, Hels. Goddamn it!" He jerks the wheel to the right and the car swerves, careening us in our seats as he pulls over to the side of the road. Millions of tiny grains of sand fly up to pelt our windows, momentarily spraying us. Somehow between blows of my fists, he shifts the gear into park.

"He had his whole life in front of him and you took it. You took it," I cry, my world fading away behind the tears that fill my eyes. "His days are gone, Mikey. All gone."

He roughly grasps both my wrists, wrestling me away from him. "It was club business. I didn't take shit. Fuck you, Hels. I didn't even know what they planned."

I have to ask; I have to know. "Did Hold know what was going to happen to Jake?" The fight dies inside of me along with Jake.

He doesn't answer at first. "No, he didn't. I thought they would only scare the kid, not kill him." Mikey releases me to move back to his seat. "You know, I've talked to Hold about you this entire time."

His words surprise me. I knew he had talked to him, but he made it sound like it wasn't about me.

"The bastard only worries about you," he says, laughing. "I don't understand it. What is it about you that turns one of the hardest asses I know into a giant pussy? I don't get it. It would fuckin' kill him to know you're hurtin' right now. He'd want to be the one here. He'd make sense out of this fucked-up mess."

To my shock, he sounds upset at the club's actions. We drive in silence the rest of the way. Nothing left to say.

Chapter FIFTEEN

May 2008

"If I get on one more spinning ride, I am going to be sick," I say, walking beside Vin. I carry the stuffed pink bear he won for me, shooting a basketball into a lopsided hoop. His fingers intertwine with mine, joining our hands. Colorful flashing lights surround us, as the smell of sweet fried foods saturates the air. The sights and sounds of the carnival unleash a youthful spirit usually trapped deep within me. Everything seems brighter and clearer than ever before.

"One more," he says, bringing the back of my hand to his mouth for a slow kiss. The entire time he stares into my eyes. "Come on." He tugs me along while I playfully whine, following him.

"I really don't think I can. You are the one who made me eat the whole candy apple."

"I made you eat it?" His eyebrow lifts, questioning my accusation.

He quickly stops, bringing our forward movement to a sudden halt. My body intentionally slams into the hard muscle of his, stealing the breath from my lungs. His mouth covers mine, and the feel of his lips makes me weak in the knees.

"I can taste the sugary coating on your tongue," he says, sampling me with every kiss.

The world goes on around us. I close my eyes, savoring the touch of his lips and the sounds of screams and laughter filling the air. The moment is one of beauty, deeply appreciated by someone who doesn't have very many happy childhood memories.

"God, you're beautiful." He moves back from me. "C'mon," he says, winking. He pulls me along with him.

The sound of a girl's tinkle of laughter catches my attention as she runs by us. She looks so much like my sister Tara. Her blonde hair flies behind her, floating on the wind. She stops, glancing back at something. Her eyes find mine, and she smiles before turning to run with her friends. I close my eyes, my heart at peace for the first time in forever.

At the sound of Vin clearing his throat, I look up to see where he is taking me. The Ferris wheel looms majestically in the night sky. It soars above all of the other rides, its cherry-red metal frame slowly revolving with its occupants seated in colorful basket chairs, swinging precariously at different intervals. He digs in his pocket for our remaining tickets before handing them to the machine operator.

Neither of us says anything as we wait in line. I am captivated by the monstrous ride, watching it slowly rotate to amazing heights. The two teenagers in front of us step up for their turn. The girl giggles as she sits down, while the boy looks entirely too anxious as he joins her. The operator steps back after latching them in and once again the Ferris wheel churns.

Finally, it's our turn. I sit down, more excited than scared. Vin sits snuggly beside me, his warmth welcomed. He takes the bear from me to lay it on the other side of us. I feel his fingers linking our hands once again.

"Here we go," he says, speaking softly into my ear.

My eyes close at the husky sound of his voice. The slow jerk of the wheel starting to turn makes my heart leap and a small sound escapes me.

"Shh," he whispers. "I got you." He maneuvers his body where he can wrap both of his arms around me. I grip the top of his thigh with one hand. His jeans brush against the side of my bare leg where my short jean skirt rides precariously upwards.

A soft breeze gently blows my dark hair that has grown out past my shoulders. The layered camisole top doesn't cover much, so I snuggle deeper into his arms. The higher we climb, the more my body becomes aware of his. I glance up to see the two teenagers making out above us. The romance is not lost on me.

As we slowly spin to the top, the entire carnival is spread out across the land below me. People rush around, living and loving every minute of it. I am learning to do that, but not until this second do I realize that it's also beneficial to step back to see the big picture. My eyes find Vin. It's him. He is the reason that I have come alive. I take my time, leaning closer to him, letting him see in my eyes what I can't say out loud. He makes me want to give instead of take, a first for me.

When my lips touch his, everything drifts quietly away. He amazes me. I am so in love with him, with the way he makes me feel. My nails scratch up and down his jean-covered thigh. I move closer and closer to him with every touch and his body reacts, growing for me.

"What are you doing?"

"Making you feel as alive as I do."

"Oh, believe me, I am feeling all kinds of alive," he says, kissing me back.

We miraculously stop at the very top. No one can see down at what we are doing inside our swinging carriage. Cinderella has nothing on me—I get the ride and Prince Charming before midnight. Our seat rocks with every little movement, especially when I turn my body so that I am facing his. My nimble fingers unbutton the top of his jeans, unzipping them with the same smooth move.

We stare at one another, not letting this moment pass us by. Both of my hands grasp the top of his jeans and boxer shorts, slightly pulling them down for easier access. I trail my finger down his exposed thick member. If his hiss is any indication, he is feeling this intensely arousing experience with me. My fingers don't waste a single second, surrounding his width, while stroking his length. He grips the sides of the chair, holding on.

At the sound of his moan, my head lolls back, enjoying the ecstasy that I am bringing him. The moon shines full and bright in the night sky, witnessing my sensual act. As I touch him, carnal images fill my mind of what he will do to me later—his hands rubbing and invading my most secret places. My body floods itself with its own juices and I have to squeeze my thighs together to calm the erotic clenching deep inside. I glance back at Vin.

We still aren't moving, so I up my game. Leaning over, I replace my hand with my wet mouth. My tongue spirals around him as I go down, increasing my suction on the way back up. I repeat my movements. My mouth must bring him insurmountable pleasure—I can tell by the subtle rocking of his hips and the glazed expression in his eyes when I glance up. Our seat rocks back and forth, intensifying the sensations rippling through my body.

The Ferris wheel jerks back to life, the movement centering him deeper in my throat. My tongue sweeps the tip with every upward movement, licking the pearly drops over the head. Our chair starts a slow descent, but I don't stop, my mouth increasing its speed. Any moment now we could be caught by other passengers above us looking down, but I still don't stop. My eyes lift to his, playing a type of chicken, daring the other to be the first to stop this hedonistic act.

"Fuck," he says. His hands grasp my arms, pulling me to him, hiding his body with mine from prying eyes. "You are crazy."

His kiss smothers my winning smile. The feel of his body, trembling with unleashed pleasure from my actions, creates a fervent satisfaction inside of me. The Ferris wheel's rotation does not stop for us to savor the experience. Time is a factor. He quickly pulls his pants up as I look around to see if anyone got an eyeful.

"Keller."

I glance over at him.

"I..." he says, stopping to look down at his hands. "I... Damn it." His hand wraps around the back of my head, pulling me to him. Our lips touch. He gives me sweet, soft kisses. "We are getting off this ride and finding somewhere to be alone."

My arms encircle him, my body completely in tune with his. He is showing me tenderness, maybe even love. Or it could be me imagining things I can only wish for. I lose myself in him as the wheel continues to spin.

"I am almost finished, Keller."

Billy finishes up last-minute touches on my new tattoo that she's been working on for the past five hours. The ribcage is one of the most sensitive spots to have a needle touching it repeatedly, but it was the best spot for the one

I designed. My body is almost at its breaking point from the regimented pain. It is designed to be a simple black and gray tattoo at first glance, until you see all the line work. It is a very heavily detailed piece.

"So I am guessing by the tattoo that things are going good," she says, speaking over the hum of the machine.

"Yeah, I guess you could say that," I say, smiling to myself. I do that a lot lately—smile when I think about Vin.

"I see that smile, girl. It looks good on you."

What can I say? If he isn't finishing up restoration on the house, he is spending time with me. He even makes me happy when we argue, which is often. He is demanding and bossy, but only because he is ensuring that I am living my life. And I miss him like crazy since he's been gone. He had some issues that he had to deal with because of the company.

"Not to rain on your parade, but have you talked about what you are going to do when he finishes the house? Are you going with him?" Billy lifts her foot off the pedal, silencing the machine.

I shut my eyes, acting like I am dealing with getting the tattoo when the truth is, I can't think about it. I know things are changing between us. When we make love, there is a desperation in the way we touch each other, almost like it will all end at any minute, which I guess it will, sooner than later. He has been different since we attended the carnival last week, quieter. Then he had to leave to go back home and since then, no phone call. I refuse to call his cell phone, even though my finger hovers over the send button daily.

Billy returns to tattooing me when I don't answer her. I wish I knew. He hasn't asked me to go with him, but I have thought about it. What better time to move on? I have stayed here longer than I expected. In fact, I have broken every cautionary promise I made. I can't regret it. He has been worth every single experience and Ginger has been the friend I have always wanted. I'll even miss Billy.

"Take a look in the mirror. See what you think," Billy says, finishing my tattoo.

My side hurts like a bitch, but I ignore the tender skin to stand and walk over to look in the mirror. Wow.

"I have to admit that is some beautiful ink," she says, standing behind me.

I nod, incredibly happy with my design and her skill: a minutely detailed Ferris wheel with small carriage seats dotting the entire circumference. The line work and shading are impeccable. This is where I realized what I felt for Vin. I look in the mirror at my reflection. The tears of happiness that appear in my eyes mark me more than the tattoo. I don't think I have ever cried because I am so happy.

Billy pats my back before turning around to clean her station, giving me a second alone. I try to imagine my life if I had stayed and I can't. I'm not sure I would even still be on this earth. There is so much I need to tell him—not my secrets that I will take to my grave, but the danger that follows me even now. No one could possibly understand why I would protect them, but I have a reason. One single, solitary reason I would sell my soul to the devil before breaking a promise.

Chapter SIXTEEN

January 2004

"So the guys are giving Hold the full homecoming with a ride, huh?"

I look over at Diamond as we sit by ourselves at Hard Ink. My fingernail is almost chewed to the quick. I was specifically told I wasn't invited and Diamond volunteered to be my caretaker for the day. It's been my life for the last several months—I can't leave the house without a chaperone.

"Yeah, they're picking him up when he is released. Then there is a huge party at the clubhouse. Mikey said that it is strictly a club deal," I say, biting a different nail.

"Quit doing that," she says, slapping at my hand. "Your nails are going to look like shit."

"I am over all this, Diamond," I say, my voice devoid of any emotion.

"Honey, trust me. You don't want to see him the first day out of the slammer. He is probably going to be horny as hell. Let him spend himself on hookers and liquor. Then you can have him when he is more rational."

"That isn't what I mean. I don't care if he takes a hundred girls to his bed. I don't want in this life anymore. I can't live like this. I am dying inside."

"Helen, honey, don't say things you don't mean. Living is sure as shit better than dying and that is the only way you are getting out of this life," she says, brushing my hair back. "Why don't you let Auntie D trim your hair? It needs it."

I shake my head no, but there is something she can do. And since the shop is empty, it's a perfect time. "Diamond, I want a tattoo. But we have to find a way to conceal it on my skin. Can you help me do this?"

She glances at me then away, before shaking her head. "What do you want?"

"I want an outline of the shape of a football and inside of it we need to do some scrolling lines that somehow secretly read the number seven. Can you do this?"

"What does it mean?" Her voice sounds tired.

"It doesn't matter and it's better that you don't know. Please."

She shakes her head, and for a second I believe that she is refusing to tattoo me. But then she stands, walking toward her chair.

"Well, are you coming or what?" She turns to look at me with her hands on her hips. "We need to finish before anyone comes in."

The tears gather in the corners of my eyes, and I show her the gratitude that I feel. I walk over and sit on her chair.

"Where do you want it?" I point to my triceps and she rolls her eyes. "You are a glutton for punishment. No. You don't want any ink below your thighs, right?"

"No," I say. It's just a personal preference. The lowest tattoo on my body is my Hell's tat.

"Okay, you never wear your hair up, so let's do the back of your neck right under your hairline. I'll actually shave a little so that when it grows back it will help camouflage. I can do it small and sneaky enough that no one will notice outright—like they would on your freaking arm, unless you plan to wear long-sleeve shirts in summertime. Geez, child. I do worry about you," she says, preparing to give me the tattoo.

It only takes her a little over an hour, but when I'm looking at the reflection in the mirror she holds up, I see the magic she created. It looks like a sleek oval with tribal markings inside, but the lines carefully and cleverly combine to create the number seven. Jake's football number. It's small enough to fit on the back of my neck and my hair hides it completely. And unless I point out the design the average person isn't going to figure it out.

"Thanks, Diamond. You are the only true friend I have."

"Hels, you could have it all. You already have the mark and the man, and if you played the game right, the money is starting to roll in for the club. What you have sure as shit beats being poor and alone out there in this big, old world. It isn't so bad here. You've just been thrust into a situation that seems desolate, but it could be so much more."

"I've tried. I only get those around me killed, D. What does it say about me if I turn my back now on everything that has happened?" I glance over at her as she cleans her area.

"It says you don't want to get your own self killed, missy," she says, looking at me like I'm an idiot. "It says that you want to have a future with a family—pretty little babies that Hold will surely give you. And the price is steep, I get that, but so is death. That is a finality that doesn't have a happy ending for anyone. Most of these MC guys love you, even after everything that has gone down. Hell, they even respect you because of your talent. You can still be the matriarch of this club that you were meant to be. It's not too late."

I watch her as she slowly walks up to me, stopping only inches away. She leans her mouth down close to my ear.

"And you want to know something? When you're queen and Hold is king someday, you get your revenge then. You hold it tight and quiet within that great, big old heart of yours, and one day you can release it for your vengeance. It's always about waiting for the right time. You understand what I'm sayin'?" she whispers.

I nod. I understand exactly what she is saying, but in this rough life that we lead, my vengeance may be extracted by someone else long before I get the chance. In my mind, I know she is giving me good advice. The problem is that I can't close my eyes or heart to what has transpired. There is one too many bodies lining up at my expense.

The next four days pass with only one message from Hold, which Mikey snidely relays. *He will call for me when he is ready to see me.* I swallow my pride. Not that I expected us to pick up where we left off, but I thought the friend in him would have missed me... because I have missed Hold. In more ways than I ever imagined. I miss the way we used to talk long before he went to jail. There is also a strange part inside of me that hungers for a taste of his body.

Mikey spent the entire afternoon detailing Hold's night of debauchery upon his return home. In fact, he says there is a certain brunette who's been warming Hold's bed every night since he got out. When I finally had enough of his gossip, I went up to my room to shut him out. I have faced a lot of hard truths since talking to Diamond days ago. Once again, I have to decide if I will try to accept this life or escape it.

I have money now, enough saved in my bank account for at least a year of running. But then a piece of me warns that when they come to drag me back, I will face a hell like I have never imagined, if not death. So now, not only am I scared to stay in this life, I am now terrified to run. My one thought since Hold has gotten out—what if he finds someone else?

What happens if he decides he doesn't want me anymore? It has to be an almost automatic death sentence. The only other option would be to black out my tattoo, which I know Badger has done to a few who have angered Ward, and pass me around as the club whore. Wow… my future is brighter than I even thought.

For a seventeen-year-old girl with little life experience, I am honestly lost as to what to do. I live in a prison with two people who'd rather see me dead, except they don't do it because of their son. As far as they know, he will never get over it should something happen to me. If I move in with Hold, I can have a chance… a chance at freedom.

I quietly crack open my bedroom door, listening to Mikey and Sage laugh over something downstairs. Now is my chance. I cross over to Hold's bedroom. In the years since he has moved out, Sage has left it the same. My hands shake as I slide the window open. I peek my head out to look down the trellis that leads to the ground. I can't believe I used to climb this willy-nilly when I was a child.

In only minutes, I make it to the ground, dropping the last couple of feet. I stand still, listening for sounds that they know I have escaped. When I don't hear any, I take off running toward my car. I hope that the keys are in the ignition. Thank goodness Mikey is an idiot who loses keys regularly so he just leaves them in the car when we're at home. I want to cry when I see them there.

It takes me only seconds to start the car and drive away. I have no clue if they heard me leave or not. I don't slow down to look. When I hit the main road, I shift to high gear and speed like a demon. For one second, I think to myself, stop by the bank and get the hell out of here. But even as the thought passes, I realize how childish it really is. Escape to where?

My foot never eases off the gas pedal until I turn onto the road to the clubhouse. The gates are open because it's during business hours. I gear myself up for the possibility that Ward or Sandman may be alerted to my absence and waiting at the door for me. My breath quickens the closer the car gets.

The front door is barren of all souls, thank God, as I pull up to the front. I let the car die, jumping out to run inside. Several of the guys look at me weirdly as I pass by them, headed up to Hold's room. My only hope is that he is in there. I climb the steps two at a time.

When I reach to turn his doorknob, it is locked. Panic overwhelms me, filling me with a sick desperation that threatens to swallow me whole. I bang my fist loudly against the door.

"Hold, open up!" I scream. "Holden, please," I yell, scared now that I hear loud voices coming from downstairs.

"What the hell?" he says, opening the door with only a towel wrapped around his waist.

I don't hesitate, falling directly into his arms. My arms wind around his neck. I bury my face against his naked chest. He smells like home. I can tell he has lost a little weight, but he is still my Hold. I sob as he holds me.

"There is my little queen," the voice behind me says. "Why don't I take her downstairs for you, Hold? I think you have your hands full as it is. We don't want to upset the future Missus," Sandman says, moving to stand next to us.

The feel of Sandman's arms grasping me from behind prompts a whimper of fear from me. I latch on tighter to Hold.

"Please let me stay with you. Please," I cry, raising my lips to whisper in his ear. The feel of his arms loosening around me, relinquishing me to Sandman, frightens me. "I need you, Hold." I place my lips against his and the physical attraction between us once again ignites. He reaches to pull me back to him, deepening the kiss. I pour everything that he has ever wanted from me into that kiss, including my heart and sanity.

His lips hungrily devour mine and return every single stroke. Every nip. Every lick. I give as much as I receive and this is nothing like I have ever experienced. This kiss is almost sinful in nature. Too sensual to be sharing in front of anyone, but I don't back away. I am too scared of the repercussions.

Hold places his hands on my butt, lifting me, and I don't hesitate to wrap my legs around him. He shoves me against the door, not slowing down the onslaught of my mouth. In the back of my mind I know Sandman is watching, waiting for his chance to take me away from him, and I refuse to give him the chance.

I rock my hips against him, grinding against his groin, enticing a pleasurable grunt from Hold. Everything is on the line with this kiss: death or escape. I can't hold anything back now. The only way to convince everyone is to turn my body on and my mind off, which I do. I whimper as I let these sexual feelings bombard me. His hand manages to force its way between us, undoing my jeans. I feel him try to tug them down, while never removing his mouth from mine.

"Hold, man. You have a fuckin' audience," Mikey says, somewhere behind us. "I don't think you want to tap that ass in the hallway."

Hold tries to move his mouth from me, but I chase it, not wanting to face the consequences of my actions. My kiss pulls him back to me, forgetting everyone around us. His hand hits the door beside my head. I jump, but never release his lips.

"Son, put Helen down. Now," Ward says.

Hold moves his head back from me, his blue eyes staring into mine.

"I need you. I need you," I cry. My body trembles from the sheer terror of what is happening.

He shifts his head to look at Ward. "Go away."

"Son, you have one bitch already in your bed. We're just trying to help you out."

Hold turns his head to look back inside of his room. My eyes follow his to see the brunette sitting in the middle of his bed, covered by only a sheet. Nothing in me cares that she has been there, but from this point forward he is mine.

"Get the fuck out of his bed," I say, looking at her.

His chuckle tickles my ear. "You heard my woman," he says.

She rushes out of his bed, wrapping the sheet around her, running by us out of the room. I glance up to look at Hold. His smile indicates I can release the sigh that is pent up inside of me. This could have ended badly. I give him a quick kiss in appreciation, to let him know I am thankful.

We both turn to look at the hallway filled with Hell's Highwaymen, including Ward, Sandman, and Mikey.

"You guys here to watch?" Hold sarcastically asks them.

"Hold, I think we need to have a meeting. Now," Ward says.

Ward does not want me alone with Hold. *Why is that?* My mind races with this question over and over.

"You go have a meeting without me," he says, turning with me in his arms and walking into the room. He kisses me as he kicks the door closed with his foot.

"Put me down so you can lock the door," I say.

"Hell, no. Not happening. Keep your long legs locked around my waist," he says, leaning over to switch the lock on the door with me still in his arms.

I happen to look down to see that the towel has long since fallen away and I am wrapped around his nude body. He traps me against the wall, his hard muscle frame holding me prisoner. This time when our mouths meet it's not as frantic. It is slower. He takes the time to savor me. I can tell the difference. He is the first to pull back minutes later.

"You want to tell me what all that shit was about? You got Ward and Sandman on your ass. What have you done, Hels?"

"You don't know? They didn't tell you?" Oh. I know now. Hold doesn't have a clue that I am being held prisoner. Mikey's words from that night ring in my ear. He said that Hold would never forgive Ward for hitting me. I am about to see if those words are true. I have everything to lose and nothing to gain by keeping quiet.

"Shit," he says, letting me go so that my feet land on the floor. He walks over to the table to grab a cigarette and lighter. He lights one up, throwing the lighter back down. "Tell me what the hell is going on."

"Do you know they killed Jake?"

His eyes go round in surprise. He coughs when he inhales instead of exhales.

"The kid we beat the shit out of? The jock that was messing with you? When?"

"Last October. And before you ask, he was trying to talk to me, but Hold, I never gave him any idea that I wanted to be with him. In fact, I always told him no. This one night he comes into Hard Ink and causes a scene and you can imagine how well that went over. The next thing I know, he's dead. I was upset at Sandman and Ward. I said something to Ward and he…" I say, stopping. I'm not sure I should finish this sentence. It changes everything.

"He what, Hels?" He moves to stand in front of me.

"He… He hit me," I whisper.

"He hit you?" Hold walks over to put his smoke out in the ashtray on the table. When he turns, I see the murderous look on his face. "You are telling me that he fuckin' hit you?" Grabbing some jeans off the back of the chair, he slides them on.

I watch him stop to rub both of his hands over his shaved head.

"Who else saw it?"

"Everyone."

"Everyone fuckin' watched him hit you? You are sitting here telling me that Mikey, who was supposed to be taking care of you while I was locked up, watched you get hit by Ward?" He turns to grab his cell phone.

I nod, watching him get angrier by the second.

"Get up here. NOW!" He yells into the phone.

Within seconds, Mikey is knocking on the door. Hold walks over to let him in and everything happens so fast. He pulls Mikey in, shutting the door behind him, then pins him to the wall in a chokehold.

"What the fuck happened to my girl?"

Mikey glares over at me, but proceeds to tell Hold in detail how everything went down. He doesn't skip over

Ward hitting me like I thought he would. The idiot even goes into detail how he heard Sandman roughed me up, which I'd planned on taking to my deathbed. He tells him how he has been my jailer for the past several months.

"Did you tell Ward that you didn't want to see me when I got out of jail?" He looks over at me, broken.

"No! I *wanted* to see you. Mikey said *you* didn't want to see *me* and that you had a brunette taking care of you."

Hold punches Mikey in the nose, blood spurting everywhere.

"Goddamn it, Hold," Mikey yells, holding his hands to his face to catch all the running red liquid. "Ward told me to."

Hold moves away from Mikey to stumble over to sit on the bed. I watch him bow his head, placing his hands over his face.

"Man, she isn't worth all this shit," Mikey says, still trying to obstruct the bleeding.

"She is worth more than any of you," he says, lifting his head to look at Mikey. "I shoulda picked her over the club years ago. Get the fuck out of my room and don't you dare open your mouth to anyone, especially Ward. You got me?"

Mikey nods. He leaves us staring at each other.

"Hels, I am so sorry," he says, his voice breaking.

I move to sit down next to him, reaching to pull him into my arms. He lets me, folding himself into my chest. My hands gently rub his back as he buries his face in the crook of my neck.

"I try to do everything right, but it comes out wrong. I tried to save Jake, Hold. He didn't deserve to die. Jake was just a kid. He had his whole life in front of him. I tried to warn him away, but he thought my fear was a joke. I'll always endanger someone in this life. How am I supposed to live like this? I wasn't made to endure it because it's killing me on the inside. Sage is so strong. She handles everything like it's nothing. I'm not built for this. You know it."

He raises his red eyes up to meet mine. "How'm I supposed to keep you in this prison, when I know what that feels like, Hels? I can't fuckin' do it."

"Let's go. You and I," I beg him. I wait for him to give me his standard, *I can't.* It is what I am used to, but I still wait.

"Hels, can you just lie here and sleep with me for a while? Like when we were kids? I haven't slept good in about a year. Even since I got out, it doesn't come easy. Can you do that for me?"

I want to argue with him; I want to scream at the top of my lungs. But I don't. He sounds so completely crushed. It kills me to see Hold like this. I do love him. I will always love him. With a nod, I give him what he wants.

He scoots all the way back in the bed, and I crawl up, following him. We lie side by side, staring at the ceiling. I realize that nothing matters at this moment but him. I turn to cuddle into him, wrapping him with my arms, snuggling deeper next to him. Hours pass. I don't think either one of us closes our eyes, but it feels good to be with him. I am hoping he feels the same way.

Eventually, we fall asleep. I wake much later to find him gone from the room. I am not sure what I should do. If I leave the room, I could be in danger, but if I stay, I'm likely in danger also. Not much of a choice. It's dark inside the room, so I lean over to turn the lamp on.

Hours pass, but still no Hold. When the clock ticks past midnight, I become frightened. Where is he? Ward wouldn't hurt Hold—he's his son. Still, I wouldn't put anything past the club, especially past Ward. I war with myself over what to do for another hour, finally deciding that Hold's safety is paramount to my own.

I open the door to find him standing there, with a brown bag in his hand.

"Please tell me you weren't going to stupidly leave my room," he says.

"I was worried about you. I couldn't leave you to wherever you were."

He shakes his head, pushing me back as he comes in. I watch him throw the bag on the bed. He walks into the small bathroom and closes the door. Minutes later he comes out.

"Sit down. We need to talk," he says, nodding to the chair that I am standing beside. "Let me carefully explain to you the situation I find you in." He sits down next to me. "You have not only pissed off our leader, but also the most deadly man I know. I hope you know that Sandman is another name for the Grim Reaper."

"I know exactly who and what he is, Hold. I am not as innocent of the club as I once was," I say.

"Well, if you're not innocent then you are just fuckin' stupid. Is that what you are, Hels? You sit here and calmly say shit like that, it pisses me off," he says, standing to walk in place. "You actually said to Ward that someone was goin' to burn him, but it wouldn't be you who'd do it? Now he thinks you're goin' to run to the Feds or somethin'."

"No! I have never even considered that. I only meant that if he kept killing off people, he was only going to mess with the wrong one," I say, standing to defend myself.

"Just so you know, you never say cryptic messages to a gang leader. That shit will get you killed faster than anything. It blows my mind that you've been raised in the lifestyle, but yet you act like you don't know how to exist in it. You let your words and actions ruin you. What the hell are you doin', Hels? Do you want them to kill you?"

"I'm tired. I can't live like this for much longer. If it's an escape… then yes, I want it," I say, letting a cry out at the very end.

"I can't be the escape you're lookin' for. I never could," he says quietly.

Somewhere inside of me, I already knew this. I think that is the reason that his words don't devastate me like I thought they would.

"I know, Hold," I say sadly, knowing it's the truth.

"If you had the chance to run, there are rules that you

need to abide by. Are you listenin', Hels? Because I will only say this once."

What? What is he saying? My heart feels like it will beat out of my chest. I nod, and he nods back at me.

"First, you can't practice tattooing anywhere. You gotta let that go, babe. The first thing Ward is goin' to do is search every hole-in-the-wall tattoo shop, if it takes him twenty years to do it. Second, you have to keep moving. Never stay in one place longer than necessary. He will put out feelers to all the clubs, putting a bounty on your head. Third, if you ever do escape and Ward finds you, he's gonna do one of two things: either kill you immediately, or humiliate you in front of the club and then kill you," he says, pausing to look down. When he looks up, he charges toward me, backing me against the wall hard. "If you ever do escape, you have to make me two promises, and I need to know without a shadow of a doubt that you mean them."

I nod, his words exciting and scaring me at the same time.

"You will never, ever speak of what you know of the club. As someone who loves you and you damn well know it, you owe me this," he says, trapping me inside of his arms. "And when we find you and you are brought back, you are mine. *If* I can even save you from Ward. There will be no more running, no trying to escape. You will have had your chance and the rest of your life will be devoted to only me… the way I always wanted you to be. If you get away, it will be the only time I will let you. I won't survive it again. I love you, Hels. It's only you for me in this lifetime."

He kisses me softly, the touch of his lips so tender. His heart calls to mine in a way it never has, and for one second, I think I can give him what he needs—all of me. But the moment passes without my speaking up. No time for lies between us anymore. He pulls back, waiting for my answer.

"I promise. I never would talk, Hold. I have always kept my mouth shut. And you know I would never betray you," I say, glancing into his eyes.

He nods, before backing away from me. "In that bag is enough money to keep you running for a while. The first couple of months, keep moving on. If you make it past a year, find odd jobs, not staying longer than six months anywhere. No one is downstairs right now. The prospect who is supposed to be on guard duty thinks I am going to be runnin' in to pick up somethin' and coming right out again. My truck is out front. It would be nice if the person that steals it would leave the keys above the visor at the bus station. Also, put on the black hoodie I have on to cover your head. Now, I'm goin' into the bathroom, because I can't watch you leave me." He leans over to give me one quick kiss on the cheek before taking his hoodie off and turning to walk away.

"Hold," I cry, running to hug him. "Please come with me. We can be together."

He catches me, holding me close. "I wish I could, but I only know this. Where you can't live here, I can't live there." His arms pull and push me away from him. "Go, Hels, before I change my mind. I don't wanna let you go."

I step back at his words, letting him walk into the bathroom and close the door. I don't hesitate, placing the hoodie on before grabbing the bag to run downstairs. The clubhouse is empty. I don't encounter a single soul. His truck is waiting for me and I ride out behind the tinted windows, past the prospect who is expecting Hold. My heart pounds inside of my chest, knowing each mile I drive toward freedom could be my last.

When I get to the bus station, I leave the truck keys where he asked before getting out. The first thing I do is buy a backpack and toiletries. Inside the brown bag is not only money but there's also fake identification. I can't believe he was able to get all of this done tonight. I ditch the bag, and find the first bus heading out of town.

I don't take a deep breath until I'm back on the road, rolling along in the large motor coach, a little old lady sitting next to me.

"What is your name, dear?" she asks.

"Helen," I tell her, not even using the name on my fake I.D. *Real smart, Hels.*

"I love that name. It always reminds me of Helen Keller. What a sad, but lovely story. You know it, don't you?"

"No, I don't think I do," I say, glancing over at her.

"Well, let me tell you about a brave, young girl."

SEVENTEEN

June 2008

"You ready for me to wrap it up?" Billy asks, indicating the Ferris wheel tattoo.

I nod. "Thank you for staying late to finish it."

"Malik doesn't care as long we lock everything up," Billy says, placing a piece of plastic wrap over it.

"Yeah." I reach for my lacy shirt and slide it on, fastening only a couple of buttons in the middle.

"Speaking of Malik, you guys good? It went from you both having this intense sexual chemistry to being all eat-shit-and-die glares," she says, smiling at me. "You know he cares about you, right? If he didn't, he wouldn't be worried."

"I know." I don't tell her that I will be moving on soon either way. It doesn't matter what Malik thinks, but I hope to resolve our issues before then.

My phone chirps with an incoming text. I reach around to the back pocket of my black denim skirt for my cell phone. My heart flutters when I see that it is Vin.

Outside the shop... I need a tattoo. Know a good artist?

"Billy, do you care if I lock up?" We all have our own set of keys.

"If you need to stay late, you can have it. I'm hitting up Lowry's for a beer. See you, lady."

I follow her to the front, unlocking the door. "Thanks, Billy. Have a nice evening," I say, smiling at her.

"You're welcome. And well, well. What do we have here," she says, looking over at Vin standing outside. "Don't do anything I would." She winks at me before leaving.

"Is it too late to get hooked up for a tattoo?" He stands with his hands on his hips.

In a million years, I would never have pictured me loving someone like Vin. He's a little too clean cut, even with his face stubble. His shaggy brown hair lies haphazardly across his eyes. I glance down at his brown loafers, tan cargo shorts, and red button-up shirt that are way too straitlaced for my taste. Nothing like the leather and jeans I am used to.

"What are you wanting?" I ask, blocking his entrance.

"Well, I've been told that the second tattoo is artist

choice," he says, stepping closer to me.

"You think it's a wise decision for me to place anything permanent on your body, considering you haven't contacted me in a week? You could walk out of here with unicorns and rainbows on your ass."

"If it would help you forgive me, I might let you." His body stands parallel to mine. His eyes stare down, trapping me in his gaze.

I don't know if it's his cologne or his day job, but he has this wonderful woodsy scent that drives me insane, especially, when he is next to me. I want to bury my nose against his chest.

"Do you not care enough to call or text? I don't understand. Are you just that busy that you don't have a minute to spare for me?" I try to disguise the hurt in my voice with sarcasm, but it's an epic fail as my words crack at the end.

"Don't say that," he whispers. "When I am away, I have to separate what is happening with us from my job, because I damn sure can't here." He brings his hands up to gently cradle my face. "Look at me. I'm an ass. It will not happen again—that I can promise you."

I watch his lips slowly lower to mine, inch by inch. When they finally touch, an electric voltage sends my senses into a tailspin. I whimper from the longing overwhelming me. My hands reach up to grab his wrists as I lose myself in his eyes and our lips do the talking for us. A deep pang of longing rocks my center, as waves of lust crash against my sensitive skin.

"I missed you, Keller," he says, breaking the spell.

My body intensely protests my retreat as I step back from him to hold open the door to Screaming Ink, inviting him in, and then locking it behind us. All of the blinds are pulled for the night and most of the lights are already turned off, except for my station. We both walk that way.

This week has made a difference that is becoming clearer by the second to me. I can't just give him my body anymore. He deserves more—I deserve more. I need to find out if I am leaving this town with him or by myself. But first things first: I need to know where we stand.

As I walk by my chair, I accidentally rub my fresh tattoo against it. I hiss, reaching for the searing pain on my ribcage.

"What's wrong?" He grabs my arm to turn me around.

"It's nothing."

He doesn't listen to me as he reaches for my shirt to pull it up. I watch him gaze at my new tattoo. His finger hovers over the covering, outlining the air above the design.

"It's our Ferris wheel," he says, glancing up at me.

"Yeah, it is," I reply, tugging the bottom of my shirt away from his hand. "Why did you come here tonight, Vin?" He visibly blanches at my words. What is the deal? It's not the first time I have noticed that something I say upsets him.

"To see you. But now I really want a new tattoo," he says, placing his hand on my hip. His grip closes the distance between us.

I give a strangled laugh. "A tattoo? Okay. What do you want tattooed?" I glance up at him. I don't miss the dire need projecting from his eyes.

"Keller, I trust you. You know what belongs on my skin. Just nothing crazy big. The pain, you know," he says, shrugging his shoulders while giving me that soul-squeezing smile of his.

How is it that I don't have some type of heart condition, with as many times that he causes it to stop and start? He turns my world upside down, and inside out, and I love it. I crave it like my drug of choice.

I know immediately what I would give him, but I need answers before I tattoo this on his skin. He needs to understand the circumstances that surround me, because he may choose not to receive the tattoo I want to give him. And I wouldn't hate him for it. I would endure the pain that would threaten to tear me apart at his absence.

"Vin, we need to talk. There are some things I need to tell you," I say, wetting my lips. My nerves are getting the best of me. "My name…"

His mouth effectively cuts off my words. This entire week disappears in a fog, the hurt carried away by the promise of this kiss. He slows down his movements, teaching and torturing me in the same instant.

"I need you to do something for me," he says, in between kisses. "I want to hear what you want to tell me, but I need you to give me one week—just one more week, before we discuss our past or future. Can you do that for me? For us?"

Alarms go off in every corner of my brain. Something is off. When we first met, he only wanted to know about my past. And now he wants to wait? "What is going on, Vin? You used to pressure me for answers about myself and now you don't want them? If you don't want me, just say it."

"It's not that. Everything is so unbelievably complicated. I am trying to work out my situation, my job, before we make any decisions. Please? Just one week?"

I can't believe what I am hearing, what he is saying. Maybe he'll know more about where he will be working next in one week, what house he will be restoring.

"What tattoo are you going to give me?" he asks on a whisper.

My throat constricts as the tears gather. "I can't tattoo what I want to without knowing there is a future for us." I search his eyes, looking for answers.

He brings his lips tenderly to mine for a kiss, before leaning back. "You are my future. No matter what you tell me, no matter what I say… you are my future."

We touch, our hands, mouth, and lips move in synchrony. I believe him. I really, really want to believe him. His words remove so many doubts, but the truth still remains between us, a gap not so easily surmounted. Our bodies know the meaning behind his words, recognizing the indescribable pleasure offered. But my mind craves more, knowing instantly that we have nothing without full disclosure.

My lips slow his, bringing the heat between us to a low-burning simmer. I try to take a step back.

"Tattoo me. Please," he says, his eyes closing as he holds me tightly to him. "Whatever your heart tells you. This is me showing you how I feel, because it's not time yet for words. We have built this relationship from broken shambles and damn it, if it doesn't work—we will start over and build it again until we get it right." He opens his eyes, "This is me telling you that you own me body and soul."

I am on a precipice, anticipating the fall. This is the first time that I don't want to take it alone. This man wants to take it with me. His eyes hold all the answers that I need.

Eagerly, I reach for the top button of his shirt and, one by one, I slowly undo them all. My hands reach under his shirt, opening it wide, and I watch my fingers spread across his hard abdomen. The heat coming off of his body makes me wet. My palms drift lovingly up his chest. He hisses as my fingertips graze each of his nipples. The corners of my mouth lift when I hear him. I want to show him how much he means to me, how much I love him. My hands slide his shirt back from his broad shoulders, pushing it down his strong muscular arms, the experience heightening my own emotions.

His eyes never leave mine as he reaches for the few buttons of my shirt. When it falls open, he takes his fingertip to press it softly to the sensitive skin below my bellybutton. His touch sets off an electric charge inside of me. His eyes lower to that one spot so he can follow his finger as it rakes up my body, stopping under the lacy pink bra. My own chin drops so that I can watch. He continues his upward ascent, between my aching breasts, and over my heaving chest, up my neck, until he rests his finger under my chin. He raises it slowly.

We stand shirtless, facing each other. My breasts rise and fall beneath my bra. Too many sensations are hammering at me—it's almost more than I can endure. I turn to gather my supplies, giving myself a minute to center my emotions. His hands circle my waist as his mouth trails across the soft skin of my neck. The touch of his wet lips breaks my concentration. I laugh, the sound so unlike me.

"I swear, my mission in life is going to be to make you laugh," he says, his raspy voice laced with the lust I feel.

It is hard to keep my focus on my equipment with him surrounding me, but I do it in record time. I turn, gently pushing his chest back until he falls into my chair. The look on his face captures my heart, and my soul yields to him. I place a hand over his existing tattoo, rubbing the place right underneath.

"Here?" I ask, waiting for his acceptance.

He nods, leaning back against the chair. It takes only minutes to prepare the area and my machine. I am not worried to free-hand the tattoo: the design blazes prominently in my mind. All of my years of experience come down to this one tattoo for him. In my head, it's like I am painting by numbers, each one representing the tears that brought me here.

I press my hand against his hard pectoral muscle,

flattening the area. My foot lightly steps down on the pedal, the buzzing hum a sweet sound to my ears. I press the sterile needle into his skin, the black ink transferring from my machine to him. He flinches, but keeps his eyes closed while I work in silence. Not a sound is made, but this haze of lust between us threatens to obliterate our surroundings. I hold myself back by sheer will. My teeth ache for the taste of him.

My design comes alive on his skin. I finish the outline and shade it all in gray. It is a small tattoo, centered directly underneath his date, both directly above his heart. Every time my hand slips, grazing his nipple, he groans. We are both on overload and the air still swells with bridled tension.

When I finish, I glance up at him to catch him staring at me. I lay down my machine, stripping my gloves from my hands. He lowers his gaze to look at his chest. For a long minute, he doesn't say anything. I watch his chest rise and fall sharply. I start to stand, fearful that it isn't something he wants. His hand moves lightning fast, grabbing my arm to pull me over him. I climb on top, my knees spread apart, surrounding his thighs. My slide-on shoes fall to the ground on either side of the chair.

His hands move to deftly undo my bra, letting it also fall to the ground as his fingers caress my back. They drift around to my chest, taking care not to touch my new tattoo. One hand moves to the heart tattoo chained on my chest above my own heart. He touches the lock, rubbing the keyhole in the center.

"You tattooed a key on my chest," he whispers, swallowing convulsively several times.

"Yes," I say, resting my hands on top of his shoulders. My nerves build as I massage the muscles that bunch underneath his skin.

"You gave me the key that unlocks your heart?"

I nod, afraid of my own words. His lips find mine, silently offering me a future I never dreamed of, a future even better than my best wish. He shifts back to look into my eyes.

"I understand now. It's beautiful ink. So much more than just a design, it is part of our story, lovingly placed on my skin," he says, knowing my soul. "It's taking every restraint within me not to ravage your body, because I want to make love to you," he says, unzipping my black skirt before bringing it up, carefully lifting it against my ribcage, and over my head.

His words are taking my mind and body to places they have never been before. He caresses his hands up and down my torso, careful of my new tattoo, making sure to tug my nipples when he comes in contact with them. His hands drift lower, and with one quick tug, he snaps the silk band of my panties. He sexily pulls them away from me before slipping them in the pocket of his shorts with a smile on his face. It is naughty and more than acceptable.

My lips find his, climbing every step of this sensual journey with him.

"I don't want your restraint. I want all of you, hard and deep, erasing everything bad in my life. I want it all replaced with you," I say, begging him as he touches and kisses me. I watch his eyes go wild from my words.

"Wait," he says, gently lifting me off of him, so that we both are standing. "How do I recline this thing down?"

It takes me less than a minute to have the chair lay completely back. He turns to sweep me off my feet, picking me up to sit me back down. The sight of him standing before me melts my insides. He toes his shoes off, then strips off the rest of his clothing, reaching into his pocket at the last minute for a condom.

"Lie back," he says, his voice commanding.

I take my time, placing my body on display in front of him. His grunt of satisfaction makes me brave with my actions. My hand drifts across my abdomen, circling my navel, moving lower. I rest it on the curls displayed at the juncture of my thighs.

"Slide down," he orders, tearing the foil packet open.

My body hums at the sound of his words. I do as he asks, scooting my butt to the end of the chair. I watch him sit on my stool, sliding it to the end.

"Spread your legs open, slowly." He licks his upper lip.

His capable hands fit themselves under my ass, lifting me to his mouth. His tongue licks me. It laps at the small nub of my clit, before spearing me entirely. In and out, he continues to stoke this lust building between us. My body writhes under his mouth. He conquers all of my fears and insecurities with actions instead of words.

He stops, kissing his way up my abdomen. My mouth is his final destination and I wait with bated breath. I feel his body climb on the chair, tasting my skin as he moves up. He sweetly places a kiss on top of the Ferris wheel that I did for him, his eyes never leaving mine.

Oh, God! I love him. He makes me feel whole, complete, something I am wholly disjointed from. When his lips reach mine, I surrender my desire, swapping it for his. The climax builds, threatening to shatter too soon. It is hard to separate myself from his touch, to slow things down. I need him; I need this.

"I love you," he says, entering me with a sharp thrust. He chants it, repeating it again and again, making it our love song.

Time stands still. He makes love to me completely. Our hands grasp each other, touching, feeling. With every stroke inside me, he reaffirms his feelings, his eyes never leaving mine. So much stored in our hearts is being conveyed. I need what only he can give me. This fire is going to consume me; only ashes will be left. When the orgasm hits, I scream, reborn as his. My body continually grips him, holding on to the streaks of pleasure pulsating though me.

He rocks into me over and over, racing to join me. I can't get his words out of my head. They keep me wrapped tightly in this euphoria. His grunt of release when he reaches his climax triggers another orgasm for me. We both give in to this tidal wave of sensual gratification. I rub my hand down his back, the sweat making it slippery beneath my fingers.

His head rests on my shoulder as he tries to regain his

ragged breathing. My body is trapped beneath his and I love it. I choose not to move or seem uncomfortable, afraid of losing this feeling of protection. He said he loves me. The corners of my mouth lift of their own accord. He said he loved me several times. A laugh bursts from my lips.

He mumbles something unintelligible against my shoulder. I am pretty sure he sung it during our lovemaking. My laugh turns into a full-fledged giggle.

"What is so funny," he says, raising up to look into my eyes.

I feel so relaxed, so... free. It is almost like I can take a deep breath and not worry anymore. His love is freeing. I bite my lip to stall my laughter as I stare into his beautiful eyes.

"You love me," I whisper, his face directly above mine.

His cheeks redden and he nibbles on his own lip, which I find incredibly sexy. "Yeah, I do. And now, I am going to get you off this table, dressed, and to my bed so I can love you some more. Is that okay with you?" He lowers his mouth to mine.

"Yeah, it's more than okay." I say in between his decadent kisses.

The sun's early morning rays slip through the window, falling softly across the bed. I hold my hand up to catch a ray of light as it splays over my fingers. My mind and naked body are fully satisfied after last night's activities. Even the soft snoring next to me sounds musical. I have lost my everlovin' mind. Happy isn't just a state of mental awareness: it's a whole new life for me.

He loves me. I stifle the laugh that builds in my chest, not wanting to wake him. I roll over to watch him sleep. He's even more handsome to me now that I know how he feels. My body responds to him and I would like nothing better than to kiss his body awake, but I can't. The clock doesn't lie and I am going to be late for work as it is.

My mind wars with whether to alert him to my absence or let him rest. I'll let him sleep. I turn to get out of bed, but his arms surround me, bringing me back to lie next to him.

"Where do you think you're going?" he asks, his voice groggy with sleep.

"Work. You kept me up all night and now I am going to be late," I say, looking up at him as he leans on his side over me. I can't stop smiling.

"You could play hooky, stay in bed with me all day," he says, leaning down to kiss my lips.

"Don't tempt me. Malik is already pissed at me. He thinks you are the big, bad wolf."

"He does? You've never told me that." He looks concerned at my words.

"It's nothing. Malik is a great guy. He's just trying to have my back," I say, leaning up to kiss his lips, before rolling away.

"Stop," he commands, pinning me against the bed on my side so I can't get away.

He reaches for the hair covering the back of my neck. Brushing it to the side, he holds it away. My eyes close at the feel of his soft, wet lips touching the sensitive skin. His fingers trace the intricate tattoo at the base of my hairline. The silence in the room belies the tension that is building directly behind me.

"It's an oval shape. Like… a football," he softly says. His voice is barely a whisper. "Is that a number seven?"

"No, it's just an oval with some line work," I say, trying to squirm away from him. Jake's tattoo is one that I don't know if I can ever share with him or anyone. My past is going to be so painful to discuss with him when it comes time.

"Be still," he says. "Please. Just lie here for a second and let me hold you."

"I'll be late," I say, sliding from his arms as they release me. I reach for my clothes scattered around the bedroom floor. It takes a couple of trips around the room before I finally find everything and am able to dress with all but my panties that he kept. I don't button my shirt because my new tattoo stings after the over-enthused bed play we partook in all night long.

"Keller, come here," he says, sitting on the side of the bed. The sheet lies haphazardly across his lap.

I walk over to him, stepping in between his legs to stand. He places his hands on both of my hips bringing his lips to my bare abdomen. My heart aches to crawl back into bed with him. He presses his stubbly cheek against the same skin.

"I am going to talk to my boss today and see if I can't disclose everything to you. I don't want to wait a week."

"You mean talk to your grandfather?" His words confuse me.

He looks up at me, propping his chin on my belly. "I love you, Keller."

"I love you, too." It slips from my mouth. The first time I have ever said it to him. I smile happily down.

He groans, then tries to pull me back in the bed. I laugh at his playful attempts.

"No. No, I have to go, Vin."

"Damn it! Stop. Don't call me…" he lets me go so that he can fall flat on the bed, covering his eyes with his forearm.

"Don't call you today?" I ask, puzzled by what he is talking about.

"Will you come back tonight? Straight here after work? Please?" He sits up, pleading with me.

"Of course," I reply, smoothing a wayward lock of brown hair from his forehead. I turn to leave before I lose my willpower. This is crazy happiness. I stroll out to my car, humming. He has me. There is no other answer.

The entire ride home, I can't think about anything but last night. A memory of him chanting that he loves me makes me grin. His lovemaking was everything and more than I could have dreamed. I don't want to imagine moving on without him. We have to make it work.

I arrive at my apartment with barely fifteen minutes to get ready for my shift at Screaming Ink. My feet hit the pavement running as I rush up the steps. It takes me less than a minute to slip the key into the lock to open the door. When I walk in, my heart crashes to the ground, taking my world with it.

"Hey, Hels."

Chapter EIGHTEEN

June 2008

"It's been a long time. Miss me?" Hold asks, sitting in the center of my tiny couch, his fingers steepled in front of him.

I glance behind me to see Mikey closing the door with a sense of finality, his demeanor diminishing any thought of my trying to make an escape. I turn back toward Hold. The man who sits stoically before me looks familiar, yet different. He seems the same, but there is nothing left of the boy I knew in that man's face. I don't even recognize those steel blue eyes that glare at me now. I swallow convulsively, scared for my life. This is going to have to play out. No one may know how I escaped that night, not even Mikey.

"Yes," I answer honestly.

He gives a bitter laugh. "Yeah, that's pretty obvious. What are you doin', Hels?"

"Living here. Not bothering anybody."

"No. What. Are. You. Doing? You should have fuckin' moved on months ago. Ward woulda never caught up to you. You broke two of the main rules: never stay in one place long and leave the damn tattooing alone. Was that so fuckin' hard to do?"

Oh, no. They have been watching me. They know my friends, my job, Vin. I have to warn him. I have to warn all of them.

"Now I see in your face you know exactly what I'm talkin' about. Ward has been having you watched for about two months. There was a reason we couldn't just pick you up. And the funny thing is, it mighta saved your life because it proved to us that you don't have a clue about what is goin' on. You're in high demand, Hels."

"What are you talking about?" I whisper, afraid of his answer.

"This is fuckin' hilarious," Mikey says, laughing behind me. "Tell her, Hold."

"Not yet. Did you pack her shit up?"

"It's in the truck. All but some clothes scattered around. We are ready to rock and roll," Mikey says, turning to open the door so that he can walk outside.

Hold stands up, his formidable stance causing me to automatically back up. My pulse beats frantically against my throat. He silently marches toward me, stopping when he is directly in front.

"Do you remember our last conversation? I know you do because we couldn't find you for years."

"I was tired of running," I say, glancing up at him.

"So you were ready for me to find you. Is that what you're sayin'? Because that's what it sounds like to me," he says, leaning down. His mouth is only inches from mine. "Do you remember your promises to me?"

I turn my face, not wanting to be in such close proximity to him after just leaving Vin. It feels... wrong. His finger finds my chin, forcing my face back to him.

"Answer me, Hels. Those promises may be the only difference between livin' and dyin'. Do you fuckin' remember?"

"I remember," I say through gritted teeth. "And I kept that promise I made to you." I stare into his eyes, letting him see the truth.

"I knew I could trust you," he finally says, leaning down to plant a light kiss on my lips.

I am too afraid to push away from him, but I don't open my mouth either. My eyes stay glued to his until he steps back.

"Let's go. Gimme your keys," he says, reaching for them.

I hand them over. *Oh, shit!* "I need to go to the restroom first," I say, realizing that I have not a stitch of underwear on... and I don't want to tell Hold.

"Hurry," he says, staring at me. "Hels, don't try anything funny... or else."

In a daze, I walk toward my bathroom with Hold close

on my heels. I pray that Mikey left me some clean undies lying around. When I reach for the door handle to close it behind me, Hold slaps it back open. He turns to face away, offering me the only privacy I am going to get. I glance around to find that nothing but a dirty t-shirt and a pair of jeans lay on the hamper. I reach for the jeans; they are better than nothing at all.

I actually make use of the toilet before sliding my pants on. My hands shake with fear, which slows my actions. He doesn't say anything while I wash my hands, but I feel him getting antsy.

"We gotta get outta here," he says, grasping my arm and pulling me out of the apartment and down the steps.

There is no question of me fighting or escaping him. I remember everything I promised him. A guy stands beside my car wearing the MC cut with a prospect patch across the back of it.

"Follow behind us," he says, tossing my keys to him. "Keep the fuck up."

He leads me to a newer Ford black truck, opening the dual cab doors. He helps me into the backseat, sliding in next to me.

"Don't get any ideas of jumping out. Child locks," he says, closing the door.

Mikey opens the door and climbs in. He looks back at us. "Hell, this ain't no Driving Mrs. Daisy."

"Just drive," Hold says, warning him.

"Alright, boss," he sarcastically adds.

I glance over to notice that Hold's Hell's Highwaymen

cut says Vice President across the patch. So he made it. I am in no way happy for him. I look down to realize that he has my cell phone in his hand.

"Okay, we call your work first since you are scheduled to be there this morning."

"How do you know?" I am completely taken aback that he knows my work schedule.

"That part is simple. We call to make fake appointments. We always knew your work schedule."

My stomach sinks at this knowledge.

"You are going to call work and tell them that you have an emergency back home and are leaving town for a while. If you mention anything out of the ordinary, we will kill the strange-hair girl up front," Hold casually says.

My heart sinks at his words. I know that he means them. I watch him find the correct phone numbers stored in my phone and dial it. He hands it over to me. I listen to the sound of several rings before someone answers.

"Screaming Ink. This is Ginger speaking."

"Hey, Ginger. It's Keller," I say, trying my best to sound normal.

"Hey, girl. Guess who had an incredible night last night? You, I'm hearing," she says, laughing at her own joke. "Where are you at? You should be here already."

"Listen, I have a family emergency. I am going to be out of town for a while."

"I didn't know you had any family. I thought you were an orphan?" Her voice sounds funny.

"It's extended family. Anyway, I'll be gone for a little

while. Can you let Malik know?"

"Uh, wait just a second," she says.

"Ginger, no. I really need to go," I say, but she is already telling someone what I just told her. Great.

"Where are you?" Malik asks, getting on the phone.

"Hey, I'm already on my way. I only found out this morning and have to rush home."

"Keller, if someone is watching you right now, just say yes, and I'll call the police," Malik says, his voice sounding worried.

"No, Malik. Really, it's personal stuff. I'll call you in a couple of days."

"Where are you going?"

"I'll call soon," I say, hanging up on him. I can't stop the tears that fill my eyes. These are my friends.

"Attachments were not part of the deal. What were you thinking, Hels, or should I say Keller? Nice one by the way," he says, winking at me.

"I wasn't thinking," I answer, looking out the windows. "Are you going to let me call him and say goodbye?" I know Hold must know where and with whom I spent last night. "He restores houses and will be moving on soon anyway."

He and Mikey die laughing at my words. What is going on? Oh, no. No. NO! What did they do? My heart sinks, knowing what the MC is capable of. I attack Hold sitting across from me.

"NO!" I scream in his face, digging my fingernails into the flesh of his arm, tearing it. "You had him killed, didn't you? You bastard!" I start sobbing as I fight him, my soul shredding to pieces.

"Stop it, Hels. Goddamn it! STOP!" He captures my arms, pinning them painfully behind me.

I continue to buck my body against his. Mikey hands him something from the front seat and he places it tightly around my wrists behind my back. I blindly fight as my heart is ripped from my chest.

"Now stop kicking me unless you want your feet zip-tied also," he says, wiping the blood away from the deep scratches I inflicted.

I slide as far on the seat from him as possible. My chest heaves from my aching sobs.

"Calm the fuck down. He's safe. In fact, that bastard is safer than you are at the moment."

"What do you mean?" I ask, sniffing my tears back. If Hold says he is safe, then I know he's alive.

"If you want him to stay that way, you are going to start from the beginning and tell me everything. How you met. What he says he does for a living. Who he talks to every day. Got it?"

I don't hesitate to tell Hold everything. If it keeps Vin safe, then I'll give him anything he wants. I start from the beginning, only leaving out the personal details between us.

A half an hour later, I finish. Mikey glances in the rearview mirror at me before staring straight ahead again. I watch him take his cell phone and call someone.

"Hey. It's Mike. Her story is exactly as we thought. Yes,

sir, we are on our way. I'll let Hold know," he says, flipping the phone closed. He turns to glance over his shoulder at Hold. "It's set up just how you wanted it. I hope you know what you're doing."

Hold nods at him, before looking at me. "He lied to you."

"What are you talking about? Vin lied to me? About what?" I didn't tell Hold that I knew Vin had secrets. Of course, I thought they were all personal secrets. Nothing like mine.

"Hand me the pictures, Mikey. What's that sayin'? Oh yeah, a picture is worth a thousand words," he says, reaching for whatever Mikey is handing him. "These were sent from one of our guys a couple of years ago when we needed information on him."

He leans over to show me an eight by ten picture. In it are a bunch of guys standing around in blue jackets with big yellow lettering that reads ATF AGENT. At first, I don't know what I am looking for, until I see him. Vin. He is the third from the left. He's smiling my smile, probably laughing at what one of them is saying while he wears his matching jacket.

Oh my God! I shudder from the pain that racks my body. The tears fall freely from my eyes. I cry from the searing pain of my heart breaking. *No! Please, no!* I lean my head against the window, wishing that I could die. I can't stop the sobs that convulse my body. The sting of betrayal is an old friend of mine. I should be used to it, but this one hurts more than all those before it.

"He's a fuckin' Alcohol, Tobacco, and Firearms agent. And that's not all, Hels," Hold says quietly beside me. "Ask me his name."

I shake my head. I don't want to know. It doesn't matter anymore.

"Ask me his goddamn name!" He yells at me.

"What?" I cry, looking at him through the tears.

"His name is Luke Carrity. Ring any bells?"

Carrity. I look away, scrabbling for oxygen.. Oh, no. Oh, NO! Jake. My eyes lift to Hold's.

"He's Jake's older half-brother."

"This can't be," I say, dazed. "I watched him restore that house myself. I saw him. He's an artist like me. I watched him use his own hands." I try to convince Hold.

"Cover story. He's obviously been undercover trying to get information. I should have known he would go looking for you," he says, throwing the pictures between us. "The bastard came to Harmony asking questions about Jake's death right after you left. He didn't lie about who he was or worked for. He flat out told me that he was working deep undercover out of the country when Jake died. When he returned home after the funeral, he found voicemails on his home phone from Jake. Evidently, Jake was in love with a girl named Helen who needed help."

"No," I whisper.

"Yes, Hels. He felt that there was more to Jake's death than the police report. He came lookin' for this Helen and found out who she was connected to. Some of Jake's teammates even thought that the Hell's Highwaymen MC had it in for him because of you. So Luke made it his mission for the next three years to make it hard on the MC until he got answers, specifically from you. He rained the fuckin' ATF down on us. All of our gun business—out the window. Sandman got hit with some stupid legal shit that Luke cooked up and spent two years in a cell. Mikey spent a couple of months up in county. He got me on a stupid technicality with my parole, which sent me back to county for another six months. Then suddenly one day he's gone. Poof. And we suckers are relieved, thinking he has given up on trying to catch us for the big stuff. Now, can you just imagine Ward for a second and who he blamed for all of this?"

"I think I should add that even before this shit went down, Ward made it his personal mission in life to bring you back to the fold," Mikey says from the front seat. "Preferably dead, but he would take you alive also."

"Yeah, Ward sent your photo out to every local chapter we have, including details of your tattoos," Hold says, next to me. "That's how we almost found you before, but shithead went and got drunk when he was supposed to be identifying you. So, Mikey gets a call a couple of months ago that one of our local chapter guys was visiting a friend that lived in Ohio. His friend wants a piercing so they go down to the local shop named Screaming Ink and he notices an artist that has a different hair color than our girl, but some very similar tattoos that he remembers reading about. Ward of course sends Sandman to take care of the problem before Mikey or I know anything about it. And guess what Sandman finds when he comes to call on you?"

"Vin."

Hold makes a low buzzer sound. "Wrong name. He finds our good friend Luke kissin' our little queen. So now the shit hits the fan because we don't have a clue if you're workin' with him or inadvertently spilled the proverbial beans. Ward decides to put a prospect tailing you and sends Sandman back to see what the fuck is goin' on. This may be what saved you from an immediate execution. Sandman observed that you obviously didn't know who Luke was and from what he gathered from people that you worked with, you didn't talk about your past."

"I never told him or anyone anything," I say, which is the truth.

Hold doesn't say anything for a while. I hiccup as my sobs slowly quiet, but other than that there is silence in the truck as we cruise down the highway. I can't believe it. Luke Carrity is Jake's brother? Everything he told me was a lie. He never loved me. He never even really cared.

All those small moments that meant so much to me: the feel of his lips against my skin, the rush of seeing him before me, making me feel like I was his world. Lies. Now so much makes sense: little things that he said, things that happened around us. How did I not see it? Was I so blinded by my love that I couldn't see the writing on the wall, his feelings toward me all a grand hoax?

My hands shake behind my back as my body convulses from the physical pain of his loss. Nothing except my sister's death has devastated me so completely. The burn of the tattoo on my ribcage representing my love is an abomination, worse than the one that was forced upon me.

"You have to call him," Hold says, looking over at me. "Let him know that you haven't been kidnapped. We don't need his or the ATF's shit around Harmony when we are getting our business back on track. Tell him you chose me."

"What?" What is he saying?

"Don't say anything about knowing who he is. Keep everything simple."

"Why didn't you let me call him before you told me then?" I snap at him, this hurt burning me from within.

He smirks at me. "Did you love him, Hels? It sure does hurt like a bitch when you love someone who fucks you, and it's all lies. Doesn't it?" A touch of satisfaction laces his voice. He lifts my cell phone up so that I can see my missed calls. "You have missed calls from Ginger, Malik, and, surprise, someone named Vin." He presses different buttons and holds the phone up to me with the speaker on.

Vin… Luke… whoever he is… answers on the first ring. "Are you okay? Ginger just showed up at the house, upset. Where are you?" He sounds panicky.

His voice tears my soul asunder. I close my eyes as a silent sob racks my chest. Only Mikey and Hold witness the pain that threatens to drown me. My face crumbles. With my hands tied effectively behind me, I unsuccessfully impede the whimper that escapes me.

"Keller! What the hell is going on?"

Hold knocks my knee with his backhand, urging me to answer him.

"I'm fine," I whisper.

"Tell me where you are," he demands.

I shake my head, knowing he can't see me, but I need to find strength somewhere inside of me to get through this. My voice breaks when I start to say his name. It's a lie.

"V… I-I am going home for a while," I say, scripting every word before I release it.

"Home?"

Now that I know the entire situation, I hear the deceit in his voice. It spoils the love inside of me, giving me the last little strength inside that I need.

"Home. You know where, right?" My eyes lift to glance defiantly at Hold.

Hold's jaw clenches as he stares angrily at me. He mouths, "What the fuck?" He grips my cell phone like he plans to throw it out the window before steadying it once more in front of me. His nostrils flare in and out, his rage visible with every breath he takes. Good.

"Florida," Luke says, lowering his tone inflection, dropping all pretenses. "Specifically, Harmony. Who are you with, Keller?"

"That is not my name," I say, my own hostility emerging.

"It is to me. Don't think for a second that what we have isn't real. It is! Do you hear me? This between us is as

302

real as it gets. It wasn't supposed to happen, but it did. I have been trying to make it right, to set the record straight, but it wasn't up to me, Keller."

"That is not my goddamn name!" I yell. "Say it!" I command. "I want to hear you say it."

The silence is deafening. My eyes remain solely on the phone.

"Helen," he whispers.

"You are a liar. I am leaving of my own free will. Don't ever come near me again," I calmly say. My voice sounds dead to my own ears.

Hold doesn't hesitate before bending the cell phone to break it, ending the call for me. He rolls down the window to throw it out. I close my eyes. How many times can I be broken before not being able to mend? The thought crosses my mind that this is it, the point of no return.

"That was stupid," Hold hisses. "Find somewhere to pull over, Mikey. Now!"

My stomach rolls with a black sickness, the insidious disease brought on by the lies that infest my life. I am infected, sullied to my marrow by my birthright. I can't possibly survive this agony smothering me.

Hands jerk me forward by my shoulders. My body slams across the seat of the truck, before he tows me outside of it. Hold's fingers gouge into the muscle of my upper arm. He half carries, half drags me toward a secluded, wooded lot on the side of the road. The ties that bind my wrists behind me, rub painfully against the sensitive flesh of my skin.

"Do you wanna die? Just fuckin' tell me now," he says, his face inches from mine. "Goddamn it!" Hold turns away from me.

He leans against the aging maple bark of one of the massive trees surrounding us. The evergreen canopy overhead shades us from the blue sky, darkening the light around us, muffling all sound. The eerie silence is only broken by the disturbance that we bring to it. I don't miss the tremble of his wide shoulders. I can't ignore the overwhelming, endless anguish that follows me, and I am tired, so exhaustingly weary, physically and emotionally.

"Yes," I whisper.

His head swings around at my answer, the blue of his eyes devoid of any trace of the boy who I remember, further exacerbating my utter despair.

A small cry escapes me at the realization of what I am asking. And his face comes to my mind. Luke. I shut my eyes, remembering the intensity when he took me, made me completely his. It was real. The love between us wasn't imagined. I felt it crack the ice that encased my heart and touch his. I can hear his voice whispering that he loves me. Luke. Vin... the name never felt right rolling off of my tongue. Every time I called him that, he became upset.

Luke. So much is clearer now. He hasn't asked me about my past in months. He didn't because he... didn't care about that. He cared only for me. My happiness. He already knew my past and loved me in spite of it.

Memory after memory, each time we were together, plays like a movie in my head: every word, every touch, every kiss. My eyes fly open. Luke loves me. The realization rocks me to the very core of my existence. I fall to my knees, the pine needles below softening the impact. My chest heaves with the onslaught of emotions as I stare at the ground.

"Is this what you want?"

I hear Hold's voice, but it is the cold metal pressing gently against the center of my forehead that garners my attention. My eyes raise to his and it surprises me to see the tears that roll silently down his cheek. He is not entirely lost, for I see my Hold still in there. This life that cages him hasn't stripped him completely of his humanity.

"Because it may be the only way that I ever get you out of my head. Four goddamn years and you still are the only one I want. I waited for you to come back on your own—not because you were broke or tired, but because you missed me. But you never came. I allowed you to go, stupidly thinking that you would find out just how much you loved me," he says, looking down at me.

Inside of me, his words war with my revelation of Luke, and the lie I uttered seconds ago doesn't apply anymore. It never did. I have fought to get away from the MC my entire life, believing there was something more to this life, and there is.

"You made a promise to me. If you ever came back, regardless of how, you were mine. Do you know why I made you do that?"

My eyes never leave his as I shake my head no.

"It wasn't because it was the only way I might could

have you. Like I said, I wanted you to hopefully come to that conclusion on your own. No, it was because I knew what Ward would do to you. If you made it back alive to the MC, I knew it might be the only way I could protect you."

"Just let me go again, Hold," I whisper. "I'll disappear this time for good. Please."

He laughs, and something about it sounds off even to my ears.

"Yeah, that's not happenin'. You see, Hels, there's a test in me being the one to bring you home. I never admitted that I let you run, but Ward knew, I could tell... and he hasn't trusted me since. I am to bring you home and give you the choice of blood in or blood out. Either way, I'm to administer your punishment," he says, his gun arm shaking, "and prove my loyalty to the Hell's Highwaymen."

He steps away from me, slowly lowering the gun. His words chill me to the bone. Proving his loyalty means that he dies if he doesn't return me. I know what the club is to Hold... it is his entire life. He never really chose me when he let me go. It only made it easier for him to exist in the MC without my interference. I see that clearly now. I know that Hold loves me, it's almost ingrained in both of us, but the MC is in his blood.

"You may not love me, but you will be mine. Death or me: they're your only two choices. I need to warn you that death is probably the less painful option of the two, and if you choose me, you may wish you chose differently. I can never be what or who you want and all those years of tryin' are over," he says, moving to me.

Hold falls to his knees, his face leaning toward mine. The touch of his lips against my mouth sours my stomach, and I turn my head to the side.

"You can hate me with your heart, while your body loves what mine does to you. I can accept that now. Your love means nothin' anyway. You fuckin' give it away to just anyone," he says, kissing his way down my neck.

A shudder of revulsion almost overcomes me. His hand tries to turn my face, but I struggle, straining my neck muscles. I don't want Hold or his body. I only have to find a way to bide my time until I can get away or until… Damn. Will Luke come for me? I can't think that way. I told him specifically not to. What have I done?

"Hold, man, we got to get outta here. Time is a tickin'," Mikey calls out from somewhere behind the trees.

Hold kisses me one last time softly on the cheek. "Don't think you've been given a reprieve, Hels. I am your future, the only one you get, and by the end of the day you will be kissin' my feet, if not somethin' else, in thanks."

I close my eyes, his words causing a chill of terror to race up my spine. He tugs me up so that I can stand, leading me back to the truck. My heart races at the uncertainty of the coming punishment. I don't doubt his words or that I will suffer before this day is through.

NINETEEN

June 2008

We arrive at the clubhouse sometime after eleven o'clock. All day we drove, not stopping to eat, getting closer to the one place I prayed never to return. I haven't spoken to Hold since our stop this morning. There is nothing I could have said to change his mind. My anxiety has risen a notch with every single mile we have traveled.

An array of vehicles is parked outside as we park directly in front. I look around to notice that nothing has changed.

"Looks like everyone is here. Let's get this shit done," Mikey says, looking over at Hold. "You have to go hard, brother. If you show her even an ounce of compassion, your deal with Ward will be off. I'll play my part to help her out." He turns the engine off and opens the door to exit from the truck.

Hold sits in front of me on the passenger side. I watch him tap the dashboard with his index finger, not saying anything.

"I am goin' to guess from this morning that you wanna live, no matter the consequences," he says, glaring at the windshield. He does not turn around as he speaks to me. "Do you want me to drug you? It won't knock you out, but it should help with what is goin' to happen."

Oh, shit! My stomach dips, the thought of the coming events terrifying me. I shake my head no. I'd rather have all my faculties at full alert than be semi-comatose.

"What is going to happen to me?" My voice comes out in a choked whisper.

"I don't know exactly, but considerin' the clusterfuck you caused… it's not goin' to be pretty. Ward would rather you take a bullet between the eyes than take your next breath. I will tell you that he wanted to smash every bone in your pretty little hands, but I reminded him that we need you tattooing at Hard Ink for the club. He said the punishment will have to fit the crime and is leavin' it up to me."

"How can you not know what exactly is going to happen if it's up to you?" I am confused by his words.

"Because I haven't decided, Hels," he says, turning around in his seat to stare at me. "Because it has to be believable or both of our lives are on the line. For the last four years I've been the lovesick fool who's moped around in your absence. It fuckin' enraged Ward. So we have to put on a show for the entire MC. They have to believe that I am committed in my actions. I have carefully masterminded your return where it didn't end with your death, but I can't see how it all will play out." He looks away to reach for the handle to open the door.

"Hold," I begin, not sure what it is that I need to say.

He either doesn't hear or chooses to ignore me calling for him. I watch through the window as he comes around to open my door. He helps me slide out. My hands and arms are numb where they have been tied behind my back the entire trip. He removes a pocket-knife from his back jean pocket and flips it open. With the sharp blade out, he leans back to cut the plastic holding my wrists captive and within seconds I am free.

The muscles in my shoulders throb from the stricture of movement for the past ten hours. I stretch my arms to circulate the blood flow. Hold moves to stand in front of me.

"Don't do or say anything stupid," Hold says, leaning down to speak softly in my ear. "Too many people in that room want a reason to kill you. Don't give it to them. Please, for me." He steps back, imploring me with his eyes.

I nod. Without Hold's help I never would have escaped. All those years ago when Tara and my dad died, it was Hold who held me and wiped my tears away. I have to trust him.

He places his hand on the small of my back, guiding me inside the building where all of this started. My breath backs up in my chest, the fear growing with every step. We enter the main room and the hushed silence is deafening. I glance around to see all of the MC guys stopping whatever they're doing to stare at me. So many familiar faces glare back with unmasked hatred, and even more surprising, is the number of new ones with the same facial expression.

Hold continues to guide me toward the bar and I realize why, when I see who is turned around on the middle barstool to face us.

"Hello, Helen. It is… *nice* to see you again," Ward says, his voice barely concealing his contempt for me.

He hasn't aged much these last several years. This is still the man of my nightmares.

"Hello, Ward," I say, stopping there. My whole system reacts to the nearness of this monster. It is a terrifying rush to be this close to him.

"You've been a busy girl. We have all just been discussing your escapades these last several months, wasting time while we've been waiting for you," he calmly says.

I try to swallow, but I almost choke. My throat is severely dry from my nerves.

Ward reaches back to grab something on top of the bar, bringing forth a glass of clear liquid.

"Here," he says, offering it to me. "Have some water. You must be thirsty after your long ride."

I glance from the glass to Ward and something inside of me screams not to drink it. "No, thank you," I say, barely getting the words out.

Several of the men chuckle around me, confirming I made the correct decision. I don't know what is in it and I don't want to.

"I guess you know by now the headache you have caused me and every other Hell's member, some more than others," he says, nodding toward someone standing against the wall.

I turn my head to see Sandman leaning back, arms crossed, staring intensely at me. He nods his head in my direction. My heart races into warp speed. I never cared to set eyes on either of these sociopaths again in my lifetime, however short that may be.

"But we have a problem, Hels. You are one of our own. There is only one way in and one way out. Those in our inner circle don't get the choice to have their tattoo blacked out to move on. I am sure you remember my preferred method of getting rid of fuckin' problems that threaten the club. There is just one complication with you though. Holden. Even after you ran from him, he still wants you," he says, staring at Hold. "It's not like the boy has a shortage of pussy, but shit, yours must be dipped in gold." His comment garners laughter around the room.

"Ward," Hold says, through gritted teeth.

Ward holds up his hand to silence Hold. He slowly stands. "Has she made her decision?"

"Yes," Hold says. "She's still alive, isn't she? You told me if you she chose to blood-in, that club justice was mine and all would be forgiven afterward. We still good on that?"

I can see Ward isn't happy with the arrangement Hold obviously made with him. If I were going on an assumption, I would say he didn't think I would return, at least not alive.

"No one is to lay a hand on her, and her death is mine and mine alone from this point forward," Hold says, glancing over at Sandman.

Sandman places a hand over his heart, nodding his head at him. Hold turns back to look at Ward. A silent standoff ensues. No one in the room speaks or moves for several minutes. Hold doesn't have to tell me that there is discord within the MC that has nothing to do with me. It is evident by the tension between these two.

"If I am satisfied with the punishment, I wholeheartedly agree. I will welcome my daughter back with open arms," Ward says.

"Fuck that," Hold says, stepping up to Ward, going chest to chest. "Don't play fuckin' games. She will suffer for the years away from me, and the shit she brought down on the club. I want your word that, following it, you will not go after her."

Ward doesn't say anything. He only glares at Hold.

"Your word," Hold says, directly in his face.

"You have my word, son," he says.

I cringe when he calls Hold *son*. He makes it sound like a derogatory term.

"Let's do this then," Hold says, stepping back to reach for my hand. He intertwines his fingers with mine, tugging me behind him.

We walk through the building with the entire MC following us. Hold exits through a door that connects to the garage. When we enter it, the cavernous building seems devoid of its usual chaos. Even the gray cement floors seem too clean for a car garage. I notice two cars at the far end, but the majority of space is clear. The back wall is lined with toolboxes and machinery that have been bunched together to provide empty space.

When I glance around, it becomes clear why. Over two hundred men fill the area to almost full capacity. Hold has maneuvered us to be in the midst of them all. Mikey brings over a metal fold-up chair, placing it directly in the center. I hear the sound of male laughter; it echoes against the high ceiling. Ward and Sandman come to stand in the front.

A terror unlike any I have ever known steals the very air I breathe. I cough, fighting to catch my breath. Hold pats my back with his hand. Tears fall down my face and I'm not sure if they're because I am so terrified or from my choking fit.

"Do you need water?" he asks, in my ear.

I shake my head, not wanting him to leave my side for anything. Better the devil you know versus the devil that you know will kill you without a second thought. It takes about a minute, but I finally regain my composure.

"I'm fine," I whisper.

"Okay. Showtime then," he softly says, for only me to hear.

He leads me to the center of the room. "Stay," he says,

loudly for everyone to overhear. "Remove your clothes."

My eyes frantically turn to search his. He can't be serious.

"Don't make me repeat my words," he says, his hand snaps out to grasp my chin painfully. "Remove your goddamn clothes."

His tone brooks no argument. *Oh my God!* What is he doing? I have the same shirt on from last night. My eyes close to him, to those who surround us. He has been trying to warn me all day and now it is time to pay the piper. I undo every button slowly, removing my blouse to let it fall to the ground. My hands tremble when I try to grab the button of my jeans. I'm wearing nothing underneath. I am afraid of stalling for too long, so I slip the button through the hole and unzip them.

Taking a deep breath, I exhale and push them down to my ankles. I remove each jean leg from my feet, tossing them down. With my eyes tightly shut, sounds seem to magnify. I hear Hold's hiss of breath and the whistles from the spectators standing barely ten feet away. My brain shuts down, not registering the actions around me. It's almost as if I am seeing everything happening to me, instead of experiencing it. In my mind's eye, I can see myself removing my bra, but I can't remember doing it.

"Mikey, gimme your belt and grab her clothes off the ground," Hold says, somewhere behind me.

He is close: I can feel his body near me. There's an instant awareness of him, being my first, but it's not sexual this time. This time it's fear. His hand caresses down my back, coming in contact with my new tattoo. He rips off the plastic wrap covering it and I cry out in pain, the raw skin sensitive.

"Shh," he croons in my ear. "I'm sorry. Did that hurt?" His chin rests upon my shoulder as he stands behind me, fully dressed against my naked skin.

His fingers dig into the flesh that my tattoo covers, callously hurting me. This time the cry that escapes me echoes around the room. My eyes meet with those of a spectator—the man who has always claimed to be my family—and the coldness that greets me is that of a stranger's. I know that what I am about to experience will change everything. Will change me. Forever.

"Do as I say, when I say it," he forcefully commands. "Turn around and put your hands on the chair behind you."

I pivot slowly on the balls of my feet. He doesn't have to tell me to grip it tightly: my fingers curve over the back of the metal chair instinctively. Thousands of tiny chill bumps cover me. I dread the thought that my naked body is on display. My heart throbs in a frantic rhythm, this moment being the torturous accumulation of years of anxiety and apprehension.

His heavy breathing sounds frighteningly close. "You are not allowed to fuckin' move."

My eyes clamp shut. I am afraid of the consequences I have wrought. My tongue darts out of my dry mouth, wetting my cracked lips. I should have taken the water when he offered it earlier. The last harrowing fifteen hours have been an emotional train wreck, and just when I think things can't get any worse, they do.

I don't hear a whisper of the leather until it rips across the center of my back, the cracking sound against my skin reverberating all around me.

"Ahhh," I yell out, the white-hot pain sucking the air out of my lungs. There must be small metal spikes lining the belt. I almost let go of the chair, until I remember his words not to move.

"That's for the year I woulda gave you my name," he says, directly into my ear, but loud enough for everyone else to hear.

I didn't think I could shed another tear, but at the sound of the pain laced through his voice, my eyes swim with them. Even after this, it kills me inside to know that I hurt him. Many seconds pass before the second strike slams across my sensitive butt cheeks. My knees go weak, making it harder for me to stand. A cry escapes me from the onslaught of the metal and leather, this one stinging worse than the last. I dig my fingers into the cold metal of the chair, hoping that I can hold myself up.

"That's for the year I woulda made our dreams come true."

So many memories assault me along with the belt, memories both sensual and evil. I want to open my eyes, but I fear what I would see in his gaze. The grief in his voice already rocks me to my core.

I loudly scream at the next two consecutive swings of his belt, and my knees roughly hit the concrete floor. My eyes open to see red splatter across my arms, staining my already colorful skin. His unerring aim catches the exact spot as the first, slicing deeper into my flesh. I choke back the bile that threatens to erupt.

"Take it easy, brother," Mikey says.

"Shut the fuck up, Mikey. This isn't any of your business. Get up," he growls at me.

I force myself back to my feet, head bowed, bracing myself for his words as much as his strikes. My tears represent the agony of defeat that I don't want to give him.

"That's for the goddamn year," his voice breaks midsentence. "I woulda gave you my child."

Any inner strength I have left vanishes at the words torn from his mouth. His feet stand before me now. I have to see him. My eyes lift from the ground to stare directly into his dark, penetrating gaze. The room and those in it fall away and I only see him. This was once my friend. My brother. My lover. My savior.

"*Our* child," he whispers through gritted teeth. He leans down to deliver a tender kiss upon my chapped lips, his tongue soothing them. His actions surprise me, the antithesis of his words. I watch him back slowly away from me. The look of desolation in his eyes is more than I can bear, so I close mine.

His backhand catches me completely off-guard. The searing pain explodes across my jawline up to my eye, staggering me backward. The chair scrapes against the floor, following me several inches. I stare at the blood-splattered ground, blinking my vision back into focus. I hear the sound of his heavy shit-kickers as he moves behind me once again.

The voice in my head screams enough. I am too close to my breaking point. I wouldn't have lived through the earlier offer of the bullet to my brain, but I am not sure I will physically or mentally survive this agonizing persecution.

My head slowly lifts to catch the evil glare as Ward stares at me. Beside him, Sandman watches on with an almost sexual intensity in his eyes. The nausea rises by several degrees—these men are fucking sickos.

The next whip of his belt catches me against the soft flesh of my legs and on the underside of my rear. My body quivers uncontrollably. I completely lose my balance, letting go of the chair. He grabs my elbow to help me steady myself. His foot kicks out to knock the chair across the room away from us. My stomach threatens to revolt at the feel of something wet and warm running down my back, down the crease of my ass, slowly over my legs. I glance down to see rivulets of crimson silently rolling over my feet to the ground encircling me. He tosses the belt so that it lands in it.

Our joint harsh panting is the only sound between us. He painfully tugs me backward to him, further lacerating my torn skin. The smooth texture of the leather rubbing against my back prompts another scream of pain. His jeans roughly grind against my buttocks.

"No," I say over and over, but make no attempt to

move, knowing it would cause him to order more of this torture.

"Do you know what it's like to pretend it's your face on every girl I kiss?" The sound of his husky voice whispers softly against my ear. "Wanting it to be your body under me every time that I fuck someone."

A violent tremor racks my system. His words make me sick and scared and I whimper as I feel his fingers brush across my wounds. They tenderly wrap around my body, and I look down to notice him painting the letters "HHMC" across my heaving chest in my own crimson blood.

"Blood in and blood out," he says, kissing my neck in between his words. "Your fuckin' choice. But know this: it is forever now my blood that runs through your veins. And I will drown you in it before I let you escape me again."

He has broken me. My body. My mind. I want him to stop. I don't know what is real and what is not. I hear him talking and I try to listen.

"Justice is served," he says to someone near us. "Now get me a fuckin' blanket."

"I would say so. Let me be the first to officially welcome her home," Ward says, his voice close.

I whimper. *Please, no!* My body trembles harder with the thought of his hands on me. I back farther against Hold. His arms gently slide around my body, holding me to him, trying his best to cover my nudity.

Ward reaches for my hand, bringing it to his mouth.

His eyes find mine. I don't miss the amusement in them. Sick bastard.

"Welcome home, my daughter," he says, kissing the top of my hand. He lets go to step back.

A blanket appears and Hold wraps me up in it. A shriek escapes me when it touches my back, but I'd much rather deal with the pain than to be naked another second. I don't miss the fact that Hold's lips or hands are touching me at all times. Something inside tells me that it's to show his affection toward me in front of the MC, so I don't protest. I have been here before and know when to keep my mouth closed.

I learned how to survive years ago and as I look out at all the prying eyes, I know I can endure whatever they are going to throw at me. Surprisingly, even to me, they haven't broken me yet.

TWENTY

June 2008

"You can't stay in bed forever," Hold says, leaning against the bedroom door.

I haven't spoken to him in over four days. Four days since he brought me back to Harmony and thoroughly beat the shit out of me. Afterward, he drove me to this small three-bedroom ranch house that he said he purchased two years ago. He led me to his bedroom, and I passed out cold from the exhaustion and pain.

The next day I couldn't get out of bed because the severely torn flesh down my back and legs was too extensive to move. I was in and out of consciousness throughout the day with some pain meds Hold gave me. I only allowed him to touch me to apply some type of salve that alleviated the burning, but other than that, I told him I would kill him if he came near me.

And even though I told Luke not to come for me, deep down I believed he would anyway. The days pass slowly with no Luke. Yesterday, I started to doubt that he loved me. Maybe it was all a believable act. The only answer was that he deceived me, lied to me. My emotional unrest compounds the physical pain.

"Leave me alone," I say, lying on my bare stomach. I turn my head on the pillow to face away from him, staring at the dingy tan-colored wall.

"Hels, I feel like shit about what I did. Talk to me," he begs. "You know I didn't have a choice. Ward was going to have you killed if I didn't make it believable. You are gonna live."

A bitter laugh erupts from my throat. I turn my head to see the agony of what he did on his face. "Says the guy who beat the shit out of me. I saw your eyes, Hold. I heard your voice. That wasn't all for show... and you and I both know the truth."

I watch him glance away, the pain evident. "My hurt turned to anger. I thought I could control it, detach myself from it enough so that I could get through that in one piece, but it burned inside of me. And it all just happened. I couldn't control my actions or my words."

"Well, I hope you and the rest of your sociopath friends enjoyed it."

"Hels, no matter what you believe, I did this to protect us. I love you," he says, his eyes pleading with mine.

"Love? I've had a lifetime of that kind of love. Get

out," I say, once again turning away. I don't want to hear another word from him.

"Hels, you've hardly eaten in four days. Don't do this."

"Get out!" I yell, lifting my head.

He turns around and storms away. I close my eyes. The pain isn't as bad as it was, but I also am afraid to test my limits. I barely am able to get up to go the adjoining bathroom, but nature calls. I don't dare look in the mirror. My back has to be a mess and my face can't be much better. The entire left side was swollen for the first two days and now I can barely touch it.

A knock on the bathroom door makes my heart jump. Damn Hold.

"Leave me alone," I yell.

"Honey, it's me, Diamond. Can I help you?"

Diamond? I shuffle across the bathroom to open the door.

"Oh, sweetie," she says, reaching out to hug me.

I am not fast enough and she wraps her arms around me. I groan from the pain.

"I am so sorry. I forgot," she says, stepping away from me. Tears fall from her eyes. "What did they do to you?" She looks me over, bending her head to glance at my back.

I shake my head no, but she already gets an eyeful. Her gasp alerts me to the severity of the damage.

"Your angel," she says, covering her hand with her mouth.

Oh, no. *My angel!* I turn my head to look in the bathroom mirror. My mother. Deep welts crisscross my back, marring the beauty of my tattoo. Some are so deep that I can see inside my flesh. I know these will scar. I slowly turn, my Ferris wheel is also marked, but it survived most of the damage. My vision blurs as the tears swamp my eyes. My beautiful tattoo.

"Don't cry, honey," Diamond says. "We'll fix it. You'll see."

I sink to my knees on the cold tile floor and cry out from the sting of the welts covering my backside. My life has never been mine—always controlled by the MC, the pain that I suffered always because of them. Those years spent away already seem like ages ago. I see myself years from now living this same life, beat down because of it. My sobs are not for the mother I lost again, but for finding and experiencing real love and knowing what it is. I am never going to have it with Hold, and I can't settle for anything less.

Diamond holds me on the floor while she tries to comfort me. Eventually, my tears subside. I can't worry about Luke. I need to get through every day the best I can, the only way I know how.

"Can I go with you to the shop?" I ask her.

"Do you think you should, hon? I am not so sure that's a good idea. You look to be in too much pain."

"Please, Diamond. I can't stay here. I need to get out."

"Let me help you wash your hair and get dressed and we will see how you feel. Okay?"

I nod. My knees tremble as Diamond helps me to stand, my body entirely too weak.

"Have you eaten?"

I shake my head.

"I am going to tar and feather that boy. Hold," she yells. "Get your ass in here."

He must have been close because it takes only seconds for him to find us.

"Get her something to eat and drink," she says, glaring at him.

If looks could kill, he would be dead, between Diamond and me. She lets me go for only a second to turn the water on. Diamond helps me undress before gently helping me bathe and wash my hair. She finds a loose sundress that falls to the ground, covering my wounds. Diamond mommies me, making sure I finish my entire sandwich and milk.

"You know, I really missed you when you left. I sorta thought of you as the daughter I never had," she says, sitting next to me on the bed while brushing my hair.

"It was last minute. You know I couldn't have told you anyway," I say, glancing over at her.

"Don't think I didn't know how much you protected me by keeping your mouth shut. I realized too late just how much you needed to talk to someone. I wish I could have been there more for you," she says, her voice hiccupping at the end.

I don't want to talk about this. *I can't.* "Diamond, let's go to the shop." I stand, showing her that I am fine now, not letting her see how I'm dying on the inside from the welts rubbing against my clothing.

"Are you sure?" She rises to stand next to me.

"Yes. Please," I say, turning to hobble out of the bedroom. The hallway leads directly to the front door, but I am stopped by Hold stepping in front of me.

"Where do you think you're going?"

"I need to get out of the house. Diamond is going to take me to the shop."

"It's not safe," he says, shaking his head. "Not gonna happen."

"You said I was fine with the club now. Which is it? Do I need to stay here in hiding?"

"There's more to it, Hels. You can't leave the house without me or one of the prospects."

"Is this your rule or your daddy's rule? Just let me know exactly who the man of the house is," I say sarcastically.

"It's my goddamn rule, because I don't trust you," he says, getting right up in my face. "And give me an hour of your time and I'll show you exactly who your daddy is."

I don't miss the flash of sexual heat in his eyes. He is still intensely attracted to me. The thought hits me that this is how I will be without Luke. I may find someone else one day, but it will never be the same intensity I feel when I am with him. Diamond was wrong all those years ago. Love makes all the difference.

Hold backs me against the far wall and I cry out as the pain flares from the contact on my abraded skin.

"Kiss me, Hels, and I'll let you go with D," he says, his lips inches away from mine.

"No," I say through gritted teeth. "They've made you into a monster, just like them. My Hold is gone. You're a monster," I whisper, flinching when I remember feeling him behind me. "You liked what you did to me. You got a hard on."

He shakes his head vehemently. "No. No. I was hard at seeing your beautiful body again, the first time in four long fuckin' years. I hated what I did. I hated letting all those men see my girl's body. I almost lost my fuckin' mind that they were whistling and disrespecting you. I saw the perversion in Sandman's eyes, the satisfaction in Ward's, and I wanted to turn the belt against them. I was their fuckin' little bitch. They had me up against the fuckin' wall, Hels, my balls in a fuckin' vise."

His arms cage me in as he places them on the wall behind me. The remorse in his voice and the pain in his eyes, hammer at my already damaged soul. I'm angry with him and confused at the same time.

"I know what I've done, what I've lost. All that ink on your body is my fault, and now so are the scars on your back. I loved you but I wouldn't turn my back on the club for you and it's cost me, big time. I'm seein' that now. I may have gotten you back physically but I've forever lost your love… the only love I've ever wanted… needed." He drops to his knees and embraces me, his shoulders shuddering.

My hands are held up and away from him, in a defensive position as I look toward D. She's standing with her hand clapped over her mouth, astonished at Hold's breakdown. The door opens and a guy pops his shaggy blonde head in. "Everything okay, boss?"

Without hesitating, I shout at him, "Get the fuck out!" I don't want him or anyone else to see Hold on his knees. When the door closes, I try to center myself, marshal my resources. I try to remember the boy I loved, the boy who saved me, who always put me first. The boy with the blue eyes. I comb my fingers through his dark hair, his face buried in my stomach as he weeps. "Right now, I hate you, Holden; I hate your guts," I softly whisper into the silence that surrounds us. "But somewhere deep inside where I can't reach her, is the girl who loved you more than life itself. That's the best I can do for you today. And it is way more than you deserve from me."

Minutes pass, precious seconds that slip once again through my fingers because of what the MC has directly cost me. The tears never come. Hold pulls back and quickly stands, turning away to wipe his eyes against the crook of his arm.

"Let me grab my cut. I can go with you," he says, replacing his emotionless mask as he reaches for his cut.

"No," I say, knowing I need some space from him right at this moment.

He turns around at my answer to stare at me. "What do you mean, *no?*"

"I need time away from all of this. From you," I say, my eyes not leaving his.

"You made a choice," he says, his fury barely contained.

"I had no choice!" I yell loudly back at him. The front door opens, once again interrupting us, as the prospect comes inside this time to investigate the noise. He is tall and skinny, with long, blonde, curly hair, and wire-frame glasses. He definitely looks out of place in the MC.

"Everything okay?" He looks from Hold to me.

"Everything is fine, Shady. I need you to take Hels, and follow Diamond over to Hard Ink for the day," Hold says, angrily staring at me.

"Gotcha, boss," he says, almost shaking in his boots.

I hobble out of the house, with Diamond and Shady on my heels. *God!* I am not ever going to be afraid of Hold like Shady. He can beat me every damn day. I stop, not sure whose vehicle I'm supposed to get in.

"Which one," I say, looking at Shady.

"Uh, my truck is over there," he says, pointing to a compact low-rider.

I look from him to the truck, wondering how he squeezes his height into that tiny vehicle.

"I'll follow you guys," Diamond says, already heading to her car.

My curiosity as to how he fits in the truck is soon answered when I carefully get in the passenger side to see him sitting down with his head tilting sideways. It rests awkwardly against the ceiling. When he cranks the engine, it is obvious where he spends his money and why he endures the discomfort. We drive in silence for most of the way, when I feel the need to ask a question.

"What kind of nickname is Shady?"

"Um, well… it's after the rapper, you know, Slim Shady, and plus I am kind of slim," he says, blushing ten different shades of red. His glasses slide down on his long nose and I watch him nudge them back up with his finger.

He hits a bump in the road and the truck bounces, the jolt magnified by the low-rider. I whimper when my body jerks against the seat, sparking painful twinges from the welts covering me.

"Are you… uh, okay?"

It dawns on me that he probably witnessed the entire event the other night. I am embarrassed at the thought of this guy seeing me nude and being abused. What must he think of me, that I let someone beat the hell out of me and then go home with him to sleep in his bed? What type of perverted fuck enjoys that? The more I think about it, the angrier I get.

"So did you enjoy the show the other night?" I ask, taking my frustrations out on Slim the shady dude.

"Y-Yes… uh… no, I mean… n-n-no," he says, his stuttering getting worse by the minute.

"Is that a yes, you saw Hold beat the shit out of me, or no, out of the goodness of what's left of your heart, you turned away? Which is it?" I know I am being uncharacteristically bitchy, but I can't help myself.

He stares at the road ahead, choosing to ignore my question. I think about goading him to answer me, but the fight just drains from my body. It's hard to be this tired and I'm in emotional overload. I am glad when we finally arrive at Hard Ink. In minutes, I'll be back inside the place where I learned the trade that would save me all these years, comforting me, and showing me there is so much beauty in this dreary life.

I step out of the truck and slowly move inside the shop with Diamond beside me. As I walk in, I note that nothing has changed. It's almost as if the years froze everything in place. Badger looks up and even smiles at me the way he used to, when I would come into the shop after school.

"Glad to have you home, kiddo," he says, returning to the customer he is tattooing.

Several of the other guys say their hellos. I don't sense any hostility, but my own builds inside of me. All of these assholes, including Badger, stood by and watched what Hold did to me. This life isn't right. It's not sane. I ignore them all. Why did I want to come here?

Diamond leads me back to her station and pulls up a chair.

"Sit," she says, pointing to it.

"I can't stay here," I say, the tears threatening to slip from my tired eyes. All my instincts scream *run*. I glance up to look out of the front windows. People walk past the shop like everything is fine, ignorant to the evil that resides in and infects this town. Or do they know and not care? My hands tremble as I pick at my dress, staring outside.

A policeman casually walks by, glancing into the shop. Something about him makes me think of Luke, and my heart stutters. Volatile emotions steamroll my senses: fiercely missing him wars with the sharp hurt of his failure to come find me. I watch the policeman look around before his eyes land on me and, for one second, I think he looks surprised, but then he keeps on walking, pretending like everyone else not to see me.

"Hels, you have nowhere else to go, honey. They will hunt you down like before and next time we both know what happens. There is no coming back. Is that what you want?" Diamond pats my knee, trying to comfort me the only way she knows how.

"This life will kill me either way. Do you honestly think I am going to stay here and play housewife to Hold? No," I reply, shaking my head.

"Listen, you can find your own happiness separate from him. You just play their game, Hels. There is so much that you can get out of this life if you're smart about it," she says, lowering her voice so that only I can hear her.

"I tried that and it doesn't work for me. He hurt me, D," I say, showing her the pain in my eyes. "You saw what he did. I don't care if Ward was going to kill me. Hold had no right, no right."

"Well, it looks like the bitch is back in town," Sage says, walking into the shop, interrupting us. She strolls up to stand in front of Diamond and myself, pushing her sunglasses back to rest on top of her head.

Sage hasn't changed one bit. And by the fire in her eyes, I can tell she isn't happy to see me.

"Sage," Diamond says, in a warning tone as she stands. "You need to leave."

"I'll leave when I am good and damn ready. Now step aside so that I can see my future daughter-in-law," she says, staring Diamond down. "Move your skinny ass, Big D."

Diamond glances back at me apologetically before stepping to the side.

"Hello, Sage," I say, looking up at her.

"Hels, it's been awhile," she says.

"Not nearly long enough," I reply, not hiding the acerbic tone of my words.

"Feeling's mutual, sweetie. Now, I am here to make sure that you understand that I don't care about anything other than Hold. If you hurt my boy again, you will deal with me. And I promise you'll wish you were dealing with Ward if it comes to that."

I laugh.

"I don't find any of this fuckin' funny," she says, glaring daggers at me.

"Your son made me strip in front of the entire MC before beating the hell out of me. Do you honestly think you can come in here and threaten me? Really? Death is almost a welcome relief. What possibly can you do to me that would hurt me any more than what I have already suffered at the hands of your family?"

"Sage, leave the girl alone," Badger says, standing behind her.

Sage continues to glare at me, a bitter laugh the only sound in the room. "This is far from over, baby girl." She shakes her head before turning to walk out. We all remain silent as we watch her get into her SUV and drive away.

"Well, I guess you win the award for bitchiest mother-in-law ever," Diamond says.

Everyone goes back to working, while I sit and watch Diamond tattoo her next customer. I can't let Sage's words bother me. For the next hour, I lose myself in watching her ink out a beautiful phoenix rising from the ashes. I have grown so much as an artist since I left, not realizing it until now. The outline needs to be a little bolder and I see areas of her shading that need a little more work. The client will not realize it, only seeing the beauty she is creating, but it makes me proud to know that I have progressed as a person and artist, something that would not have happened if I didn't run that day.

"Shit! We got trouble," Shady says, interrupting everyone in the shop.

I glance up, looking out of the windows to see a local cop car and a black Jeep Grand Cherokee park across the street from the shop. The police vehicle doesn't have its flashing red and blue lights turned on. An officer slowly gets out of the car, waiting for whoever is behind the Jeep's darkly tinted windows to exit.

We all stand to look outside, waiting to see exactly what is going on. Finally, the door to the Jeep opens and out steps its sole occupant. I gasp, my heart lodging securely in my throat. My hands fly to my chest. Luke.

Chapter TWENTY-ONE

June 2008

He came. *Shit!* With the police. What was he thinking? I watch him walk over to speak with the officer.

I run toward the front door. Badger yells for someone to call Hold, while Shady steps in front of me, effectively blocking my exit.

"I have to wait and see wh-what Hold wants to do," he says, pleading with his eyes for me to listen.

"Don't be stupid, Helen. You don't want to get another person killed, do you?" Badger stands beside me, looking outside.

His words wash over me, chilling me to the bone, halting my forward progress. He is telling the absolute truth.

"I have to see what he wants. You don't want them

coming into the shop, Badger. You've got customers."

He pauses, taking a deep breath before nodding. "Shady, follow her outside."

I take a deep breath, steeling myself for whatever is to come. He might not be here for me. And even if he is, Badger is right. I can't think of all that now. I step through the door to the outside.

The sun shines overhead, highlighting the white clouds that float lazily across the clear blue sky. Birds chirp in the distance making everything seem peaceful in Harmony. The sidewalk is empty of anyone save me and Shady, who stands behind me, blocking the doorway. Luke has his back to me, still speaking to the local cop. I watch as he stops, and turns his head slowly to look behind him.

Our eyes meet, my plain brown to his russet-colored ones. Every single cell in my body calls for him. *Damn him!* I have never felt such a love; it connects and binds us completely. I feel the pain of him seeing me like this.

"Motherfuckers! What did they do to you?" He yells, jogging toward me, stopping only short of running into me.

At his words, I remember my face. My hand rises to my cheek, barely touching it. I remember seeing the pale green bruising from my mouth across my cheekbone in the mirror this morning. Not exactly the look I would like to be wearing to see him again.

"I'm fine," I say, lost for an explanation. I can't tell him what happened. It could get us both killed.

"You're sure as shit not fine. Tell me what happened, Kell..." he stops when he realizes what he is calling me. "This is a mess." He rubs his hand over his heart, where both of his tattoos reside.

I'm not sure if it's on purpose, or an automatic response.

"My name is Helen. And your name is Luke," I say, my voice not hiding the overwhelming hurt of his deceit.

"I never wanted to cause you any pain. From the very beginning it felt wrong to lie to you. Every single damn time, it became infinitely harder to look you in the eyes. I have worked undercover for years and never have I wished so badly that my cover be blown. It was killing me."

"You slept with me, knowing it was only false pretenses between us," I whisper. I don't miss that we have an audience. Badger now stands beside Shady and opposite them is the police officer, both parties observing our conversation. "Was that part of your job?" I am dying to know.

"Helen, I..." he says, looking away.

No! I see the truth in his eyes before he turns from me. When he glances back, his eyes are slightly glassy.

"I was to obtain information by any means necessary. That is my job wherever I go, Helen. But from the first time, it was never like that with you. And you damn well know it," he says, stepping forward to whisper into my ear. "You stole my heart. I already knew your background, guessed the hell you probably went through, and I watched you keep on fighting to have something normal.

You appreciated every scrap of happiness that came your way. And, God, I wanted to give you more than you could handle."

"I don't know what is real and what is fake. I watched you restore that house for hours at a time. Your love for it was genuine. I know it was," I say, searching his eyes for the truth.

"It was. My grandfather does own a company that restores old houses. When my mother and father divorced, my mother took me to live with him and he taught me everything he knows. When I needed a cover story, it was a believable one, but I swear to you that my passion for it was real. So real that I want to quit my job now and restore houses for the rest of my life."

"Jake?"

He shakes his head. "Jake was my younger half-brother. Look, I don't want to discuss all this in front of everyone," he says, looking around us. "Can you please just come with me? We need to talk."

"Hels," Badger warns behind me.

I love this man standing in front of me. No matter the circumstances that brought us together, my affection is pure and real, more solid than the bruise that colors my cheekbone or the welts that mar my back. And I know that I would rather die than have any harm come to Luke. I might try to run again, but it will not be with a bounty on his head too. I know how capable my family is. His father has already lost one son because of me.

"Go," I say, glancing away from him. "You don't belong here."

"I belong with you," he whispers, reaching for my hand to link our fingers. "Wherever that is, I want to be."

Oh, God! I won't survive this, but he can. "You lied to me. I can't do this," I say, removing my hand from his.

"Well, damn it. You know what? You lied, too! I told you we built this relationship on shambles and do you remember what I said would happen if it fell apart?"

I know exactly what he said, but I shake my head. Tears swim in my eyes as I try to keep them back.

"Yes, you do. I said we would rebuild it again. And if that falls apart, we will keep rebuilding it until it works for us. That is how bad I want this relationship to work. Failure is not an option. Ending it, is not an option. Do you hear me, Helen?" He reaches for me once again, but I step back.

Every teardrop I release is a tiny piece of my soul, staining the sidewalk. I turn to walk toward the shop. I can't do this. My mind begs for me to turn back and go with him, but my heart loves him way too much to deliver his death sentence.

His fingers slide around my wrist, gripping it tightly to spin me around. A ragged cry escapes me. He stands before me, more beautiful than the art that decorates my body, his love shining clearly in his eyes. It outlines my heart and colors my soul: he is my artist. I have to protect him.

"We are through," I say, the blasphemous lie torn from

the depths of my soul. The words scald my lips with their falsity. I see the anger in his eyes, before he pulls me flush against his body.

"We aren't through. We will never be through!" His mouth captures mine, letting me know exactly whom I belong to. It's not even a competition. Luke owns me heart and soul. And my life has no meaning without him in it. Our tears mingle as they slide down both of our cheeks.

His hands slip around me and I whimper in pain when he accidentally grazes my injuries.

"Helen? What is it?" He steps back, his voice sounding pissed and concerned.

"I…" I start to say.

The roar of a motorcycle engine shatters the silence. I turn to watch an unmistakable Hold ride down Main Street, stopping directly in front of us. He quickly dismounts from his bike, slinging his helmet to the ground.

"Get your fuckin' hands off of her," he says, walking toward us.

His eyes blaze with anger, directing them solely at Luke. I don't know what to say or do. My heart is torn between fighting to be with Luke versus surrendering to keep him safe. The cop and Shady join our tight little circle.

"You don't want to do this, man," Luke says, pointing at Hold.

"What? You here to bring somebody else in on some bullshit charge? Or you just need the protection, pussy?"

"No, the officer is only for insurance." He nods toward Shady. "The same as your boy standing behind you. My business is concluded with your little club... unless I find out you have hurt her in any way. Then I will hunt you down like the dogs you are," Luke says, stepping toward Hold.

"Hels, you don't want to involve him," Hold says, his threat very clear to me.

"We need to talk, you and I," Luke says, looking directly at Hold. "I'll send my guy back to his vehicle if you send yours. Let's contain this and protect Helen." He turns to the cop and nods his head for him to return to the car, which he does.

At first I don't think that Hold is going to agree. He looks entirely too enraged to discuss anything in a calm manner. My eyes frantically volley between these two men: this volatile situation is on overload, tempers are obviously at peak levels, and I can't see it ending well.

"I got this, Shady," he says, nodding his head at him. "Go inside."

Within seconds, the three of us are left standing on the sidewalk, Luke's hand tightly gripping mine. A delicate silence exists among all of us.

"I took a chance coming here like this, but you wouldn't let me see her when I came to your house," Luke says.

His words shock and surprise the hell out of me. "You tried to find me?"

"Of course, I tried to find you," he says, swinging his

head to glance at me. "I will always find you."

He turns back to glare at Hold. "I knew this was the only way I could talk to her. I didn't want to involve the local police, but I also didn't want to end up a missing person. We both know that I have friends who wouldn't be very happy about that."

"I don't give a fuck where we are. Business is business and she is mine." Hold angrily stares back.

"She was yours. Now she is coming with me," Luke says, giving my hand a tight squeeze.

"The fuck she is," Hold says, his voice lethal.

"I love her," Luke says.

"You love her? You don't know a goddamn thing about her. She has been with me since we were kids. I fuckin' know her. I fuckin' love her," Hold says, pointing to his chest. He reaches for my arm that isn't linked to Luke's.

Luke steps in front of me, cutting Hold off. Hold's fist grabs a handful of Luke's shirt, jerking the material toward him.

"Go ahead and beat the shit out of me," Luke says. "It will only land you in a jail cell. Either way, she ends up leaving with me." Luke doesn't retaliate by laying his hands on Hold. He calmly utters every word. "I came here four years ago seeking the truth about my brother's death and when I didn't find it, I made things hard for your little motorcycle club. And that's what it is... a small operation. The only reason my department allowed me to investigate you guys is because of your contacts with bigger fish. I walk out of here, you have no more ATF problems, unless you do something incredibly stupid."

"Well, hit the road." Hold's face contorts with his hatred for Luke as he speaks. "But she stays."

"Not going to happen. Do you hear me? I will place myself so far up the MC's ass that I'll know every time you take a shit. And if you try to eliminate me, my friends will know who did it and keep coming." Luke turns his head to me. "Don't let him threaten you with my life. There is no doubt that he or one of his lackeys can take it, but they'll wish they never did."

I watch Hold become increasingly upset by the second. It scares me because I know what he is capable of, and if not him, any of the other MC'ers inside the tattoo shop. In fact, I would bet there is a gun trained on us as we speak.

The sound of several motorcycles somewhere in the distance alerts us to the coming danger.

"God... damn it!" Hold lets go of Luke and steps back. "You fucked up now, Hels. I won't be able to save you."

"Don't worry about it. I will protect her," Luke says, pulling me beneath the protection of his arm.

"Oh, yeah? You've done a shit job of it so far. I can see why she should trust you, considering you lied to her and manipulated her. Not to mention, fucked her completely over." Hold turns to glare at me. "How could you trust this piece of shit over me? I am the one that got you outta here in the first place. And then made it so you could come back without dealing with Ward."

My own anger spikes listening to Hold. "You made it

so I could come back? Are you fucking kidding me? What you did sickens me, and to know that you took some type of perverted pleasure in it is unforgivable," I say, pushing away from Luke to confront Hold. "How did you think this was going to work out, Hold? Did you honestly believe I was going to let you fuck me when I loved someone else?" I shake my head. "You should know me better than that. I am through being a whore for you or the MC."

"I never asked you to be my whore. I only ever wanted your love," Hold whispers, his anger dissolving before my eyes.

"But your mom made it very clear when I was only fifteen what I was to you. And as long as I live here, that will be the case or I risk my life every day."

"Tell me then, Hels, how do I let you go for good? When I look at you, I see my future. I swore that if I got you back, I would never let you out of my hands," he says, moving to stand in front of me, placing his mouth inches from mine. "How do I say goodbye when I love you so damn much?"

His words normally would soften my heart and mind, but he broke something inside of me. Any emotional bonds left from before were severed with every lash he gave me.

"Please let me go," I beg softly.

"It's not up to me. You know too much... you're a liability we don't need," he says, stepping back, retreating behind his emotionless mask.

"I'll never tell him or anyone what I know. You should know that by now. My feelings for you right at this moment aren't in a good place, but I couldn't live with myself if I got you in trouble. That isn't something that I could ever do. Hold, you have to realize that if the club keeps dealing in illegal stuff, that something bad is going to happen. I will be the least of your worries."

We all turn when a handful of motorcycles blocks the entire road, and the MC crew swings off of their rides in unison. Luke's police officer gets out of the car and all of the men inside of Hard Ink file outside. I automatically back up to stand beside Luke and he reaches for my hand.

"It's going to be okay," he says, trying to reassure me.

I don't voice my opinion that it's not in our favor to walk out of this alive. Ward and Sandman are at the head of the group that walks slowly toward us.

"Well, what do we have here?" Sandman says, looking over at Luke. "Seems like Mr. ATF Agent has come a callin' on his girlfriend, our recently returned little queen." His head turns to me. "It was nice seeing you the other night, Hels. You sure have grown up," he says, with a smirk on his face and a wink of his eye.

My stomach revolts at the mention of what Hold did to me the other night. I remember seeing Sandman's facial expression and the thought that he enjoyed it sexually seriously makes me ill.

"What we got here, boys?" Ward steps out in front. "I thought you were headed out of town after not finding any gun shit on us?"

"I lost something and came back to retrieve it. Now that I have her, my business here is concluded. We will leave your town," Luke says, not backing down from Ward.

Ward laughs. "She belongs to the MC. I'm sure you saw her tattoo. We'll give you a pass this time, considering you don't know what that certain tat means, but know that it marks her as one of ours. And I think she's smart enough to realize the ramifications should she forget what that tattoo means," he says, shifting his beady eyes to look at me.

I don't miss his veiled threats and neither does Luke. His body stiffens next to me. My hand grips his tighter, trying to convey to him to be cool about this. This is all I have ever known. Threats and intimidation have been the only love this family has given me, and I now use that to my advantage.

"You know, Ward, my family taught me to keep my mouth shut and I have done that my entire life. It would be a shame, though, for that to change. I am sure I can find a whole network of people to listen."

Out of the corner of my eye, I see Sandman moving to position himself beside Luke. Ward's face turns several deep shades of purple. He is completely surprised by my threat—I'm not the timid girl he used to know. Ward's eyes stray down to Luke's side and my eyes follow. Sandman has a gun pressed secretly to his ribcage. He hides it from the police officer in plain sight by the angle at which he stands.

Luke doesn't look concerned. He turns casually toward Sandman. "Get the goddamn gun off of me, before I bring all kinds of hell down on your town. Don't be stupid."

"We'll take out the cop before he even knows what hit him," Ward says, leaning in to whisper to Luke. "You and Hels here will come with us, quietly or in a bloody spectacle—your choice. Tell the cop to get in his car and go. You don't need him anymore."

I am unbelievably calm, Luke's strong presence beside me a factor in my bravery. He gives me strength not to roll over for the MC.

"You going to shoot us in the middle of the road in broad daylight? Seems to me you're getting sloppy, Ward." My words hit their mark, enraging him, I can tell, by the not so subtle facial expressions.

"You fuckin' bitch. I should have killed you the moment we found you. But I may get my wish after all."

A black, unmarked van pulls up on the other side of the motorcycles. The side door slides open and the black-tinted window rolls down for me to see that Mikey is driving it.

"You will get in the van, or I promise that everyone you have come in contact with these last several years will die. I will make it my personal mission in life," Ward says to me.

No! I can't risk my friends' lives. My eyes shift worriedly to Luke's.

"What do we do?" I can't ask him to give up his life for people he hardly knows. But I know that I can't leave here if there is a possibility that I could inadvertently cause Ginger's, or Malik's death.

"I won't leave you," he says, turning toward the cop. "We are all good here. You can go on back to the station."

Nobody in his right mind would believe a word of that, so either the cop is stupid or he's already on the MC's payroll because he turns to get in his car.

"Smart man," Ward says, looking at Luke. "Stupid bitch," he concludes, staring directly at me. "Let's take a little ride."

"You heard the man," Sandman says, poking Luke in the side with his gun to guide him toward the van.

Luke grasps my hand tightly as we slowly move away from the sidewalk. My heart sinks when I think about what is happening. He can't die because of me. I turn to see Hold walking beside us. He stares at me and I try to plead with my eyes what I can't say out loud.

My feet stumble clumsily over the hard concrete, and I intentionally fall into Hold, letting go of Luke. Our stomachs touch as he holds me close with one hand. His gaze encompasses so many emotions, but out of them all, I see love. This is the one person who has been there for me, protected me, when everyone else has left.

"Please," I quietly beg him. Looking into his eyes, I visually see the internal struggle deep down in his soul. Our hands touch between our bodies, and he presses something heavy into mine. My fingers wrap around the cold metal. A gun. I glance up into Hold's blue eyes. The tears he will never release tell of the toll our love has cost him.

"Go with Mikey," he mouths back.

My heart aches with the weight of the moment, but I don't have time to say what is left to be said between us. I don't hesitate, turning swiftly, and moving behind Ward. My fingers tremble with what I hold in my hand, but I don't stop what I plan to do. I push it noticeably into Ward's back, letting him feel exactly what I have against him.

"You gonna shoot me, girl?"

"Maybe," I say, maneuvering Ward so that my back is to the hard door of the van. "Drop the gun Sandman. I am not afraid to use this."

"I don't believe you, little queen," he says, smiling at me, while keeping the gun on Luke.

Almost on instinct, I whip the gun out from behind Ward and shoot at the ground at Sandman's feet. The bullet pings loudly off of the cement, ricocheting into Ward's motorcycle. Small hard chunks of cement spray those standing near. The sound of all the men cursing fills the air. Luke doesn't waste precious time, slamming his fist into Sandman's face and taking his gun.

"Get into the van," I yell at Luke, as I climb in, too. I point the gun at Ward daring him to follow us. Luke slams the door shut and Mikey takes off like a bat out of hell.

"I hope you know where you're going, because in two seconds we're going to be swarmed by motorcycles," Mikey says, from the front seat.

"Head straight and take a right at the corner," Luke says, reaching for his cell phone to call someone. He speaks loudly into it. "Plan B is in play. Yeah, not too good. I need a roadblock at the end of Dade Street. Now! No, I need a car waiting and call the airfield to have a plane ready for takeoff. Thanks."

When he looks at me after getting off his cell, I raise my eyebrows at him.

"Hope for the best and plan for a fucking catastrophe," he says, shrugging his shoulders while answering my unasked question.

We hang precariously on to the back of the seats inside the empty cargo hold. Mikey drives the van like a racecar, speeding around every corner. Each bump jars my aching body, but everything is happening so fast that my injuries are the least of my worries.

"Why are you helping us?" I quietly ask Mikey, knowing that Luke can hear me.

"Not for you. For Hold. He told me that if anything went south, it was my duty to protect you, no matter what. Ward didn't know that when he asked me to drive the van. If you're harmed by the MC, that fucker will lose his shit and no more Hell's Highwaymen. He will burn our chapter down to the ground," he says, looking in the rearview mirror. "We got company."

I turn to look out of the back window and notice the fast-approaching motorcycles racing toward us.

"Hey, if they catch us, you better believe my story is that you have a gun to my head."

"We will be fine as soon as you turn onto the next street. Don't slow down," Luke says, looking ahead.

We corner on two wheels when Mikey takes the turn too sharp, but the sight at the end of the road is a welcome one. Police cars line the road. We come to a screeching halt beside them.

"I am going to tell them that you were giving us a friendly escort out of town," Luke says to Mikey. "You tell Ward that not a word about what just happened will be relayed to any of the authorities, only because I don't want Helen to have to stick around to testify. We are disappearing. He is best off forgetting we exist, and that *we* includes anyone she has met these past couple of years. If something happens to any of us, there will not be an MC left in Harmony. I promise him that," Luke says, opening the door to help me out.

He ushers me inside the backseat of a police car, speaking to one of the cops at the same time to explain the situation. After his statement, he slides in beside me, staring out of the back window toward the commotion we're leaving behind.

The beat of my heart pounds loudly in my head. My adrenaline rush burns itself out quickly, leaving me emotionally back at ground zero. Every single second of the last hour seems almost too incomprehensible for words. I can't believe Hold sacrificed himself once again for me. What is Ward going to do to him?

The memory of seeing his love as he looked at me, and his knowing that I'm leaving again, softens my heart. I shut my eyes tightly, the pain in my soul questioning if I can leave him at the mercy of the Hell's MC. Even after what he has done to me, I don't know if I can be the one to walk away this time.

I glance over to see Luke staring at me. He doesn't seem too affected by the turn of events.

"I guess in your line of work this is just another day?" My sarcasm belies my anxiety.

"Used to be. Now I am just an unemployed carpenter," he says. A smile threatens at the corners of his mouth.

My cool façade finally cracks. "Can you be serious for just one minute? We were almost shot to death. I almost lost you." A hiccup hides the hysteria that halts my words for a minute. "What about Hold? He gave me the gun. He's the reason we got away before ending up in an unmarked grave," I cry, my voice breaking at the end. "How can I possibly protect Malik or Ginger from the MC?"

"I *am* serious and there wasn't a chance in hell that you were going to lose me. I plan on having the next fifty or so years to make you laugh," he says, leaning to pull me next to him. He captures my lips with his, holding me tightly against his chest. "Don't worry about Hold. He's a big boy. I'm sure he will take care of himself. And I've already arranged to have Malik and Ginger warned and protected." This time his kiss shoulders some of my worry.

The touch of his mouth makes every single dangerous minute that we've been through worth it. I touch my tongue to his and deepen the emotional bond we are rebuilding. My hands wrap around his strong arms, holding on for dear life.

"Where are we going?" I pull back to ask, knowing that no matter what, the MC is coming for us.

"For now, we'll travel overseas. Let shit settle. I thought I would take those tattoos of yours to see some exciting places," he says, softly caressing the side of my face.

My lips turn upwards, smiling at his play on words. I search his eyes, finding everything I am looking for deep within them. He gives me a huge grin in return.

"Maybe we should start over," he says, scooting back against the seat. "Hi, I'm Luke Carrity. I'm twenty-nine... I know, older than you thought, but remember, experience goes a long way." He offers me his hand, trying his best to stifle the laughter that obviously threatens to erupt.

I give a soft chuckle. This man in front of me is more than I have ever wanted.

"Hello. My name is Helen Rudder. I'm a former tattoo artist who is currently on the run from her psycho MC family."

Acknowledgements

Merely two years ago, I would never have dreamed of writing full time and so many people have made that possible. Thank you, dear reader, for your loyal support. I am forever grateful to you!!

To all the bloggers who have supported me throughout my journey, thank you from the bottom of my heart. None of this would have been possible without your support. Please know that I appreciate everything you do for me (even when I don't see it). Denise T., Denise S., Lisa, Christine, Kim, Kathy, Theresa... all of you ladies are so important to me!!!

Trina, you are without a shadow of a doubt, my sanity in this book world. You keep me grounded. And when things do not make sense, you bring clarity. I thank God (and Maryse's Blog) that you came into my life. Books equal friends. Thank you for being the best beta reader and boss there ever was. No matter what, I am thankful for you.

Hang Le, your covers ROCK, but it's your friendship

that means more. Thank you for all the hard work and time that you devote to me. It's unbelievable.

Kirsten, your input when it comes to beta reading my books are spot on and amazing. Thank you for always dropping everything to devote the time and energy in me. I am so very thankful for you and your friendship.

Ena, you have been one of the most important people in this book life of mine. Thank you so much!! I am so happy and proud of you and wish you much success.

Lisa Aurello, I am completely humbled and forever in your debt with the time and love you took editing Beautiful Ink. You helped me bring this story and its characters to life. Thank you seems inadequate for how I feel, but thank you from the bottom of my heart!!

Erin Noelle, I love you. No, really, I love you!!

Tyler Seielstad Photography, your photographs are art and inspirational. Amazing!!

Sheena, I appreciate the love you have shown me this past year!! Big kisses!!

Danielle, thank you so much for your support. I love you bunches!!!

To my Reed's Street Team ladies, thank you all for your continuing support and love. You guys ROCK!!

My road team, Lynn and Christan, you are more than family. Thank you for all that you do!! Mom... I love you. Who cares if we never see "eye to eye"... we keep it real!! Heather & Penny, I'll have you reading yet.

To my Dad who is always supportive, even if I don't let him read my books.

Shannon, Cannon, Reese, and Madi Grace, it has been a rough year, but we keep it going because we are family. Thank you for taking care of me throughout. I love you all!!

About the Author

Nicole Reed is the New York Times Bestselling Author of *Ruining You*. She is a true Southern girl, enjoying life with her husband and three children in the peachy state of Georgia. As a child, she discovered another world between the pages of a book. In 2012, she self-published her first book *Ruining Me*, and then followed it with *Ruining You*, *Cake*, and *Wasted Heart*. Her books have also been listed on the overall Top 100 Amazon and Barnes & Noble Bestselling list. She is represented by Ginger Clark with Curtis Brown, LTD. You can follow her on Facebook https://www.facebook.com/authornicolereed, Twitter @nicole1reed, and her website www.nicolereedbooks.com.

49577468R00203

Made in the USA
San Bernardino, CA
29 May 2017